The Family Business 3

The Family Business 3

Carl Weber
with Treasure Hernandez

www.urbanbooks.net

Urban Books, LLC
97 N18th Street
Wyandanch, NY 11798

ISBN 13: 978-1-60162-635-6
ISBN 10: 1-60162-635-5

First Hardcover Printing February 2015
Printed in the United States of America

10 9 8 7 6 5 4 3 2 1

*This is a work of fiction. Any references or similarities to
actual events, real people, living or dead, or to real locales are
intended to give the novel a sense of reality. Any similarity in
other names, characters, places, and incidents is entirely coin-
cidental.*

Distributed by Kensington Publishing Corp.
Submit Wholesale Orders to:
Kensington Publishing Corp.
C/O Penguin Group (USA) Inc.
Attention: Order Processing
405 Murray Hill Parkway
East Rutherford, NJ 07073-2316
Phone: 1-800-526-0275
Fax: 1-800-227-9604

This book is dedicated to my Pops,
Carl Weber Sr., the man who taught me more
about how to run a business than all my
business school teachers combined.

Dear Reader,

I hope you enjoyed *Family Business 3: The Return of Vegas*, as much as I enjoyed writing it. Here at Team Weber, we are presently working on the next four installments of the Duncans' saga, which will begin in the summer of 2015 with *Grand Opening*, a *Family Business* prequel about how LC, Chippy, and Lou first got started the business; then we return with *Family Business 4: The Search for Ruby* in February of 2016; *Finishing School : The Education of Nevada Duncan* in 2016; and *No More Mr. Nice Guy: The Introduction of Niles Monroe* in 2016.

For fans of my other series, look for *Married Men 2*, coming in 2016.

All the Best,
Carl Weber

Prologue

Junior Duncan walked into the Waldorf Astoria looking handsome yet uncomfortable in his navy blue Brooks Brothers suit. His awkwardness was not apparent to most of the other hotel patrons. However, it was so obvious to his lovely, full-figured girlfriend, Sonya, that she made a mental note to herself to give him a very special treat in bed later that night for being such a trooper. You see, despite the fact that Junior and his family were as rich as anyone in the building, he was more comfortable in a pair of jeans or coveralls than he was in a suit. Still, today was the one-year anniversary of their first date, and he'd promised her a night out on the town, and he planned on living up to that promise.

The couple held hands as they walked through the lobby toward the Zagat-rated five-star Bull and Bear Steakhouse. There they were greeted by the maître d', a dark-haired Frenchman who seemed to know Junior personally.

"Ah, good afternoon, Mr. Duncan. Your table is ready. Right this way." He led them to a very private table in a corner, handing them menus once they were seated. Less than a minute later, a wine steward arrived with a very expensive bottle, which he opened and allowed Junior to taste.

Savoring the wine, Junior nodded his head like he'd seen his father LC Duncan do at fine restaurants like this one a hundred times before. The wine steward filled their glasses, and Junior lifted his, toasting, "To the prettiest woman I've ever met, and the most wonderful year of my life."

Overwhelmed by the moment, Sonya blushed as she tapped her glass politely against his. This was like a dream come true for her, but what she didn't know was that Junior had much more in store for her.

"Excuse me, Madame." The maître d' interrupted their moment, laying a domed silver tray on the table. "I believe this is for you."

"But I haven't ordered yet." Looking up at the maître d', she missed the look of pure satisfaction covering Junior's face.

"The gentleman has taken the liberty of ordering your first course." He motioned to Junior, who nodded his approval. The maître d' swiftly disappeared, leaving Sonya staring at the silver tray.

"Is there a Lexus with a bow parked outside for me? Are there keys under this thing?" Sonya asked, lifting her head to see Junior's smirk.

"You're never gonna know unless you take off the cover."

She drummed her fingers over the lid nervously and then snatched it up, revealing a small jewelry box covered in rich leather that told her whatever was inside was expensive. Sonya's hands flew to her mouth and her eyes started to water. She looked from Junior to the box and then back to him.

"Oh my God. Is that what I think it is?" she murmured.

Junior picked up the box and dropped to one knee.

"Oh my God, this is really happening!" Sonya felt herself trembling. She knew she loved him and he loved her, but never in her wildest dreams had she expected him to propose.

"Yes, baby. It's really happening." Junior opened the box, revealing a three-carat, heart-shaped diamond. "Sonya Brown, I've never loved anyone as much as I love you."

They were so caught up in the moment that neither of them noticed the three large men wearing bow ties and old-man suits headed their way. The maître d' tried to block the men from interrupting the couple, but a menacing look from the one in front was enough to not only silence the Frenchman, but send him scurrying off toward the kitchen.

"Will you marry—"

"Excuse me," the leader of the bow-tied group interrupted Junior in a very polite and proper tone. "Are you Junior Duncan?"

Junior looked up at the clean-shaven man with schoolboy glasses, quickly evaluating him and the two men who flanked him. They weren't cops; of that he was sure. There was no doubt in his mind, however, that all three were armed. Unfortunately, this was the rare occasion that Junior wasn't.

"Yeah, I'm Junior Duncan," he replied, rising to his feet. He glanced over at Sonya, who was no longer focused on him, but on the men hell-bent on interrupting them. The uneasy look on her face really irritated him. This was supposed to be their most special moment, and these three clowns had come along and ruined it for his woman. He tried to comfort her with his eyes before staring down the five foot ten man in front of him.

He was expecting the man to at least look intimidated by his size, like most people, but neither the man nor his associates showed the slightest bit of concern. "Who are you?"

"Who I am is not important," the man replied.

"Oh, no? Then why are you here?"

"I was sent to deliver a message."

"A message from whom?" Junior asked, losing his patience.

The man looked past Junior, directly at Sonya, as he spoke. "A message from Brother Xavier."

Sonya let out a loud sigh. Junior turned and saw the worry on her face. If this went on much longer these men were going to ruin his entire night, he thought.

He puffed out his chest. "I don't know a Brother Xavier. Now get lost so I can get back to my woman."

The man continued, clearly not taking orders from Junior. "Well, you can be assured that Brother Xavier knows you."

Junior didn't like the sound of that, but he tried to remain calm. He needed more information to assess this situation.

"So what's his message?" he asked gruffly.

"The message, Mr. Duncan, is for you to stop fornicating with his wife." He delivered the words in a deep, strong voice. In fact, his speech was so intense that the noise level of the restaurant was reduced to a hum as patrons gave up pretending that they were not listening to the scene taking place in front of them.

Junior stiffened. "What did you say?"

"I said Brother Xavier wants you to stop fornicating with his wife." This time he looked at Sonya as he reiterated his message.

"And what if I don't?" Junior asked, taking a step forward to force the man's attention back to him.

The man shook his head, as if he were disappointed in Junior's response. "Well, then I would get my personal affairs in order as soon as possible, because your time amongst the living is not going to be very long."

On that note, all three men turned with military precision toward the door and exited the same way they'd entered. Junior's eyes landed on Sonya, who was shaking. This was definitely not the way either of them had expected this night to turn out, he thought as he looked down at the ring box still in his hand.

Vegas

1

My brother-in-law Harris rode shotgun as Junior drove the Land Rover up Third Avenue toward 125th Street. I was in the backseat watching the streets of Harlem pass by like they were my own personal TV show. Queens might have been my home, but Harlem had been my playground since I was a teenager hanging out with Daryl Graham. I don't know why it had taken me so long to get back uptown. I'd been home for almost six months, and this was the first time I'd stepped foot higher than 65th Street. I just wished it was for a happier occasion.

By the time Junior wheeled the car in front of the impressive Strivers' Row brownstone, I had mentally prepared myself for our meeting. I would let Harris take the lead, hanging back with Junior for security purposes, but I had known from the moment the old man told us who we were going to see that I would have to let my presence be felt.

At the door, we were greeted by a middle-aged black woman, clad in all white from head to toe. She had been expecting us, and Harris, always the arrogant fuck, walked right by her like he owned the place. Junior and I, on the other hand, shook the woman's hand politely then gestured for her to lead the way. Despite his overbearing size, Junior had always been the most respectful of my mother's children. With that being said, I could tell he was nervous from the way he kept tapping his suit jacket to make sure his gun was still there.

He did, however, remain composed and alert, which was good. One of the first things my Uncle Lou had taught me as a teenager was that you should always be concerned about the unknown.

Junior's nervousness told me that he understood that he was way out of his element. We'd entered a different world by coming here, and neither Harris nor my brother knew what to expect—but I sure as hell did.

The woman led us down a long, wood-paneled hallway that reminded me of something out of an old horror film. She eventually left us in a room that I assumed was a library because the walls were covered by bookcases bearing thousands of old books. Harris immediately took a seat at a large antique table and began rummaging through some papers in his briefcase. Junior, obviously still out of his element, began fiddling with his phone like it was an extension of his hand, most likely texting his girl Sonya.

With no imminent threat, I bypassed the chairs, walking across the room to the bookcases to look through a few of the old books. I was impressed that most, if not all, appeared to be written by people of African descent, and that the large majority of them were first editions. Most people didn't know this about me, but I was a book enthusiast, and had read a multitude of books even before I went to prison. I also had several highly collectible first editions of my own, though nothing like this.

As I skimmed through an original copy of J. A. Rodgers' *From Superman to Man*, the library door opened. Two large, suit-and-bow-tie-wearing brothers entered, posting up on either side of the door like sentries. A few seconds later, a very short, dark-skinned man in his seventies stood in the entryway. I recognized him right away. His name was Minister Aariz Farah, and despite his diminutive stature, you could tell he was to be respected.

Harris, ever the brown-noser in the presence of powerful people, rushed over to Minister Farah like a bitch in heat, with his hand stuck out in greeting.

"Minister Farah, it's a pleasure to meet you. I'm Harris Grant, legal counsel for Duncan Motors. You spoke to my father-in-law on the phone earlier." Without saying a word, Minister Farah took Harris's hand, giving him an unimpressed once-over. "I'd like to introduce you to my brother-in-law, Junior Duncan."

"Nice to meet you, sir." Junior walked over and shook his hand. From the cold, hard stare Minister Farah was giving them, it did not look like our meeting was going to be very productive.

Harris gestured toward me. "And over there in the corner is my other brother-in-law—"

"Vegas Duncan!" Minister Farah's surprisingly strong voice boomed, and his eyes turned to mine. His hard face broke out into a wrinkled smile as he came into the room, arms outstretched, to welcome me into a brotherly hug that barely reached my middle. "As-Salaam-Alaikum, my friend. It's really good to see you."

"Wa-Alaikum-Salaam. It is better to see you, Brother Minister," I replied, pulling back. We stood there, grinning at each other for a moment. I can't begin to tell you how good it was to see him after all these years. His face brought back memories of a forgotten past.

"It has been too long. My God, what's it been—ten years?"

"At least. I left the school in 2003." Minister Farah had been one of my instructors and the associate headmaster at Chi's Finishing School in Europe.

"I've heard your name spoken many times over the years through the grapevine. You've made quite a name and reputation for yourself. Your incident with the Armenians was quite honorable. I am very proud of you," he said.

"Thank you, sir," I replied humbly. "I've tried to utilize what you and the others taught me." Over Minister Farah's shoulder I could see the surprised expressions on Junior's and Harris's faces.

"So, what brings you uptown? You slumming?" he asked with a laugh.

"Heck, if this is slumming, the poverty line must have been raised considerably while I was away," I joked. "But in all seriousness, Minister, my brother Junior has a problem. I think it's with one of your people."

Minister Farah was one of the most respected members of the Nation of Islam. For years he had run the Fruit of Islam, or FOI, their security force.

"Then let's talk and see if we can solve this problem." He patted my back, prompting me toward the table. The four of us sat down.

"You say your brother is having a problem with one of my people?"

I turned to Harris, who flipped open his folder and said, "Do you know a man by the name of Brother Xavier? His government name is Charles Brown." As soon as Harris said the name, a look of concern crossed Minister Farah's face.

"Yes, I know him. He is not a man to be trifled with, but he is not one of my people. Not anymore."

"He's not? What did he do? Why did you break ties?" Harris questioned in rapid-fire succession.

"For many years Xavier was an important man in the Nation. I actually appointed him head of the New York FOI myself. He was a hardworking, honorable man who moved up the ranks swiftly, until he lost his way."

"Lost his way how?" Harris chimed in before I could interject. Minister Farah shook his head, looking worried.

"Without any of us in the hierarchy of the Nation realizing it, he was committing robberies along with the men he was supposed to be leading closer to Allah," Minister Farah's tone sounded like he had tasted something terrible. Just the memory of it infuriated him.

"Wow, now that's what I call a gutsy move," Harris added, stopping short of sounding impressed. I glanced at Junior, who was still taking it all in.

"Obviously we couldn't allow him to continue to represent the Nation or the FOI. We released him from his position, and he was shunned from our community. We believed that would be enough to bring him back in line, but we were wrong."

"In what way?" I asked.

"Instead of humbling him, it led him to create his own organization, the Islamic Black Panther Party, a very powerful, radical group that he now runs very successfully from a jail cell."

"Whoa! The Islamic Black Panther Party is run by Brother X. You're telling me this Brother Xavier is the same man they call Brother X in prison?" I stared at Minister Farah uneasily. All of a sudden his level of concern was nothing compared to mine.

Minister Farah nodded. "Yes, I've heard him called Brother X before."

"You know this guy, Vegas?" Junior asked.

"I never met the man, but if we're talking about the same person, we have a much bigger problem than we thought. The IBPP are known for carrying out the majority of the paid prison hits in New York, New Jersey, and Connecticut. They pride themselves on being able to get to anyone, anywhere in the prison system. Last year they got those three guys the Feds were holding in protective custody for that big Mob trial. To this day nobody knows how they got in those cells. The Russians, the Jews, and the Italians use them extensively." I finished with a shiver. I literally had goose bumps on my arms.

Minister Farah ran his hand across his face. "They have over a hundred highly-trained men in the prison system at any time, and have at least that many on the outside. They are as good as any of the people trained by the FOI, and a hundred times more deadly because they have no conscience."

"Jesus Christ, what the hell has Sonya gotten us into, Junior?" Harris got up and started pacing nervously, reminding me of why I hated his punk ass so much.

Ignoring Harris, Minister Farah turned to Junior, full of apprehension. "Young man, I must ask you, what is your business with Xavier?"

Junior glanced over at Minister Farah hesitantly, lowering his head. "I'm sleeping with his wife."

"And he's not very happy about it," Harris added.

Minister Farah sat back in his chair, "Oh, that's not good. That's not good at all. Did you know this woman was married?"

"Of course he did," Harris cut in angrily. He'd stopped pacing and was standing in front of Junior, staring down at him like a father about to chastise his child. "It was the rest of us who didn't know. He could bring down the whole damn family with this. And for what—some other man's pussy?"

"Shut up, Harris!" I growled. Junior remained silent, but I could tell from the way he was glaring at Harris that he was about to take his past few days of frustration out on our brother-in-law. As much as I might have liked to see him knock Harris on his ass, we had too many threats from outside sources to start fighting within the family. "Did you hear me? I said sit down and shut up!" I repeated through gritted teeth.

"Why, Vegas? We all know I'm telling the truth. All the man wants is for Junior to stop screwing his wife. We wouldn't even be he here if he'd just jettison the bitch!"

That was when Junior snapped. He jumped up and grabbed Harris by the throat with one hand, lifting him off the ground like a rag doll. His other hand was pulled back in a fist, ready to unleash his fury onto Harris's face. All of a sudden, my big-talking brother-in-law looked like he wanted to shit his pants. He glanced at me, but I had nothing for him. I'd already warned him. He should have known better than to call Sonya outside her name.

"You call her a bitch again and I'll make my sister a widow. You understand me?"

"Yeah, yeah, I was just trying to make a point," Harris squealed, barely able to speak.

"So am I." Junior released him, and he fell to the floor. "I'm gonna get some air. I'll meet you at the car, Vegas."

Minister Farah sighed, leaning closer to me as we watched Junior head out the door. "You do realize your brother-in-law is right. You must convince your brother to end this affair. This woman is married, and Allah considers that sacred. Now that your brother has been warned, Brother Xavier will have no choice but to end his life and the lives of anyone who stands in his way, if only to save face."

The displeasure on Minister Farah's face was pronounced. It was one thing to have a business problem where the most you could lose was money, but this was personal. The one thing the old man taught me back in the day was that personal things always lead to trouble with a capital T. I stood up, and so did Minister Farah.

"I need your help on this, old friend. I need to know that my brother can walk the streets and be safe. Can you help me?"

He reached out and patted my shoulder like the friend that he was. "I will do what I can. We still have people who are close to Brother Xavier's people. However, it may be of little help. Islamic law is very clear on adultery. It is not to be tolerated."

I nodded, trusting that he would do whatever he could to help me. "Thank you, Minister. All I can ask is that you try."

He nodded, reaching into his breast pocket and pulling out an envelope. "I was asked to give you this if I ever ran across you." He handed it to me.

"Who's it from?"

"I think you will get all the answers you need when you open it."

I studied his face for a brief moment, but he gave away nothing, so I tore open the envelope. Inside was a single postcard with a picture of Israel. I turned it over and saw that the only thing written on the back was STM3482. A lump developed in my throat as I turned the postcard back over to the picture.

Sasha

2

"Oh God! Oh my God! I'm about to come! I'm about to come!" my cousin Paris announced to the world, way louder than necessary.

Now, don't get me wrong. Stavros's fine ass *was* eating the hell outta her, but then again, Paris had a knack for being overly dramatic. I can only imagine how over the top she would have been if she'd known I was standing in the doorway watching. They were, however, putting on quite a stimulating show. I was getting hot just watching her hold onto his head and ride his face like a bucking bronco. When she lifted her ass off the bed and started screaming, I could almost feel her satisfaction.

"Shit, I'm coming! I'm coming! I'm fucking coming!"

She eventually released his head like a hot potato, collapsing on the bed, totally spent. That's when Stavros noticed me in the doorway. He didn't saying anything; he just stared at my bare breasts, waving his hand for me to come over and make their little party a threesome. I had to admit the thought was very appealing. He certainly was fine enough, and from the size of his dick, I knew he had the equipment to handle two women. Only problem was that Paris didn't play well with others when it came to men, especially not when it came to me. Besides, I had already fucked his cousin Felix less than an hour ago.

So, instead of heading to the bed to join them, I walked over to my knapsack to retrieve what I had come down from the top deck for in the first place. As I pulled out my suntan lotion, Paris was still blissfully recovering from her mega-orgasm, and Stavros was still grinning at me hopefully as he mounted her. Of course, his grin faded quickly when I pulled out my silenced .45, pointing it at his head.

"Oh shit!" he murmured in that sexy Greek accent. Paris opened her eyes just as I pulled the trigger.

Thunk! Thunk!

Two silenced bullets hit Stavros in the head, killing him instantly and splattering blood all over Paris's naked body. From the look she gave me, I could tell she was not a happy camper about me killing her new lover, and even more pissed about the blood.

"Really, Sasha? Really! You had to kill him now? You couldn't stick to the plan and wait until after I fucked him?" She pointed to his still hard cock, shaking her head in disappointment. We both hated to see a good dick go to waste.

"Sorry, but we don't have time for that. Our timetable's been moved up," I was trying not to give away my concern about the message I had just received on my cell phone.

"Yeah, yeah, yeah. Hand me a towel so we can get the fuck out of here."

I loved the way she could go from zero to not giving a fuck in two seconds. I threw her a towel and watched her climb out of bed.

"What about his partner?"

"Oh, Felix," I replied. "Poor Felix is dead."

"Good, but I bet you fucked his ass before you killed him, didn't you?" She glared at me jealously as she toweled off the blood. All I could do was smirk because she was right—and he did have some good dick. "Bitch!" Paris replied when she noticed my satisfied expression.

"Look, this is not the time or place to get petty. We still have a job to do."

"I know that. It would have been easier to do at night," she replied, slipping into her bikini bottom. "I just don't know why Orlando's always upping the timeline on our asses. We weren't supposed to make a move on anyone until tonight. Why can't he just let me do my job?"

"It wasn't O who texted me. It was Aunt Chippy. She wants us home on the first thing smoking."

"My mother?" Paris was puzzled. "My mother doesn't get involved with operations or troubleshooting."

I shifted my head in her direction, slipping on my knapsack. "Exactly! So you know what that means, don't you?"

"Yeah, something's going down in New York. Come on. Let's go find that fat bastard LaSalle. It's time to take our asses home." She reached into a knapsack similar to mine and pulled out a silenced Glock. By taking out Stavros and Felix, I had made our job that much easier, but taking out LaSalle was not going to be anywhere near as simple as killing his horny nephews.

We left the cabin and made our way down the hall, trying our best to hide our guns. It wasn't easy, considering we were wearing only bikini bottoms and knapsacks. When we arrived at the master stateroom, Paris took out the sentry with one shot.

Thunk.

Taking a deep breath, I counted down on my fingers: *three, two, one.* On one, I opened the door and we stormed the room with guns blazing. What we found, however, was far from what we expected. Oh, LaSalle was there all right, but he wasn't in any shape to be a threat to us. In fact, his fat ass was tied up to a four-poster bed, naked as the day he was born, with a sock in his mouth.

What the fuck? Paris and I shared a confused look, with guns still drawn, until we heard a familiar laugh.

"What took you so long?" We turned to the voice, and there was my flamboyant cousin Rio, sitting in a captain's chair with a cell phone to his ear, sipping a glass of red wine like he didn't have a care in the world. At his feet was an opened briefcase filled with money

"Rio!" Paris shouted with relief. Rio was her twin brother, and half the reason we had been so worried about LaSalle was because we knew Rio was with him. "You were supposed to seduce him—not tie him up!"

"I did. I seduced his ass right into those ropes. I'm sorry, I don't do fat or smelly, and he's both." Rio looked repulsed, waving his hand past his nose. I couldn't help it; I had to laugh.

"Please, Sasha. Don't encourage him," Paris snapped at me before turning her attention back to her twin brother. "Ree, we need to get outta here."

"I know. I got Ma's text. I'm talking to the pilot right now. The jet should be prepped and ready to go in an hour."

"Good. What's this guy's status? He say anything?" Paris walked over and pulled the sock out of LaSalle's mouth.

"Other than threatening to chop me up into little pieces and shove me back up my mother's womb, nothin'."

"And I'm going to do the same thing to you, bitch!" LaSalle spat like a maniac.

"Well, I guess that would make sense, considering we're twins." Paris pointed her Glock at his temple. "Just one problem. How you going to do all that when you're going to be dead in ten minutes?"

His facial expression softened, but his voice remained strong. "Then my nephews will avenge me. They will kill you all!"

"Oh, I doubt that." Paris giggled, waving me over. I made four long strides, pointing my .45 at his other temple. "You see, Sasha here killed Stavros and Felix."

His eyes were now wide open, his expression a mix of anger and fear.

"A month ago, four masked men stole a shipment of pure black tar heroin from a car carrier in South Carolina. That shipment surfaced in Detroit last week. The entire crew who brought it is dead. Sasha killed them too." Paris grinned, tilting her head. "Oh, from the look she's giving you right now, I'm pretty sure she wants to kill you too."

Gone was the anger from his face. Dude could no longer hide his fear. I smiled at him then shouted, "Boo!" and he let out the stinkiest fart I'd ever witnessed. It was so nasty you could almost taste it.

"Oh my God, Sasha. What the hell you do that for?" Rio snapped, covering his lower face with a handkerchief and waving his hand. "This fool's been eating onions and hot dogs all day."

"Well, I'm about to take him out of his misery." I cocked the hammer on my gun.

"I'm sorry," he said in this whiny, pathetic voice. "Please don't kill me."

"You want to live?" Paris asked. LaSalle nodded. "Okay, then you got one chance, and if you as much as think about lying to me, she's gonna blow your brains all over these nice silk sheets."

"I'm not going to lie. I swear. Anything, anything you want. I'll tell you," LaSalle stuttered.

"I just wanna know who told you about the shipment."

Without hesitation, LaSalle gave up the information. "Niles. His name was Niles Monroe."

Paris's face became an angry, contorted mess and she flew into a rage. "You lying piece of shit! Niles Monroe is dead!" She pulled the trigger and then stormed out of the room.

I glanced over at Rio, who had closed the briefcase and was about to follow Paris out the door. I grabbed his arm. "What the fuck was that all about? Who the hell is Niles Monroe?"

Rio's face went soft and sad. "Niles Monroe is the only man Paris ever truly loved. And the first person she ever had to kill for the family."

Sonya

3

"So I guess you got my message?" My husband's voice sounded overly calm considering the message that had been delivered.

As he stared at me from across the table, I was wishing I was anywhere but there with him. I could feel his eyes undressing me, slowly and intentionally removing all the layers I was wearing. Guess it didn't matter how hard I had tried to cover myself up; he knew every single contour of my body too well to be thrown off by baggy clothes and no makeup. There was a time when that look he was giving me would have made my clothes melt away so I could jump his bones right there, but those days were long gone.

"Oh, I got your message loud and clear," I replied sharply, looking up at his smug face for the first time. It had been three days since his men entered the Bull and Bear restaurant, threatening Junior and me like modern day Stormtroopers. I'm sure Junior thought it was about him, but I knew that confrontation had been my husband's way of reminding me that I was his wife and that playtime was over, regardless of the fact that he was behind bars. "Why else would I be here?"

He turned the chair around and sat in it backward, his eyes narrowed in anger. I had no doubt that if the guards weren't watching our every move, he would have slapped me for using that tone of voice with him. A part of me wanted to jump up and run. I could write him a letter when I got home instead of doing this face to face, I thought. Deep down, though, I knew that would never work. Not if I truly wanted to be with Junior. Besides, I hadn't taken a five-hour bus ride just to turn tail the moment things got uncomfortable. I needed to confront him. It was the only way he would respect me enough to give me my freedom and leave Junior alone.

"I'm not sure. I'm hoping you've come to your senses," he finally said.

"Yes, I have come to my senses. I want a divorce, Charles."

He sat up straighter, clearly taken aback by my words. "My name is Xavier—and I love you, so that's not going to happen. You knew when we first got married that Islamic law has no provision for divorce other than death. I'm your husband. Your only husband!" He spoke with finality, the same way he did when he was giving orders to the countless men who were always at his beck and call. The problem was, he seemed to forget that I wasn't one of them.

"Really?" I shot back defiantly. "And what kind of husband have you been the last five years?" I said it loud enough for half the people in the visiting room to hear.

"I've been a faithful one. Can you say the same?" Most people would have stopped at that moment, frightened by his steely calm, but I had come this far, and I was going to have my say.

"No, I can't, and that's why I want a divorce. You can't do anything for me locked up in here, Charles. I'm a woman. I need to be held at night. I need to be made love to. Hell, you stay in so much trouble that we can't even have conjugal visits." I stared at him, refusing to back down.

He reached out for my hand, but I moved it away. I didn't want him to soften my resolve. "I understand, and I'm sorry," he said, sounding more sincere than I would have expected. "I can fix that. Get my conjugal reinstated. I know this hasn't been easy on you, but I can make this right. Sonya, baby, I love you."

I shook my head. "It's a little late for that, don't you think? You're not a husband; you're a responsibility. A responsibility I don't want anymore. I just want to be free."

His eyes flashed with anger. "The only way for you to be free from me is for one of us to die. And I don't plan on dying anytime soon. You get where I'm going with this?"

"I don't love you anymore!" I pleaded. "I'm in love with someone else. What part of that don't you understand?"

"None of it! Because it's not happening and that's that," he barked so loudly that I saw people from the next table flinch. Their eyes shot toward us, but they looked away just as quickly. Even the other men in prison jumpsuits wanted to pretend they hadn't heard anything. They were all so afraid of him—but I wasn't.

I clenched my jaw and sat straight and motionless, letting him know that I wouldn't let him intimidate me with his yelling. First he looked frustrated, like I was a hardheaded child he was trying to discipline, but then he just looked confused. He wasn't used to anyone pushing back against his authority.

"You love this man. Is that what you're telling me?" His eyes were tearing up, and I realized that beneath his hard exterior, he still had feelings for me. This was the most vulnerable that I'd ever seen him. Unfortunately, it was a little too late for that.

"Yes, I love him," I replied with tears now falling from my eyes. "I'm sorry. I didn't mean for it to happen, but it did."

He angrily swiped away a tear that had escaped and began to run down his cheek. "You do understand that I will kill this man—and any other that stands between us."

Just like that, the hard-as-nails husband that I knew was back. If I had thought for a second that he was going to let me go easily, I realized now that it was a foolish notion.

"You're serious?" I asked.

"Very serious. As far as I'm concerned, he's already dead." His voice was barely a whisper as he dropped that bomb; then he stood up and walked out of the visiting room.

Paris

4

There's this magical moment that I always try to savor. It doesn't happen very often, and it only lasts a few seconds at the height of my orgasm, but when it does, there's no other feeling that can compare. That's where I was as I slid up and down on Niles's thick penis. I was trying to hold on to that phenomenal sensation, but it quickly slipped away. Don't get me wrong; I wasn't mad that it had subsided. I was still enjoying the after effects of my orgasm. I just wish I could have held that sensation a little longer.

A few seconds later, Niles palmed my ass cheeks, pulling me all the way down on his dick so I could feel him explode.

"Damn, that was good," I murmured as I collapsed on top of him. This man knew my body as if he were a part of me. God, I loved him.

"Where are you going?" he asked as I rolled off of him and started dressing.

"With you."

"Paris . . ." he said warily.

I stifled a laugh. "No, no, no. I'm going to drive you to the airport. I think I deserve a sappy good-bye." *Or perhaps a chance to talk you out of leaving,* I thought. "Besides, I need to get my ass out of here and back to Spain. Left all my shit there."

"Is this some ploy so you can go along?" He got up, revealing all the reasons I wanted to just throw him back on the bed.

"If you were going to any other city, then maybe, but I'm not tryin'a show up in New York."

"Yeah, I get it. I'm gonna go jump in the shower. I would ask you to join me, but we'd never get out." He laughed as he grabbed me around the waist and planted a deep, wet kiss on me.

"I'm not showering," I said. "I want to smell you on me all day. Maybe I won't shower at all until you come back."

"That is so fuckin' nasty and hot, you dirty girl," he joked as he headed to the shower.

"Hey, since you fixed my tire, we'll take my car. I'll transfer all your stuff into it," I said.

He turned around and smiled at me, cocky as hell. "See, this is why I'm keeping you. You're like a sexy ninja Girl Scout." He took a step in my direction, like he was ready to start round two of our lovemaking.

"Go! I don't want you blaming me for being late." I pointed him to the bathroom. As soon as I heard the shower turn on, I got to work gathering everything I would need. Twenty minutes later, we were headed out of the compound.

"You know, you're the first man I ever loved," I said as I drove.

"So you love me?"

"Yes, very much." I wanted to turn and face him, but I had to keep my eyes on the road, so I pulled over to the side.

"Why are you stopping?" He placed his hand on top of mine.

"What if you don't come back?" I asked.

"Then I will reflect on the wonderful moments that I've shared with you in way too short a time," he said softly, caressing my face. "But the main thing I'm gonna do is my job, and do it effectively."

I understood. I knew that I couldn't ever change his mind. The job was what he did, and he would no more walk away from unfinished business than I would. I reached out for his hand and held it tight, wishing this moment had never arrived. I wanted to tell him the truth, but I couldn't bring myself to speak.

"Hey. I've got something for you." He interrupted my thoughts. Reaching into his waistband, he pulled out one of his karambit blades and extended his hand to me. "It's for you . . . until they're reunited."

"What . . . why?" I questioned as I took the blade from him.

"Paris, you make me nervous like a little schoolboy. I'm not used to feeling all open and shit, but I do believe fate brought us together back in Spain. I love you with all my heart, you crazy, sexy woman, and I'm ready to commit to you. When I get back, we'll lay it all on the line, me and you, and see how things go."

I was stunned. On top of my frayed emotions, this left me speechless.

"Just something I needed to get off my chest," he said, "on the off chance that something does happen to me and I don't return. Tomorrow's never promised, but I need you to know that my love for you is."

Niles kissed me tenderly. As he pivoted, I locked my grip on the single blade, mad at myself for enjoying the kiss. When we finished, neither of us spoke. I drove away from the side of the road and let him direct me back to the private airstrip. I pulled my car up to the plane and let him out. God, I didn't want to. I wanted him to stay here with me. He unloaded his bags and then turned to face me.

"I need to know something before I leave. Are you all in, Paris?"

"Yeah. I am," I said solemnly.

"Good. Because I know you know who my next assignment is," he stated, startling me. "Just wanted to show that I trust you with my business . . . no matter who says I shouldn't. No secrets. I love you, ma," he said, oblivious to who I really was: the daughter of the man he was hired to kill.

"I love you too," I replied. "Always."

"Then we're on the same page." He gave me a quick kiss on the lips, holding me around the waist. As his hands fell away and he began to move, I grabbed his arm, holding it firmly. At first he looked confused, because my grip had intensity, but when his eyes met mine they were soft, smiling.

"Do you trust me?" I fought back tears.

"Yes, and that's not something that comes naturally to me," he said, holding my gaze.

"Then believe me when I say you can't go. You have to walk away from this job." I heard my voice catch from the emotional hell swirling deep down at the core of my heart.

"Babe, it's gonna be all right. I'm not leaving you. Plus, I need to finish this job so that I can walk away from Nadja."

"I don't care. Do another job for her. I need you to stay with me." I knew the begging wasn't sexy, but I couldn't just let him go. He reached out and swooped me up in his arms and held me close, but by the time he put me down, I knew he'd made his decision and nothing I said would deter him.

I watched as he walked toward the plane and stepped up the ladder, disappearing into the G5. Just like that, he was gone.

I climbed back into my car, and with trembling hands, I donned a pair of gloves that I'd hastily stowed in my pocket in anticipation of this moment. From the opposite pocket, I produced a wireless transmitter and removed the safety with a flick of my thumb. I waited until the plane had taken off, imagining him there in the cockpit, thinking about me the same way that I was here thinking about him.

Taking a deep breath, I closed my eyes and counted to three as I fought back tears. In the end, the outcome was predetermined from the moment I had looked in that file back in a cheap motel in Valencia.

Niles had once taught me a valuable lesson about having to make hard choices when he wanted me to prove I was "about this life." *Well, I am*, I thought as I opened my eyes and pressed the trigger.

"I love you, Niles," I spoke out loud, although he was miles in the air by now.

Only when I saw the flames of the airplane lighting the sky and falling into pieces over the hill was I convinced of my success. However, success was synonymous with misery as the transmitter fell from my open hand and I closed my eyes again.

"Niles!" My chest heaving, I screamed at the top of my lungs, but there was no one there to hear it. I opened my eyes, and suddenly it was all gone. No smoke, no fire, no plane, nothing. Just Rio and Sasha sitting across from me, looking at me like I was a fool.

"You all right?" Rio asked, leaning as far as his seat belt would allow.

It took me a second, but I finally got it together and realized it was all a dream, and that we were on the ground, buckled up in the company G5. I glanced out the window as we made our way to the hangar.

"Paris, you all right?" he repeated.

"Yeah," I said, angry about where my mind had taken me. "That motherfucker LaSalle fucked my head up. I was dreaming about that last day with Niles."

"Damn, that must have been some good-ass dick! You still dreaming about him after he's dead."

"Shut up, Sasha," Rio and I said in unison. "Shut the fuck up!"

Brother X

5

"Two ninety-nine, three hundred." I finished my last pushup just as the sound of the cell block changed from the normal jailhouse chatter to a hushed whisper. This could only mean one thing: there were more than the usual number of corrections officers, or *screws*, as we inmates called them, on the floor. Within seconds of this observation, two of my most trusted associates, Brother Muhammad and Brother Jules, were posted outside my cell.

"Jefferson and Nugent are headed our way, Xavier," Brother Muhammad said without moving from his post.

"It's cool. I've been expecting them," I replied.

I stood up and adjusted my kufi then whistled at Lenny and Squiggy, my two pet rats, who scrambled up my arm and onto my shoulders. I'd raised them from babies after I killed their mother for chewing into a pack of Oodles of Noodles I'd stashed in my cell. There was only one thing in the world I cared about more than those two rats, and that was my wife Sonya—who, unfortunately, didn't seem to share the same feelings for me anymore.

As I fed Lenny and Squiggy peanuts, two white-shirt screws, Sergeant Jefferson and Captain Nugent, stepped in front of my cell. They might have been employed by the state, but both of them were on my payroll as well, and occasionally did a job or two on the outside when the price was right. Jefferson, a brother, stepped in my cell and almost killed himself tripping over Nugent to get out when he saw Lenny and Squiggy perched on my shoulders.

"Jesus Christ. What the hell are those things doing in there?" he asked once he was safely back outside.

"What's wrong, Jefferson? You don't like rats?" Nugent laughed as he walked into my cell. Unlike his darker counterpart, he didn't seem to have a fear of my pets.

"Fuck no. If it wasn't for the money he's paying, I'd have those nasty motherfuckers exterminated. If you don't mind, X, I'll stay right here."

"Suit yourself," I replied.

Unlike his partner, Nugent was always careful not to implicate himself in anything illegal, so he spoke in a low tone, making sure that only he and I could hear what he was saying. "The Italians just got word that their little problems in Attica and Rahway were taken care of. They send their thanks."

"Tell them that prompt payment is thanks enough."

Nugent nodded then made his way out of my cell. A few seconds later, Jefferson poked his head back in and said loud enough for the entire tier to hear, "Hey, X, I need you on a work detail over by Cell Block C. Deputy Warden Martinez said I can buy you some KFC if you finish it today. What do you say?"

I smiled. "Long as it ain't swine, I'm down."

Five minutes later, Jefferson and I, minus Nugent, were walking down the main corridor of my cell block. Jefferson was keeping his distance because I had Lenny and Squiggy hidden in my orange coverall pockets. That didn't stop him from talking, though.

"X, man, what the hell would make you wanna mess with nasty-ass rats?" Jefferson asked.

I wanted to stab him in the neck with the shank I was hiding for talking about Lenny and Squiggy like that, but I also knew I needed his diarrhea-of-the-mouth self, so I kept it lighthearted. "They wouldn't let me have a dog," I replied.

Jefferson laughed, continuing to talk about nothing as we turned down another corridor and walked until we had no choice but to stop at a gate. I'd never seen this part of the prison, but I had no doubt he was taking me to where I needed to be.

"On the gate!" he yelled, smiling at the female screw behind the glass. She pushed a button, triggering a loud buzzing sound, and then the gate opened. We'd already gone through five similar gates, and not one screw even raised an eyebrow. This was the power of the white shirt, and the reason why I paid fools like Jefferson and Nugent so much. Guys like them gave me and the brothers carte blanche to move freely throughout the prison to do our jobs.

Twenty feet after the gate, we went through a door that led outside to a long, barbed-wired path, which led to another building. I stopped and let the sun touch my face. Something I had always taken for granted when I was outside in the world was now considered a luxury.

Halfway down the path, Jefferson, who had somehow retrieved a rake on his way out of the building, interrupted my thoughts and started talking again. I swear that dude loved to hear the sound of his own voice.

"X, when we get around that building, I want you to take this rake and start cleaning up the leaves. It's a blind spot in the camera network, so the only people who will be able to see you are me and the other COs on the yard and in the tower. He should be around here in about twenty minutes, so I'll keep them occupied. When that time comes, I'm sure I don't have to tell you what to do."

I nodded in confirmation as he escorted me to the spot where I would be raking.

After five minutes, Jefferson wandered off to talk to some other screws on the other side of the small street, so I let Lenny and Squiggy out to play in a pile of leaves. As I raked, my thoughts wandered to Sonya. I still couldn't believe she was having an affair. I wasn't one to explore my emotions—hell, some people might say I didn't have any emotions—but every time I thought of Sonya with another man, I became overcome with an intense jealousy.

"Motherfucker, I want my fifty dollars!" I turned around at the sound of a fight starting. This was nothing new. In prison, dudes fight every damn day. What made it different this time was that it was two COs who were beefing. Jefferson was pointing a finger at another white-shirt screw who was almost half his size. He was yelling loudly enough for half the prison to hear him.

"Get your finger out my face. I don't owe you shit!" the pint-size screw yelled back.

I had to stifle a laugh when Jefferson pointed his finger and poked him in the nose. What happened next surprised me, and probably all the other screws, because no one would have expected the short screw to punch Jefferson in the face. A melee ensued, and every screw on the yard came running.

When Jefferson had told me he'd take care of the screws, he wasn't playing. I whistled at Lenny and Squiggy, scooping them up. Less than a minute later, I spotted him coming my way, and my heart rate sped up, my body tensed, and my palms became sweaty. This was the moment I'd been waiting for. I glanced over at the screws, who weren't paying any attention to me or him as they tried to break up the fight.

When I looked back, he was less than twenty feet away. I tensed, tightening the grip around my shank, ready to spring into action. This was do or die time. I was on a mission, and I wasn't going to let anyone stop me from accomplishing my goal.

"Get in and bring the rake," he ordered when he was in front of me. He had parked the prison van to block the view of both the tower and the COs.

"I have to admit, Nugent, I didn't think you had the balls to pull it off." I jumped in the van and hid behind the seat. He threw a blanket at me, and I covered myself.

"I didn't, but you gave me half a million reasons to grow a pair." He chuckled as the van moved toward the gate. Next stop for me: a visit to my wife and Junior Duncan.

Chippy
6

Even as I listened to LC fill Paris, Sasha, and Rio in on the Brother Xavier debacle, I felt like I could finally breathe again. For the first time since Junior told us about Sonya being married, I had my entire family safely under the same roof. As a mother, nothing was more important to me, especially after Vegas informed us that our situation with Xavier was far worse than we'd expected. In spite of the fact that Minister Farah was a high-ranking member of the Nation of Islam and a mentor to Vegas, it turned out that there was little he could do to help us other than make a few pointed phone calls. For all intents and purposes, we were now on the verge of war with a lovesick Islamic radical who had an army of well-trained Black Muslim hit men at his disposal.

As LC spoke, I felt a pair of strong hands massage my shoulders. I turned, smiling at Orlando, my middle child and our company's CEO. He leaned down and kissed me. My momentary calm was interrupted as Harris stomped into the room with a scowl. Not that it should have worried me. As legal counsel and the only immediate family member who wasn't born a Duncan, Harris always seemed to have the weight of the world on his shoulders. Today was no different, except his facial expression and body language told me that something was horribly wrong.

He motioned for Orlando to join him then headed across the room to LC. "We've got a big problem."

"What now, Harris?" I could hear the stress in LC's voice. This whole situation had him under a lot more pressure than he wanted to admit, and it was starting to show.

"I just got a call from one of my guys with the New York State Department of Corrections. Charles Brown, aka Brother X, escaped from prison four hours ago."

"What do you mean, he escaped? I thought we had people with eyes on this guy twenty-four/seven, Orlando?" LC turned to our son.

"We do, Pop," Orlando replied, maintaining his calm. "At least we're supposed to. I'll check with our people."

"You do that," LC demanded. "Harris, how reliable is your source?"

"Very. He's one of the deputy commissioners."

"Yeah, I'd say that was pretty reliable." My husband scanned the room, making eye contact with everyone present. He had their attention. "Okay, nobody leaves the compound without a bodyguard and my consent. And that especially means you, Paris. We're the hunted, not the hunters this time. I don't want anyone going off the reservation until we know what we are up against. Is that understood?"

LC locked his gaze on Paris until she nodded. "Yeah, I understand," she said, "but why don't you just let me and Sasha take his ass out? I don't like the bitch, but she does come in handy in a fight."

Sasha rolled her eyes as LC answered Paris. "Because killing him will only make him a martyr to his men. The last thing we need is for them to take up his cause. That would be even worse than blindly following his orders like they do now."

"He's right, Paris," Harris said. "But what I wanna know is where the hell is Junior? It'd be nice if we had our head of security to coordinate things, considering this is his mess."

"He drove Vegas and Marie to the airport about an hour ago, Daddy," Paris replied.

My heart sank as I realized that I did not, in fact, have all of my children safe at home with me. No one had even told me that Junior and Vegas were going out.

Apparently LC was not pleased either. "Rio, get Junior on the phone. I don't want him taking any detours on his way home," he said grimly.

"What is Vegas doing at the airport?" I was trying to stay quiet and listen, but I didn't like the direction things were going. With this man Xavier escaping from prison, I didn't have to be a rocket scientist to realize his next stop was to put a bullet in my son's head. This was not one of those times I was going to sit back and shut up.

"All I can tell you is that Marie was sporting a dope-ass DKNY sundress, Tory Burch sandals, and a fly-ass pair of Prada sunglasses, like she was going somewhere warm," Paris offered.

Sasha stood up and handed LC what looked like a postcard. "Uncle LC, Vegas said to give you this if you asked where he was. He said you'd understand."

LC glanced at the postcard then over at me. He hesitated for a moment before he said, "I need to speak to your mother alone for a second." His tone and facial expression told everyone in the room that he was not to be questioned right now. Still, that didn't stop them from protesting silently with frowns and worried glances. Orlando went so far as to open his mouth, but LC shut him down before he could get a word out. Orlando left reluctantly with the others.

When we were alone, LC walked over and sat on the arm of my chair then turned the postcard toward me. It took me a second, but I gasped when I realized what the picture of Israel meant. "Jesus Christ, is this for real?"

"Evidently Vegas thinks so," LC responded. "Otherwise he wouldn't have taken off."

"You do know this could be a trap. We should call the pilot and have him turn that plane around," I said desperately. I grabbed his arm, pleading with him to get my son out of harm's way, but he just sat there, stone-faced. "He's just come home, LC. I don't want him getting himself killed. I worked too hard and pulled too many strings to get him home in the first place—no thanks to you," I added bitterly.

"I know that, Charlotte," my husband countered. "But we both know we can't stop him. He'd never forgive us."

"Then let's send Sasha or Paris to back him up," I implored.

"I wish I could, but you know I can't. Not with this Brother X on the loose. We spread ourselves too thin and a man like him will pick us off one by one. With Vegas gone and Junior's head in the clouds, Sasha and Paris are our best offensive and defensive weapons. Have you forgotten the man has just escaped from a maximum security prison?"

"I haven't forgotten a damn thing. It's all I can think about," I snapped angrily. "I don't want any of my children hurt over this, LC."

"Neither do I, but this Brother X is not like the people we usually deal with. This isn't about money or power to him. This is a matter of principle. More importantly, it's a matter of the heart."

"What about the Russians or the Italians? Can't we go to them? They're the ones who employ the man, and we put a lot of money in their pockets."

"I already tried," he said. "All of our mutual friends and contacts say this is a matter amongst Blacks. They don't want to get involved. Frankly, I think they're just as concerned about Brother X and his army of killers as we are."

"You do know there's only one way to avert this, don't you?"

He shook his head. "I know what you're thinking, but I thought we decided—"

"No!" I cut him off, giving him a pointed look as I stood up. "*You* decided! I kept quiet because you said you and the boys would come up with a solution. Well, you don't have a solution, and I'm not keeping quiet anymore. I'm putting a stop to this craziness, whether you or anyone else likes it. I will not allow my family to be sitting ducks for this man."

He didn't bother to try to assert his authority over me. We'd been married long enough that he knew I meant every word I said. I would stop at nothing to ensure the safety of my family, regardless of what anyone said to try to talk me out of it.

"Have you even thought about the consequences of what you're suggesting?" he asked.

"Of course I have, and compared to the alternative, I'll take them every day." I turned toward the door.

"Charlotte! Charlotte!" He called after me as I left the room, but he didn't follow. He might not have liked it, but I was sure he knew, just like I did, that what I was about to do was our only way out without bloodshed.

I walked into the kitchen, where my oldest daughter, London, was preparing the last touches of dinner with Sonya. They turned in my direction when they heard me enter with a loud sigh. I'm sure they knew I was not a happy camper, but each kept to her task and remained silent.

"London, honey, could you give Sonya and me a minute, please?"

Sonya's eyes were pleading with London not to leave her alone with me, but my daughter was smart enough to know not to get in the middle of what was to come. She gave Sonya a sympathetic glance but turned to me and said, "Sure, Ma. These are the last plates for dinner anyway." She lifted the tray of steaks and headed for the door, leaving Sonya to face me without backup.

"I'm not going to pretend like I'm happy about anything I've heard the last few days. Now, I've done everything in my power to make you feel welcome, because I like you and I know you love my son and he loves you. Besides, I'll be the first to admit that we're not your average family, and it takes a very special person to be a part of it." I could see her relax ever so slightly, but I wasn't finished with her yet. "You could have told me that you were married," I snapped, stepping closer.

"Mrs. Duncan . . ." I didn't let her get more than a few words out before I shut her down. She was taken by surprise when I pushed her against the refrigerator, snatching up the knife London had been using and pointing it at her throat.

"Don't bother trying to explain," I hissed at her. "Now, you may not know this, but your husband has escaped from prison." Her eyes went wide with fear. "So I don't have the time or the patience for you to be sugar-coating shit." I pressed the blade against her throat.

As I saw tears welling in her eyes, part of me felt sorry for her. I really did like Sonya; however, she was the catalyst for a very dangerous situation, and all I cared about was protecting my son and family, even if it was at her expense. "I have some questions that need to be answered, and I need them answered now."

Her voice cracked with emotion as she asked, "What do you want to know?"

"Your husband, is he planning on killing my son? Is Junior in any real danger?"

Tears fell from her eyes. "Yes, I think so."

"What about the rest of my family? Are they in danger?"

I could see how much it pained her to admit the truth. "If any of you get in his way, he will kill you all. He's relentless when he puts his mind to something."

I lowered the knife, about to lay down the law, but she spoke up first. "I'm not going to put you or your family in danger, Mrs. Duncan."

"And how the hell do you suppose you can promise that?" I barked.

"I'm leaving Junior. I love your son too much to risk his life and the lives of everyone he loves. I couldn't live with myself if something happens to him or to any of you. I'm just going to need you to keep him away from me."

I laughed out loud at her naïveté. "You don't have to worry about that. I'll keep him away."

"I want you to know I love your son. I love him more than life itself."

I knew she meant it, but my family was in danger, and there was no time for sentimentality. "Well, then I'm sorry things didn't work out," I said curtly. "But you're making the right decision. I'm glad this didn't have to get any uglier than it already has. Can I call you a cab?"

Vegas

7

I got out of bed carefully, so as not to wake Marie. The last thing I wanted was for my girlfriend to start questioning me about where I was going. It had taken four good orgasms and a sleeping pill in her wine, but she'd finally fallen asleep. Being the boyfriend of a beautiful madam with an ultra-high sex drive was fun, but not an easy job. When it came to sex, Marie was more like a dude than any woman I'd ever met. She wanted it when she wanted it, and that seemed to be all the time. Since I'd been released from prison six months ago, we'd end up doing it two or three times a day—four, if I'd let her. Now, don't get me wrong. I was flattered that she loved the dick, and the pussy was outstanding, but there were other motives behind her trying to drain every drop out of me. Marie wanted to have my baby, and getting pregnant had become her top priority. Not that I was putting up any stop signs. I loved the idea of having a kid too.

I slipped on a black wife beater, pants, and sneakers, along with a white button-down shirt that I kept open, before heading out of the hotel room toward the elevator. It was quarter to one, which meant I only had four and a half hours of darkness left to accomplish my real mission in Saint Martin. I'd already spent two days more than I should have away from home. By now I was sure Sasha had given the old man the postcard Minister Farah had given to me. Pop hadn't blown up my phone or sent anyone down to stop me, so he must have approved of, or at least accepted, my plan of action.

I stepped off the elevator and was greeted by a very attractive, exotic-looking, short-haired sister behind the front desk. I'd caught her sneaking a peek a few times when I was with Marie over the past few days. Now that Marie wasn't with me, there was no shame to this woman's game. Her gaze followed me from my first step off the elevator, so I thought it only right that I returned the favor, locking eyes with her. By the time I reached the counter, the poor woman looked like she was about to melt.

"Good evening, Mr. Duncan. You're up rather late." She spoke in the heavy Caribbean accent that made my blood hot. "Can't sleep?"

"I've got a lot on my mind. Thought I'd put the top down and take a drive along the coast. It's a full moon tonight."

"It is. Too bad I don't get off for another hour, or I'd take that ride with you."

I chuckled. "I don't think my companion upstairs would appreciate that."

"Her name is not on the reservation. Yours is," she said, her voice dripping with sensuality. "The hotel management has made it very clear that you're a VIP on the presidential level, so my job is to make sure you have the best experience this resort can offer. And I'm very good at my job." She gave me a smile that could have tempted an angel. No beating around the bush for this Caribbean chocolate drop.

"Oh, I can only imagine. But I'm good for right now."

"Okay, then," she said, not hiding her disappointment. "How else can I help you tonight?"

"There should be a package down here for me." I handed her a luggage receipt.

She typed something into a computer then nodded. "Yes. Just give me a moment to retrieve it." As she turned and walked away, I couldn't help but follow her perfectly round ass as it went through the door. If I didn't have a woman like Marie upstairs, I would have loved to play in her playground.

A few minutes later, she returned with an oversized briefcase. "Is this what you were expecting?"

"That's it," I said, taking the case from her. "Thank you."

"You're welcome. My name is Kimberly. If there is anything I can do to help, just call." We both knew that she truly meant *anything*.

I walked out of the lobby and into the warm Caribbean night, headed toward my rental car, a black-on-black European edition BMW 650 convertible. Placing the briefcase on the passenger seat, I let the top down and pulled out into the night air. Not long after, I was crossing from the Dutch side of the island to the French side, headed to Orient Beach.

When I found a quiet place to park at the beach, I discarded my white button-down under the seat and scanned the area for the occasional late night dog walker, or perhaps a couple looking to get in a moonlit quickie on the beach.

With nobody in sight, I turned my attention to the briefcase, lifting it onto its spine. Running my fingers along the lock, I spun each wheel until I had the proper combination, then pushed the two buttons on either side of the briefcase. The locks clicked open, and I was soon staring down at my two guns, Bonnie and Clyde, which were securely placed in foam cutouts next to clips, cartridges, ammunition, and other accessories. Bonnie was a Smith and Wesson M&P 9mm, which I favored over the Glock 9mm, while Clyde was a .500 S&W Magnum, by far the most powerful commercially made handgun in the world.

At the top of the case, there was more ammo and a custom-made double shoulder holster, which I slipped on. I screwed a silencer onto Bonnie and snapped in a clip before placing her in my holster. I then reached for Clyde and snapped in a five-bullet cartridge before sliding the gun into my holster. There was no need to silence Clyde, because when I reached for him, I didn't care who heard me. The next five minutes was spent tucking clips, cartridges, and ammo into their various homes on the holster. Once all of that was done, I took a deep breath, feeling complete for the first time in years. It was now time to do what I did best. I stepped out of the car and slipped into the shadows of the warm Caribbean night.

Brother X
8

We'd finally stopped moving after nearly two hours. I wasn't sure if this stop was a good thing or not, because the driver had gotten out of the car and was talking to somebody. From my vantage point inside the trunk, I couldn't make out what they were saying. I remained hopeful, but I still tightened my grasp around the shank when I heard the trunk being unlocked.

After two days in a safe house in Albany, we had headed south toward New York City, switching vehicles at least four times. I knew this was the last time as soon as my eyes adjusted to the light and I recognized the man helping me out of the trunk.

"Elijah," I muttered, pulling him in for a brotherly hug. Elijah had been my friend and right hand man since I headed the FOI New York for the Nation. He was also more loyal than any other man I'd ever met and twice as deadly.

"As-Salaam-Alaikum, Xavier," he smiled, squeezing me.

"Wa-Alaikum-Salaam, my brother." He released me from our embrace. Looking past him, I noticed three cars and ten brothers standing with military precision thirty feet away.

"You've done well, my friend. What about my wife? Do we know where she's been?"

"Yes, she's been at home the past couple of days. Alone."

"Alone?" He nodded. "And what about this Junior Duncan?"

"He's been holed up at his family home in Far Rockaway."

"Interesting. Have you completed what I asked?"

"Everything is exactly as you instructed, except that the Jew wants to meet. I can debrief you in the car."

"Good." I patted him on the back then turned back to the trunk, whistling for my rats, who quickly came out of their hiding place.

I picked them up, giving each a kiss before I placed them in my pockets and followed Elijah toward the car.

"X! Yo, X!" I turned in the direction of the familiar voice.

It was Jefferson, who was leaning against the car, wearing civilian clothes. Nugent was sitting on the hood, arms folded, his eyes hidden behind aviator sunglasses. In my exuberance over being with my men, I'd practically forgotten about these two.

"Well, X, you're free," Jefferson stated. "So you know what that means . . ." His broad smile revealed every last one of his teeth.

He turned his attention to Elijah. "Cash on delivery. That was our deal, right?"

Elijah stared at him blankly, but I had to give credit where credit was due. They'd planned and executed something I honestly didn't think they could pull off. I said to Elijah, "You got their money?"

He nodded, waving over Samuel and Adam, two of our men who were posted closest to us. Each man was carrying a green duffle bag. Samuel handed a bag to me, and I opened it, pulling out a thick stack of money for all to see.

"As promised, half a million dollars each." I put the money back in and tossed the first bag to Nugent, who caught it on the fly. He opened the bag, showing Jefferson the contents with a smile.

"Hey, what about me?" Jefferson rubbed his hands together greedily.

"Don't worry, Jefferson. I got yours here too." I turned to Adam, who handed me the bag he was holding. I tossed the bag to Jefferson, who unzipped it and pulled out a thick wad of cash.

"Now, that's what I'm talking about." Jefferson's greedy ass started doing the happy dance.

The distinctive sound of rounds being chambered stopped Jefferson's dancing. He and Nugent looked up to see Samuel and Adam pointing their firearms at the two screws.

"Motherfucker, you got to be kidding me, X!" Jefferson shouted. "Are those guns?"

"First of all, my name isn't X," I stated for clarity. I glanced at the 9mm pistols Samuel and Adam were pointing at them. "Secondly, yeah, they look like guns. What do you think, Elijah? They look like guns to you?"

Elijah nodded. "Definitely guns."

"What's going on here, Xavier?" Nugent dropped the bag and raised his hands. There was no question about it; he was scared, but he remained cool as a cucumber. "We've done a lot to help you and your people, including putting our livelihoods on the line helping you escape. All we want is our money and to go home. I thought we were all friends here."

"Friends," I replied. "I don't think so. I like to think of us as business associates whose association has come to a conclusion. And for the record, I really appreciate all the hard work you've done for the cause, especially breaking me out. Regrettably, you know entirely too much about me and my organization, and your partner talks entirely too much. Eventually someone's going to figure out your involvement in my escape. So your services are no longer required." On that note, Elijah and I turned toward the cars.

"X, you son of a bitch! You're not going to get away with—"

Bam! Bam! Bam!

I never looked back, but I can assure you those were the last words Jefferson ever spoke.

Vegas

9

Twenty minutes after I left my car, I stepped out of a wooded stretch of land and was met by the fence that surrounded an expensive gated condo complex. I hopped the fence, staying in the shadows as I made my way toward the buildings. Earlier in the day, Marie and I had visited the place as prospective buyers. Of course, she had no idea I was really scouting the place out for tonight's business, but as the realtor took us around the property, I was able to get the lay of the land, so I knew exactly which condo unit I was headed to now.

I crept my way around back, climbing up the trellis onto the balcony with Bonnie in hand. It was dark inside the condo, and if I was lucky the occupants were asleep, but that didn't mean they were to be taken lightly by any means. I took a moment to catch my breath and evaluate the situation, and then I placed Bonnie back in her holster and pulled out a small tool kit, which allowed me to pick the lock on the sliding glass door in a matter of seconds.

Opening the door just wide enough to slip inside, I simultaneously reached for Bonnie. Inside, I remained motionless for a good sixty seconds, letting my eyes adjust to the darkness of the room as I tried to ascertain if I'd alerted the occupants to my presence. So far, so good, but I could hear the sound of a television and some snoring off to my right in another room, which meant I definitely wasn't alone. I would go check on the identity of the sleeping person in a while, but I wanted to gather some information first.

I made my way over to a desk in the corner, confident there'd be some sign of what I was looking for amid the contents of the makeshift home office. I scanned the top of the desk the best I could in the dark. There was nothing telling, just some bills for a Mr. Curt Bunn. The name didn't ring a bell, so I moved on to the laptop. I wanted to turn it on, but the light and the sound may have woken my snoring friend. Pulling out the desk drawer, I discovered a nine millimeter handgun very similar to Bonnie, but without the silencer. Just as I reached out for it, I heard the unmistakable sound of a round being chambered in a gun, followed by the sensation of cold steel on the back of my neck. How the fuck I could have let someone sneak up on me, I don't know.

"I'd put both of those down if I were you." It was a determined male voice, and he was whispering as if he didn't want to wake the person in the other room.

I did as I was told, letting go of the gun in the drawer and slowly placing Bonnie down on the desk.

"Where I come from, people get killed for shit like this—without even giving it a thought. So consider yourself lucky that I haven't plastered you brains all over my brand new desk." He pressed the gun firmly against my neck for emphasis. "Now, you damn sure better have a good reason for being here."

I stared off into the dark, speaking to my unseen enemy. "I'm here to find out if the rumor is true."

"Rumor?" he whispered. "Most people don't go breaking into houses looking for rumors."

"The rumor is that Daryl Graham, who supposedly died in a fire back in New York, is really alive. You wouldn't know anything about that, would you?"

There was a slight pause before he answered in a slightly louder voice, "No, I wouldn't. As you can see from the paperwork you were snooping around in, my name is Curt Bunn."

A smile spread across my face as I turned around slowly, looking into the face of the man with the gun. "Curt Bunn, huh? Well, you sure as hell look a lot like Daryl Graham, Curt."

"Then this Daryl Graham must be one hell of a handsome motherfucker, Vegas." Lowering the gun he had been aiming at me, my best friend since I was six years old spread his arms wide to give me a brotherly hug.

"Man, Daryl, it's good to see you, brother. I missed you," I said, getting a little misty-eyed.

"It's good to see you too, V." Daryl was just as choked up as I was. "I missed you more."

"You know, you really had me fucked up when I heard you were dead. I was crying and the whole nine."

He broke the hug. "Sorry about that, man, but it was important that people thought I was dead."

I didn't press for details, because I knew Daryl well enough to understand that just like mine, his life was complicated, and sometimes things were on a need-to-know basis. If and when he wanted to tell me the full story, I was sure he would.

Daryl and I had met in elementary school. It was a school that someone with Daryl's address shouldn't have been attending, but his mom, who was a maid, wanted so much more than his local public school could provide. So, she secretly enrolled Daryl into one of the better suburban schools using the address of one of her employers. She wanted Daryl to rub elbows with kids from a different socioeconomic class. One of those kids just happened to be me, and from the moment we met in Mrs. Moran's first grade class, we were pretty much inseparable.

Pop had taken such a liking to my new playmate that when the school system busted his mom for faking their residence and kicked him out, Pop took it upon himself to find her a place in the district. He later paid for Daryl to study abroad at Chi's Male Academy with me. He then hired Daryl as the family's troubleshooter when we graduated. It was a job that he excelled at, until this chick Crystal aborted his baby. He kind of went off the deep end emotionally for a while, and decided to go out on his own. Unfortunately, it didn't take him long to get himself hemmed up in some trouble and land in the city lockup. By the time he got out, I'd been sent away for a while myself, so Daryl and I hadn't seen each other in a long time.

"I knew you'd understand my postcard," Daryl said. I looked down at the Star of David he wore around his neck and had to laugh. Daryl was a Black Hebrew Israelite, or, for lack of a better word, a Black Jew. In Chi's school, his code name was Israel, and mine was Nevada. That's why, when I received the postcard with the photo of Israel on the front, I knew it was him—or a death trap. I sure was glad it turned out not to be the latter.

I tucked Bonnie back down into my holster. "Man, I can't believe you're alive."

He clicked on the low wattage lamp on the desk. "And I can't believe you're out of jail," he said, shaking his head. We stood there for a minute, grinning at each other like two long lost brothers finally reunited.

"This is a cause for a celebration." He walked over to the mini bar, grabbed two glasses and a bottle.

"Hennessey," I said as I watched him pour his favorite drink. "You always did like this ghetto shit."

"You know it." He turned around with a glass in each hand. "Sit." He nodded toward the small couch. I walked over and took a seat, while he sat across from me in a chair.

In spite of the time that had passed since we last saw each other, Daryl and I were close enough that I knew I didn't have to bother with formalities. I skipped all small talk and got right to my point.

"Dee, I really need your help. My family needs your help."

He raised an eyebrow as he downed another sip of Hennessey. "What kind of help? What's going on, man?"

"You ever heard of a dude named Brother X?"

Daryl almost choked on his drink, which confirmed much of what I'd already suspected about the man we were up against.

"Yeah, I've heard of him," Daryl said. "He's one bad- ass dude with a lot of bad-ass dudes behind him. Y'all aren't doing business with him, are you? This bastard ain't nobody to play with." He placed his empty glass on the table and poured himself a refill.

"Then you can imagine how he's reacting to Junior screwing his wife." I gulped down the last of my drink.

"Screwing his wife?" Daryl shouted, then glanced over toward the bedroom door and lowered his voice. "Damn, never a dull moment with the Duncans."

"Tell me about it," I replied in frustration. "So you can see why I need you to come back."

Without taking even a moment to think about it, Daryl shook his head. "I wish I could, bro. I really do. You know I'd do anything for the fam, but—"

"Honey? Is everything okay?" A female voice came from the bedroom.

We both turned toward the sound, and I saw the silhouette of a woman standing in the doorway, bathed in the glow of light from the television that was now turned on in there.

"Everything's fine, baby. Come over here. I want you to meet somebody," Daryl said.

The woman who walked into the room and placed a hand on Daryl's shoulder was thin and frail. She looked to be about sixty years old. If I didn't already know his mom, I would have guessed that this lady was Daryl's mother.

"Vegas Duncan, I'd like you to meet my wife, Connie."

It took a lot of effort to conceal the shock of hearing that my boy was married to this little old lady. Back in the day, Daryl could get pretty much any chick he wanted, and he usually went for the hottest ones around. This woman was a far cry from that.

"Nice to meet you Vegas, I've heard so much—" The woman started a coughing fit that I watched Daryl coax her through with more love than I'd given him credit for. I was honestly impressed and more than a little surprised.

"It's nice to meet you too, Connie," I said, taking her frail hand when she stopped coughing.

"Well, I'm going to leave you boys to talk." She kissed Daryl's forehead. "Love you. Don't stay up too late."

"Love you too," Daryl said. "And please make sure you turn the oxygen on, babe."

Even after she closed the bedroom door, I could still hear the sickly woman coughing. My uneasiness must have been written on my face, because Daryl came to her defense in a hurry.

"Don't judge her. I love her."

"Enough to marry her?"

"Yeah, can you believe it?"

"Honestly," I said, "I can't."

A deep sadness passed over him. "She's got cancer, Vegas. She only has a short time to live, and I'm going to be here for her, no matter what. Which is why I was about to tell you that I can't come back."

I pressed a little harder, not wanting to accept his decision as final. It may sound cold, considering how sick his wife was, but my family was in dire circumstances. "Dee, please. The family needs you. I need you, bro."

"I'm sorry. She's been too good to me. She's been there for me when I needed her most. You know you and the family mean the world to me. I owe you all more than I could ever repay you in a lifetime, but I won't abandon her, man. She's my family too."

I have to say I was a little disappointed in Daryl. As tight as we had been, and as much as my father had done for him over the years, I never would have expected him to say no when I came looking for him. But I saw that he wasn't going to change his mind. Daryl had family of his own now, and he needed to tend to her. I decided to let things rest—at least for now.

Sonya

10

You know, I never used to understand people who talked about committing suicide. I just couldn't wrap my head around the idea that anything could be so bad you'd want to take your own life. Well, that had changed, because in the past few days I'd come to the conclusion that without Junior, life just wasn't worth living anymore. There is something so brutal about having that kind of love and losing it; it's almost better to never have had it at all. What made it even worse was that I knew he still loved me as much as I loved him. If he'd abandoned me or left me for another woman, I could have wallowed in my anger. Instead, I had left him. Not that I'd been given a choice, with Xavier threatening to kill him and his entire family. So, I'd been seriously considering taking my life to get this intense pain over with.

I didn't want to go out bloody or suffer in any way, so this morning I'd laid out a bottle of sleeping pills next to my favorite bottle of wine. I figured it wouldn't be that hard; all I had to do was take a couple of handfuls of pills, chase them down with wine, and then go to sleep and never wake up again. In all honesty, the only thing holding me back was the fact that my death wouldn't guarantee the safety of Junior or his family. Xavier hated losing anything that he considered his property, and it would be just like him to try to make Junior pay for my final choice. He'd never consider that he was the one to drive me to take my life by keeping me away from the man I loved. No, that would never enter his mind because that would mean he was at fault, and he had too much of a God complex to ever admit he was wrong about something.

I walked wearily over to the table and poured myself a drink as my phone started to ring. I stared at it, wanting to pick it up because I knew it was Junior. He'd been calling constantly ever since I left his house, but I hadn't answered any of his calls. I couldn't. Whenever I felt myself growing weak, I recalled the image of his mother's desperate face as she held that knife to my throat, and I let it ring. I did not want to have to face that woman again and explain to her that I couldn't stay away from her son, even though I had promised to never go near him again. I couldn't risk it, knowing what Xavier would do to that family. In the years since my husband had gone to prison, he'd become far more dangerous than he'd ever been before, and the types of people he dealt with would do anything for him, including wipe out an entire family if he asked.

I sipped my wine, making my way over to the living room window to peek out. The blue sedan was still parked across the street with someone sitting in the driver's seat. I didn't know if they were staking me out in shifts or what, but that car hadn't been moved since I came home from the Duncan estate three nights ago. They weren't even trying to hide their presence from me. No, like everything else, Xavier was trying to send me a message, letting me know I was a prisoner in my own home.

"I'm not going to let you win, Xavier," I said out loud, finishing off my wine then heading to the bathroom to take a much-needed shower. In the three days since I'd returned from Junior's, I hadn't showered or slept, and I had barely eaten. I'd called my job and taken a leave of absence, because the last thing I could imagine was taking care of anyone else right now. As a nurse, I was accustomed to being the calm in the storm, but if I walked into that hospital in my current state, my boss would probably try to admit me into the psych ward.

The shower helped to revive me enough that when I emerged from the bathroom a while later wearing the tightest, most revealing dress I owned and plenty of makeup, I felt a new determination. Everything about my attire was chosen to be a gigantic "fuck you," and for a second it actually made me laugh. On my way to the front door, I stopped and scooped up the bottle of pills from the table. I wasn't a hundred percent sure how this was going to go down, but if I had to die tonight, then so be it. I planned on making sure Xavier would witness it firsthand.

I stepped out into the night and sashayed across the street so that the driver of the blue sedan could see my every move. When I reached the sidewalk, I surprised him by approaching the car, opening the passenger side door, and sliding in next to him.

"Take me to your boss," I demanded. The poor kid couldn't have been more than twenty-two, and he looked like he was about to shit his pants.

"Ma'am, I have to call and see if it's okay," he mumbled.

"Then make the call. I don't have all day," I said, sitting casually back in my seat.

A half hour later, I was being led down a long, echoing corridor with a dark sack over my head. My guide stopped to open a door, and my knees almost gave out when I heard Xavier's voice. I still wanted to confront him, but the reality of being around him with no prison guards in this unfamiliar place was starting to take its toll on me.

"Sit," someone said, forcing me into a chair and then taking off my mask.

"Hello, my beautiful wife. Nice of you to come." Xavier smiled at me, and I swear I saw the devil in his eyes. "What was so urgent you had to see me?"

"I've ended my relationship with Junior Duncan, so you can call off your dogs. I won't be seeing him again."

"Is that so?" I could tell from his tone that he didn't believe me. I shouldn't have been surprised, because aside from Junior, Xavier knew me better than anyone. He knew how much I loved Junior, and I wasn't one to give up on the people I loved. Hell, look how long it had taken me to come to my senses about Xavier, as bad as he was.

I opened my purse, and I guess the quickness of my movement caught him off guard. He jumped, and the next thing I knew, his hand was clamped down on my purse, grabbing it out of my hands.

"What is wrong with you?" I screamed at him.

The door flew open, and two gun-wielding men dressed in black stood in the entryway.

"It's all right. Just domestics." He waved them out.

"So you thought I was here to kill you?" I laughed. "Then that means your men didn't do their job of patting me down properly."

"My men would never put their hands on my wife." His voice was full of simmering rage. He smashed the contents in my purse between his fists, and I guess that was enough to satisfy him that I wasn't carrying a weapon in there. He handed it back to me.

"Don't worry, Xavier. I didn't come here to kill you." I opened my purse and pulled out the bottle of pills. "In fact, I don't want to be here at all."

"What is that?"

"Sleeping pills. I kept thinking that I could be done with you . . . by any means necessary," I said, using a phrase I'd heard him use a million times.

"No! You will not kill yourself. It is not the way of Allah." He reached over and snatched the pills out of my hand. "You will not get these back," he said, as if that was the last word on the subject.

I shook my head. "You forgot what I do for a living. I have access to pills, as many as I need, but you know what?" He narrowed his eyes in anger, and I knew it meant he felt his control of me slipping away. "It doesn't have to be this way. You want me not to kill myself? Then leave Junior—and me—alone. I have left the man who I love, and that needs to be enough. Do you understand that?" Looking into the eyes of my unpredictable, psychotic husband, I could only hope that my threatened suicide would be enough to keep him away from Junior and his family.

Brother X

11

"I want to know every move Junior Duncan makes," I demanded of Elijah the second Sonya walked out the door. "I don't believe for one minute that he's going to give her up. Or that she's going to give him up, for that matter."

"You may be right," Elijah replied. "But from what we can tell, he hasn't left the house in days."

"Well, keep an eye on him."

Elijah frowned. "Actually, I had to move our people off the surveillance of the Duncan compound this morning."

"Why?" I snapped.

"They hired a private security force. They've got cars and dogs patrolling the interior and exterior of the property, and Muhammad spotted them installing infrared and heat-monitoring cameras. These people are way more sophisticated than anyone we've ever dealt with."

Every muscle in my body tensed up. "Stop making excuses, Elijah, and get the job done."

"I'm not making excuses. I'm just informing you that we need more time. This is not some prison hit or some random guy off the street you have us stalking. These people are millionaires with all kinds of resources, and we've lost the element of surprise."

"I don't care! I want Junior Duncan dead by the end of the week. It's the only way she's coming back to me." My voice lost its power as I referenced Sonya, my one weak spot.

Samuel entered the room and whispered something to Elijah, who then turned to me with a look of displeasure. "The Jew is here."

"What does he want?"

Elijah shrugged. "I don't know, but it must be important. As you can see, he tracked you down, and he's not taking no for answer."

"Okay, Brother Samuel, send him in." I gestured to Elijah to take a seat. "This should be interesting."

A few moments later, eighty-year-old Bernie Goldman and two rather tough-looking Jewish men in yarmulkes entered the room. Bernie was a frail, dark-suited Hassidic Jew adorned with the standard hat, long beard, and curled sideburns.

"Xavier, it's good to see you among free men," he said, his Yiddish accent as strong as ever. He took the seat directly across from me, and his two bodyguards positioned themselves behind him like pillars.

"You've come a long way, Bernie. To what do I owe the pleasure?"

"You know we do not like to get into your personal business; however, it has come to our attention that you're planning on killing a man by the name of Junior Duncan."

Bernie claimed not to like getting into my personal business, but he damn sure made it his business to know what any one of his associates was up to at all times. Hell, he hadn't become as powerful as he was for no reason. Knowledge was power. For that reason, I wasn't tripping over the fact that he knew what was up.

"You can already consider him dead," I said nonchalantly.

Bernie erupted in a coughing fit, and one of the bodyguards patted him on the back. It took the old man a minute to stop coughing and catch his breath before he spoke again. "I think that would be unwise."

"Who are you to tell us what to do? We don't take orders from no Jews." Elijah flexed his muscles, challenging Bernie's bodyguards to make a move. He hated white people more than anybody I'd ever met, but more than anything, he hated Jews.

Bernie sat back in his chair calmly, dusting off his hat before addressing Elijah like he was a child. "If you don't know who I am and who I represent by now, young man, then perhaps it's time you replace Xavier in prison and find out. I can have that arranged for you by week's end if you'd like." Elijah's face went blank and Bernie, satisfied, turned to speak to me.

"I know this situation with your wife is important to you, but our mutual friend is concerned about what a war with LC Duncan will do to what we have built."

His comment had me confused, and Elijah said what I was thinking. "LC Duncan is a car salesman. He's no threat to us."

Without glancing at Elijah, Bernie leaned forward and said to me, "LC Duncan wants you to think he's a car salesman, but if you kill his son, you will see that he is much, much more."

"What are you saying?" I asked, pissed off and a little embarrassed that I had badly misjudged this situation. "Are you trying to tell me the Duncans are connected?"

Bernie shot a dismissive glance in Elijah's direction. "I'm saying that for a very smart man, you allowed your right hand to make two crucial mistakes. Number one, he should have spoken to us first. We would have told him—and you—who the Duncans are. Two, if you were going to kill Junior Duncan, you should have just done it and not let him or his family know you were coming. Your arrogance in this matter has exposed you and us immensely. Now they've had time to prepare."

"So if they aren't just a bunch of nigga-rich car dealers, then who are they?"

He paused, looking up toward the ceiling as if he would find the right words to describe them up there. "How about the most respected drug distributors on the East Coast? They have ties to the Italians, Russians, Mexicans, Dominicans, and Asians, as well as with me and my people. And you should know that they've reached out to all of their allies about their recent problem with you and your organization."

I glanced over at Elijah, who was avoiding eye contact at the moment. Bernie was right; he should have known who the Duncans were. I would deal with that mistake later. For now, I had to learn all I could about what I was up against.

"And what has been the response from his allies?"

"Nobody wants a war. It's not good for business. Most of them have decided to stay on the sidelines for now, but if they had to choose sides, I don't think you would fare well. You provide a necessary service, but the Duncans are a cash cow that makes us all a great deal of money. Although . . . I'm sure many of them wouldn't mind seeing the Blacks kill each other off so they can pick up the scraps, if you know what I mean."

I knew exactly what he meant, but it didn't change the fact that I was going to kill Junior Duncan. "And you? What do you and your people want?"

"That is an interesting question. To be quite frank, we want what you want, but we want you to do it smart."

"I'm listening."

"You want to kill Junior. Well, we're suggesting you make life easier for yourself—and us—by eliminating his father first."

"You want us to kill LC Duncan?"

Bernie leaned back smugly in his chair. "Who are we to tell you anything, Xavier? You've always been your own man. Still, logic dictates that if you cut off the head, it's much easier to kill the rest of the snake."

I shook my head. "Bernie, you are one cold piece of work. Here I am thinking you've come to stop me from killing Junior, and instead you tell me to kill his whole family." We laughed together briefly, but I cut it short, announcing, "It's gonna cost you one million dollars."

"Huh. A million dollars for what?" He sat up, looking pained at the thought.

I explained my price, though he knew damn well what the million was for. "A million dollars to kill LC Duncan."

"This is your problem, not ours."

Elijah noticeably stiffened, and I can't say I blamed him. It was taking everything in me not to go off on this old Jew for insulting me this way. If Bernie was anyone less powerful I might have snapped his neck on the spot. Given his position of power, though, I kept my temper in check as best I could.

"I don't understand why you think I'm so stupid, Bernie," I said through gritted teeth. "You didn't come here to give me advice. You came here because you want us to do your dirty work—and I'm telling you it's going to cost you one million dollars. I'll throw in the rest of LC's sons, especially that homewrecker Junior, for free. But I want a million dollars to take out LC."

Bernie bit down on his lip. To be honest, I didn't think his cheap ass would go for it. He looked like he was in actual pain when he finally said, "Fine, we'll pay one million dollars, but I must have your assurances that nobody will know me or any of my people gave the order. And I mean nobody."

"We don't talk about our clients or the jobs we do for them. You know that."

"Just make sure you kill the one they call Vegas too. Otherwise we'll all have to sleep with one eye open. He's a very dangerous man." Bernie got up from his chair with a little help from one of his bodyguards. "Let me know when the job is done."

I nodded. "So before you leave, you wanna tell me why you want the old man dead?"

Bernie turned to me with an annoyed expression. "For a million dollars, I don't think I should have to tell you shit. Just get the job done, Xavier."

I watched Bernie and his goons head out the door.

"What, Elijah?" I asked. I couldn't see his face, but I could feel his gaze.

"I don't trust him," Elijah replied.

I turned to face him. "Neither do I, my friend. He's hiding something, I just don't know what it is yet."

"You want me to look into it?"

"No. I'll deal with Bernie Goldman. You go speak to our people on the street. I want to know everything there is to know about LC Duncan and his family." I grabbed his arm. "And this time, Elijah, I want to know *everything* there is to know about the Duncans—both legal and illegal."

Paris

12

Bam! Bam! Bam!

As I descended the basement stairs I could hear the distinct sound of a .38 being fired, and I knew exactly who was shooting before my feet hit the ground. I touched the cold steel of my nine, heading toward the gunfire. I probably should have gone back upstairs to get Sasha, but it had been a long time since I'd had an opportunity like this, and I wasn't about to let her outshine me.

Bam! Bam! Bam!

As I turned the corner, I watched my father take aim and then place three rounds dead center. LC Duncan wasn't one to go into the field anymore, but he was no joke with that .38 he always carried. I slipped in beside him, taking out the target next to his with three rounds of my own.

Bam! Bam! Bam!

He glanced over at me and smiled. We used to do this type of thing down in our basement shooting range all the time, before my son Jordan was born and I was still considered his baby girl. You can't even imagine how much I loved my daddy.

He took off his protective ear covers.

"What you doing down here shooting, Daddy?" I asked.

"With everything going on, I figured I better make sure I keep my skills sharp. You never know."

"True that," I replied. "Orlando said you wanted to see me?"

"Yeah, where's Sasha? I wanted to see you both."

"She'll be down in a minute."

"Good. That'll give us a little time to talk." He put his headphones back on and started to shoot, taking out his target's head.

Bam! Bam! Bam!

"Talk about what?" I asked, though I wasn't sure if he'd heard me through the gunfire.

Lowering his gun, he turned to me and pulled the ear covers behind his head. "I'm worried about you, Paris."

"Why? What'd I do now? I got my shit together." He shot me a disapproving look. "I mean, I got my *stuff* together. I'm taking care of Jordan, being responsible, doing my job."

He placed an arm around me. "I know that, but you don't have to do anything for me to be worried, little girl." I loved it when he called me his little girl. "Sometimes a father just worries."

"You really worried about this mess with Junior, aren't you?"

"Yeah, but not in the same way I'm worried about you."

I looked at him, confused. "Huh?"

"Rio told me what LaSalle said about Niles," he said.

Just the mention of Niles' name still caused my stomach to flip, but I couldn't let Daddy know that. "Fuck LaSalle," I shot back. "Niles is dead. I killed him myself, Daddy. Just like I killed LaSalle's fat, lying ass." Suddenly, I was on the verge of tears, and I wasn't doing a very good job of hiding it. Daddy pulled me in close, wrapping his arms around me.

"It's okay, little girl. Let it out. I know how you felt about him. I'm sorry it had to come to that."

Usually I prided myself on being one ultra-tough bitch, but it felt good to be held in my daddy's strong arms for a minute, just like I was a little girl again. I pulled back in a hurry, though, when I heard footsteps approaching and then my brother's voice as he came into the room.

"I just got word that Vegas's plane landed, Pop. Oh, and you were right. Junior's gone," Orlando said. He glanced in my direction, but if he had noticed me wiping away the last of my tears, he didn't react.

My father's face was grim.

"Where the fuck did Junior go?" I asked, not happy that I'd been kept out of the loop.

"Where do you think?" Orlando said.

I shook my head in disbelief. I knew Junior was head over heels for this chick Sonya, but I couldn't believe he'd be stupid enough to go see her when she was the cause of all this drama in the first place.

"That bitch gets my brother killed and there won't be a rock she can hide under," I seethed.

"Calm down, baby girl," Daddy said. "It's not just her. I told your mother that Junior wasn't going to give her up, and he's certainly not going to get over her right away."

I couldn't believe that he was taking this all so lightly. Daddy was acting like he'd been expecting Junior to go to her all along, while I was ready to go find him and smack the shit out of him for being so stupid. Then again, I was always the hotheaded one in the family.

"What do you want us to do, Pop?" Orlando prodded, staying much calmer than I was.

"Where's Sasha?" he asked.

"Here I am, Uncle LC." We turned to see her coming down the stairs.

Daddy looked at her and then at me. "I've got something I want you two to do."

I preferred to work solo, so I wasn't necessarily thrilled about being sent on a mission with my cousin. Still, if it meant getting the hell off the compound, I was down. "Sure, Daddy. Just point me in the direction of whoever I've got to kill," I said, only half joking.

He ignored my attempt at humor and said, "With Vegas back we have a little more room to maneuver. Orlando, you and me are going to the office for a meeting. Paris, you and Sasha—"

"I know. You want us to find Junior."

"No, I'll send Kennedy and Rio to do that on their way to the airport to pick up Vegas. I want you two to find Brother X—and do it subtly. I know he's somewhere in New York. Concentrate first here in Queens, then in Long Island and Brooklyn. Orlando will get you copies of all the information we have on him. Be careful, and read the file."

"What do you want us to do with the body?" I jumped in, itching to handle my business.

He glared at me sternly. "I didn't say I wanted you to kill him. I just want you to find him before he finds Junior."

"Don't worry, Uncle LC. We'll find him and just run surveillance," Sasha stated smugly, always trying to brown-nose Daddy.

Daddy caught me rolling my eyes at her, and he put me in my place. "You need to keep your attitude in check, Paris, and work closely with your cousin. This isn't some ordinary guy you two are looking for. Brother X is a killer on another level, who trains men to kill."

Sonya

13

As soon as Xavier's men put me back in the car and pulled away from the curb, my phone started vibrating. I pulled it out of my purse to check the caller ID. "Junior," I whispered sadly as I rejected the call. His name on my lips would be the closest I'd ever be to him again. The pain of that realization was intense, and suddenly I was wishing that Xavier hadn't confiscated my pills.

Within seconds the phone was vibrating again. Each time I ignored the call, it would almost immediately start vibrating again. Junior blew up my phone during the entire ride home. By the time the car pulled up in front of my house, I'd given up and turned off the phone. As I slid it back into my purse, Xavier's driver opened my door, extending his hand to assist me out of the car.

"I don't need your help. I don't need shit from you," I snapped angrily as I stepped out of the car and slid past him. "You work for him, not me, so don't get it twisted. I sure as hell won't."

"I understand exactly who I work for, Mrs. Brown." I hated it when his men called me that.

"Look, I've had a long day, and the next time I look out of that window"—I nodded toward my house—"I don't want to see you or anyone else sitting outside, unless you want me to call the cops. You got that?" I poked him in the chest, but it had no effect, since the mountain of a man was four times my size.

"You finished?" he asked with an eerie calmness.

My courage dissolved quickly as he stared me down. I stood there, trying not to shake in my stilettos as I prayed that he wasn't the type of man who would hit a woman. When it came to Xavier's people, I couldn't be sure. They may have called themselves Muslims, but those murders had no moral compass whatsoever.

"You can call the cops, the National Guard, or the Marines. I really don't give a damn. Ain't no one going to stop me from doing my job." With those words, he walked back to the driver's side of the car, giving me the side-eye the entire way.

"Fuck you. I hope you die." Though I wasn't brave enough to say it louder than a whisper, it still felt good to curse him. With my fists clenched tightly, I marched into my house and locked the door behind me.

Leaning up against the door with my eyes closed, I took a few deep breaths in an attempt to steady my nerves. With each exhale, I hoped to release some of my pain, but my heart still ached intensely. If I didn't have the pills that would end it all, at least I could get drunk enough to forget for a few hours, I thought, as I went into the kitchen and headed straight for the unfinished bottle of wine.

A sudden movement behind me sent a shot of adrenaline coursing through my veins. I gripped the neck of the wine bottle and flung myself around, prepared to attack whoever had invaded my home. Then I saw him, and the bottle fell from my hands, crashing to the floor.

"Oh my God, Junior. Your mother is going to kill me. What are you doing here?"

"You haven't answered my calls for days," he said. "Then I get here and you're nowhere to be found. Are you back with him?" he asked, looking as vulnerable as I had ever seen this gentle giant.

"No. I hate him." I should have lied, but I couldn't bear to hurt him like that. I wanted Junior to leave, but there was no way I wanted him to believe that I could go back to my husband, or that my feelings for him weren't real.

He took a step closer, and I could feel the heat rising off his body. It took every ounce of my willpower not to throw myself into his arms. Every nerve ending in my body was craving his touch, but I knew it wasn't safe for either of us.

"You can't be here," I said, stepping away from him. The broken glass crunched under my shoes. "They've got people following my every move. They're probably following you too."

He shook his head. "Baby, you know what I do for a living. Ain't nobody following me if I don't want them to." He read my expression, which told him I was still worried. "But if it makes you feel any better, I cut through your neighbor's backyard to make sure I wasn't seen."

"I'd feel better if you left," I told him. "This isn't smart, and we need to be smart."

He shrugged. "I've never been known for my brains," he said. "I'm known for my heart, for the way I react when someone close to me is in trouble, and the way I am when I love someone, so I'm not going anywhere."

Junior placed his hand on my cheek, and for a moment, I allowed myself to cherish the sensation of his skin on mine. I closed my eyes and inhaled. When he pressed his lips against mine, a small moan escaped from me before I came to my senses.

"No, I can't." I pushed him away. "We can't. I promised your mother." Turning away from him, I fought back the tears that were threatening to pour down my face. "It's over, Junior. I'm sorry, but you have to go . . . and never come back. It's for your own good."

He dropped his hands to his sides, a wounded expression on his face. "Tell me that you don't love me, and then I'll go. I will go and you will never see me again."

I stared at him wordlessly, unable to form those words. I opened my mouth, but still no words came out. Looking into Junior's eyes, I saw all the love I felt for him reflected back at me. I'd never known love like this before, not even with my own husband, and the fact that we weren't able to be together felt entirely unnatural. I was mad at the universe for putting us in this impossible situation, and I took my anger out on Junior.

"God dammit, Junior! I can't say that and you know it!" I shouted as my tears began to flow freely. But I couldn't be selfish, I told myself. I had to set him free. I shook my head. "Xavier is crazy. He's never going to let us live in peace. And I promised your mother that I'd keep you safe. Don't you understand that?"

"Yes, I do, and that's why I'm here. You think I came over just because I couldn't stand being away from you?"

"It's true, isn't it?" I questioned.

"Yes, but that's not all of it. The last couple of days I've been watching my family prepare for a war. A war that is starting because of me . . ."

"No, because of me," I corrected him.

"Shhhh! Let me finish." I shut up and allowed him to continue. "One of my best traits is that I know how to listen, and so the last few days, I've been like a fly on the wall. I overheard Vegas talking to my father about Minister Farah, an old family friend. Apparently Vegas went to see him about this situation before he left. Minister Farah suggested very strongly that I should disappear. That *we* should disappear. See, the thought is that if we disappear, your husband will lose all interest in my family."

"How can you be sure?" I asked him. It made sense, but I also knew my husband, and he was a vengeful motherfucker.

"I can't be sure, but what other options are there? This war; it's on. My family is prepared, but there's nothing anyone can do to stop it at this point. What I do know is that if we leave, the battle will be a whole hell of a lot shorter, and less blood will be shed."

I was still skeptical. "I don't know, Junior. I don't see Xavier stopping until he's brought down your entire family."

"I hear you, but no matter how jealous or possessive you say he is, he's still a businessman. Minister Farah suggested that once we're gone, the family can approach Brother X and offer him some kind of olive branch. Give him money, or allow him to use some of our contacts. Truth is, our businesses could help each other."

It was starting to make sense, and part of me wanted to believe it could work, but one thing still didn't feel right. "I don't know, Junior. I mean, there must be a reason your family didn't take the advice. No one came to you and told you to leave town, but your mother just straight up threatened me and then kicked me out. She doesn't want you to leave; just me."

He smiled. "Yeah, my moms is intense that way, but one thing I do know about her is that ultimately, she wants nothing more than for her kids to be happy. After we get through this, we will be happy, and she will come to accept us being together. I promise."

"You make it sound so easy." I walked into the living room, checking out the window to see Xavier's thug still parked across the street. That man would never let me go, and not because he loved me, but because in his mind, he owned me.

Junior came up behind me, and I dropped the curtain in a hurry. "All we have to do is get on a plane and leave, Sonya. Maybe go to Europe or Asia, somewhere they'd never think of looking for us. I can keep us safe. Don't you see that we have no choice?"

"You think your family is going to just let us disappear? We're talking about your mother, the woman who insists that all of her grown children live under her roof. Besides, let's just say we manage to get away somewhere safely. Then what are we supposed to do for money? I can't be a nurse on the run. Xavier's men will track us down and kill us."

"That's not going to happen." In spite of my attempts to come up with all the reasons his plan couldn't work, Junior remained calm. "I've got a few million stashed away for a rainy day. We should be able to survive on that for a while. I'm not like my brothers and sister: I don't need much other than you."

I wasn't sure I'd heard him correctly. "You have millions stashed away? You say that like that's normal."

"Every Duncan has a rainy day plan, Sonya." He planted a kiss on my lips, and this time I didn't push him away. "Now, get dressed. We have to go."

And that became the moment I decided to put my life in the hands of the only man I had ever truly loved.

Paris

14

As Sasha and I rode up Guy R. Brewer Boulevard and turned down 110 Street toward Forty Projects in her sky blue Bentley convertible coupe, we were looking fly as hell, as usual. I was sporting all white, from my eyeliner and lipstick down to my diamond-studded toenails, and Sasha was rocking sky blue with navy blue accessories to match her $150,000 dollar car.

She parked in front of building number five, and we got out of the car like we owned the place. Sasha leaned against the door, and I posted up along the hood of the car, looking like we were on a photo shoot. It didn't take long for damn near everyone on the block to notice us, especially the dope boys. Just as we knew they would, a couple of them sitting on the stoop got up from their place of business and approached us.

"What do you think? The one on the right's kinda cute," Sasha whispered to me as they headed our way. Leave it to Sasha's horny ass to point out the obvious.

Dude wasn't cute, though. I mean, he was fine in a Drake kind of way and had plenty of swagger, too, but he wasn't for me. I'd been craving a dark chocolate thug like his boy walking next to him for a minute. Too bad he was a little young.

"They a'ight," I replied, "but let's keep it professional. We're not here for dick. We're here on business."

She nodded, leaning back on the car.

"What up, ma?" the Drake lookalike said, looking at me like his dreams had come true—kind of like a little boy imagining that the pinup girl on the poster in his bedroom had come to life.

I almost felt sorry for Sasha. She'd basically called dibs on him, yet the brother was staring so hard at me that he hadn't even noticed her. Sucked for me too, though, because his pretty-ass dark chocolate friend was paying more attention to the car than to either of us.

"How can I help you ladies on this fine day?" he said with those little-boy dreamy eyes of his.

I wasn't moved by the attention he was showing me. I could get the same attention just taking out the garbage in my robe and slippers. But I did want something, and so I played up to it. I gave him this knock-'em-dead flirtatious smile I'd been working on. "Either of y'all seen Lojack?" I gave him a sexy once- over.

They exchanged a knowing look before the Drakelooking one said, "Oh, you two must be working girls. That nigga Lojack be buying some pussy like a motherfucker." He rubbed his hands together and licked his lips. "But damn, I'm sure your two fine asses is setting him back a grip."

"What the fuck you say?" I snapped, totally losing my cool. I'd been mistaken for a lot of things in life, and yes, I was a high maintenance kinda bitch, but I was not to be confused with a street-walking hooker. I was about to open a can of whip-ass on this punk-ass nigga, but Sasha stepped in.

"Yeah, we working girls," she said, throwing her hands on her small waist. "You want some of what's under this skirt?" She leaned in, slowly running her tongue across her upper lip. "I'll give it to you for free." She lowered her hands to the hem of her skirt, and the dudes got so excited they looked like they were about to jump out of their skin.

Sasha lifted up her dress just enough for them to see her thigh holster and her .45. She popped the strap of leather that held the gun in place, and then touched the grip like she was massaging a dick. I know she wanted to blow the light-skinned one away for not paying her any attention.

"Oh, shit! She's strapped." Dude fell backward trying to get away like a little bitch. His chocolate partner looked shook too, but at least he stood his ground.

"What's wrong?" I chimed in. "Y'all ain't never seen two bitches with guns?" I lifted my skirt and showed him my 9mm, but got no response.

"Yo, ma, ain't nobody mean no disrespect." The dark-skinned one lifted his hands in a gesture of surrender.

"Good, no disrespect taken," I said then got right to the point. "Now do me a favor and tell Lojack that Paris Duncan is outside. We don't have time to play with little boys."

"No problem." Dude went running toward the building.

I looked over at Sasha, giving her a smile that said *See, wasn't that easy?* Of course, as everyone knows, shit ain't never that easy.

A minute or so went by, which was a minute too long. I looked up and saw someone peeking through the shades in one of the apartments. Getting Sasha's attention, I patted my gun as a sign to let her know to be prepared, just in case something unexpected went down.

A few moments later, Gerald Mann, aka Lojack, stepped out of the building. Lojack was one of New York's most notorious thieves, but he sure as hell wasn't looking confident right about now. His nervousness was due to the beat down Junior and I had put on him about two years ago for stealing one of our cars. He'd pretty much been our bitch ever since, and a great source of information.

He went into defense mode before I could say a word. With hands raised, he started. "Paris, I ain't stole no cars in over a year, so if y'all shit is missing, it ain't me."

"Calm down, Lojack." I stepped closer to him. "What's the matter? Can't a woman stop by to check on a good-looking man like yourself?" I reached out and touched his face, running my hand down his chest, past his stomach, and along the outline of his package. His dick jumped to life. I have to admit that I really like being a woman, a hot-as-hell, ass-for-days, attention-getting bitch. It usually comes in handy in my work.

"Sh–sh–sure," he stuttered. "But what's really up? I doubt this is a social call."

"We thought we'd give you the opportunity to enjoy a little Duncan cash." Nothing got Lojack's tongue wagging like a few Benjamins.

Sasha pulled out some cash, peeling off a few bills, and I watched his eyes get wide.

"What you wanna know?" He reached out to grab the money, but she held it back.

"Motherfucker," I snapped. "You know the rules. You don't get paid until we get the information. Come take a walk with us, Lojack."

I looped my arm through his and nodded for Sasha to follow. We walked to the alleyway behind the building, where Lojack leaned up against the wall, still trying to front like he was all casual. I stood in front of him, planting one hand on each side of him, with my palms flat against the brick wall.

He had a hopeful grin on face, as if the existence of a benevolent God was about to be proven by me getting down on my knees and sucking his dick—then handing him a wad of cash. Poor fool had no idea that a miracle like that would damn sure never take place.

"Tell us what you know about Brother X," I said.

That grin exited his face so fast I thought I was going to have to catch his bitch ass from fainting. Just hearing X's name had made him tremble. He made a movement like he was considering trying to dip out on us, but the distinct sound of a round being chambered into Sasha's .45 made him think better of that.

"L–look, I don't know shit about X or any of his people." Lojack always stuttered when he was lying. Did he not think that I knew his ass by now?

I leaned over and took the money from Sasha, waving it in his face. "Then I guess I'm just gonna have to go on a shopping spree with this grand." I looked into Lojack's eyes as Sasha raised her gun to his head. "I was hoping to give it to you, though," I said with a shrug as I went to tuck it away. "I guess we'll have to give you a bullet instead."

"Wait," Lojack said, swallowing hard. His eyes stayed focused on the money. I could see the wheels churning in his head: *fear or money*? As a girl who loves to shop, I see where he could be conflicted.

"Look," he started, tearing his eyes away from the cash to look at me. "All I know is that X escaped and is back on the streets. Word is it's the warden who let him out. Made him a very rich man and shit."

"You hear where he landed since his escape?" I asked.

He fell silent again, so the same way a dog's owner gets it to do tricks by waving a treat in its face, I held the cash under his nose. Money is like an aphrodisiac to a snitch. I thought Lojack was gonna bust a nut right through his pants.

"You didn't hear this shit from me, 'cause I ain't trying to piss him off, but the word is he's coming after your brother Junior hard. Now, why anyone would want to go after that big motherfucker is a mystery to me."

"Good," Sasha said, "'cause that ain't none of your business. Now, where can we find X?"

Once again he clamped his mouth shut, so Sasha pointed her gun at his temple. "You better tell this fool who I am, Paris, 'cause I'm about to blow his brains out his fucking head."

I shook my head slowly. "Lojack, Lojack, Lojack, I think I would tell her what she wants to know, 'cause she's the crazy one in the family, not me."

He looked at Sasha's determined face as she kept her gun aimed at his head, and he started talking. "Brother Samuel is one of X's key guys. He trusts him with his life. If you can find him, then you locate Xavier."

"So where the fuck do we find him?" I shouted. I didn't have time for the games. This was my brother's life, and every second counted. I'd already been here long enough.

"Well, publicly Brother Samuel is a good Muslim man. Married, with a couple of kids. Not so publicly, he has a taste for the girly-boys, even set one up in his own place when he got out of prison." He looked disgusted by the thought.

"You think women have big mouths?" he continued. "Talk to the swishy ones. They love to brag about their conquests: who has to have them, and all that shit. Well, this one lives in a fly-ass, high-end spot in Brooklyn, which is the perfect place to hide your secret. You know those Muslims don't go anywhere near that place. Too many white people."

"And you know the address?" I asked.

Perhaps I was asking too much of Lojack. He froze up again. "Lojack, I understand you're a little fearful, but sometimes you've gotta deal with the devil who's right in your face versus the one who's around the block."

Lojack looked down the barrel of Sasha's gun. Sweat beads had begun to form on his forehead. Still, he remained silent.

Deciding he needed a little more encouragement, I pulled out my gun and pressed it against his groin area. "I hear you like to spend your money on pussy, Lojack. Well, if you don't keep talking, you won't have this money to buy any pussy with, or a dick to fuck it with, even if it was free. You feel me?" I pressed the gun harder into his nuts.

He exhaled hard then began talking like the snitch I counted on him to be. "All I know is that he works at a salon on Montague Street. Loud-mouth little PR with blonde hair, goes by the name of Darlene. Rumor has it that he might be skinny, but he's packing. I don't think a day goes by that Samuel ain't try'na connect with his sidepiece. Darlene is not the most faithful type, so there is a mighty short leash."

I palmed the cash into Lojack's hand, and we lowered our guns and turned to leave. We were almost out of there when he stopped me. "Wait, you want me to keep an eye out for Xavier? I can ask around. That's worth something, ain't it?" he begged, desperate to get his hands on some more cash.

"What the hell." I handed him a couple more hundreds and we were in the wind.

Rio

15

Despite everything that was going on with Brother X, I could hardly contain myself as we rode to Sonya's house to look for Junior. I was beside myself at the fact that Pop had actually sent me on a mission with Kennedy, our top security guy. Kennedy and James, my father's driver/bodyguard, had been with the family for years. If Kennedy was involved, it meant this wasn't just a task to keep me busy and make me feel like I was part of the family business. This was some serious shit. I hadn't been sent off to some fancy killing school to get trained like my twin, Paris, or my cousin Sasha, but it felt good knowing that Pop trusted me enough to ride shotgun with a man like Kennedy. He didn't consider me just some flaming fuck-up.

If there was anyone in the Duncan organization I respected, it was Kennedy. He never showed any sign that he cared about my sexuality one way or the other, unlike some of our other employees, who were so bothered by my homosexuality that they refused to even make eye contact with me. One dude always took a slight step away from me, like my "gayness" was contagious. I tried not to take it personally. Those were their insecurities, not mine. But it definitely made me appreciate Kennedy more, because he was secure enough that he had no qualms one way or the other. When Pop gave us our instructions, Kennedy didn't even question the fact that I was the one he was on this mission with instead of a more experienced Duncan. Hell, London only got her hands dirty when she had to, but those other dudes still would have rather had her by their side than me. Not Kennedy.

Okay, now if I'm being completely honest, the fact that Kennedy was so nice to me was kind of a turn-on. I mean, what gay man wouldn't get excited about going on a mission with someone so fine that he could just as easily have been a movie star instead of the hired gun he was? It took some effort on my part not to reveal my crush, but I did what I had to, because I didn't want to embarrass myself or make things awkward for him. Just because he wasn't homophobic didn't mean he was down with the program, if you know what I mean. Considering the fact that we were entering a potentially dangerous situation, now was not the time to be distracting Kennedy with sexual advances, whether they were unwanted or not.

"Here we are," Kennedy said as we pulled up to Sonya's house. While my mind had been wandering, his serious expression told me he was totally focused on our mission. "You ready for this?"

I shrugged. "Sure. Are you?"

"You know I get paid to stay ready. You, on the other hand . . ." His words trailed off.

"What?" I suddenly wondered if I'd misjudged him. Maybe he was just as homophobic as the rest of them.

"Well, I'm used to this kind of thing, you know, dealing with unexpected trouble. Clubbing someone over the head if I have to. And you. Well . . ." He looked me up and down, his eyes traveling over my vintage Versace shirt and leather loafers.

"What about me?" I challenged, daring him to call me a sissy or something.

"You know. You just like to club. I mean, look at you. Your Pops gives you an assignment that could be deadly, and you show up in your Versace shirt and some six hundred dollar leather loafers." He laughed. "You look like you just stepped out the pages of *GQ* magazine. All handsome and shit."

I rolled my eyes at him. "Mm-hmm. Thanks for the compliment."

His laughter ceased when he realized I might have been offended—which I wasn't. If anything, I was flattered by the fact that he'd noticed what I was wearing. I was just playing coy by refusing to look at him now.

"Anyway, you strapped?" he said.

I snapped my head in his direction. "Am I strapped? I'm a Duncan. That's like asking a stripper does she know how to slide down a pole."

"I guess you got a point there."

"Besides, all we came to do is see if Junior is here. Either he is or he isn't. That shouldn't involve a weapon," I said casually.

"It shouldn't, but you never know." Kennedy unlocked the doors and stepped out. I followed behind him, up the walkway and to the door.

"Whoa. Hold up." He put out his hand, which just so happened to press flat against my chest. I knew he didn't mean anything sexual by it, but that didn't make my heart beat any less rapidly.

"What?" I asked, hoping this man would leave his hand right where it was just a little bit longer. So what if he was straight? A boy can dream, can't he? The way he looked at me sometimes, I refused to believe that he might not play for the other team every now and then.

"Check that out." He removed his hand from my chest and pointed at the door, which was slightly ajar. I might not be in the heart of the action most of the time, but any fool knows that an open door is not a good sign.

Kennedy took out his gun and held it in front of him, so I did the same thing. Just to prove I wasn't scared, I made a move to step around him. Once again he stopped me with a hand on my chest.

"Let me go first," he said.

I sure was grateful that he was in charge. If anything jumped off, it would land on him first. Not that I wanted to see anything happen to Kennedy, but I loved myself too much to want to risk my life. Truth be told, no matter how happy I was that Pop was including me, I was too damn cute for this shit. However, if anybody heard me admit my true distaste for violence out loud, I'd get my Duncan card revoked, so I just nodded at Kennedy and stepped back.

Kennedy crept up to the door and pushed it open, pointing his gun from left to right, then straight in front of him again. After a few seconds, he looked over his shoulder at me and nodded that it was okay for us to enter.

Kennedy went in first, and I was right behind him. The moment I stepped my black ass through the door, we were ambushed by three men.

"Rio, run!" Kennedy shouted as he let one off, hitting one of the men in the chest. That man fell to the ground.

This fired up the other two, who immediately began shooting. At first I was going to follow Kennedy's orders and make a mad dash for the car, but he'd been protecting me since the moment we set foot on the doorstep. It was time I returned the favor. I started shooting at the two guys left standing—even if I did position myself slightly behind Kennedy. Don't hate! Hell, his gun was bigger.

I swear it was like a crazy Western scene. It was two against two, and no one was backing down. Within seconds, another man inside Sonya's house was down, and then finally the third.

"Hell, yeah! That's what the fuck I'm talking about!" I cheered. This was bananas. We'd actually had a face-to-face shootout with three of X's men, and both of us were left standing. That was some shit.

Kennedy turned around and looked me in the eyes. "You did good, Rio. I might have to buy you a drink after we pick up Vegas from the airport." I thought I saw him fighting to keep the corners of his mouth from rising into a smile.

This man had done everything in his power to protect me. What I really wanted to do was run into his arms and thank him, but I played it cool. "Thank you, Kennedy. I might just take you up on th—"

Before I could get the last word out, I heard a gunshot. Next thing I knew, I saw blood seeping through Kennedy's shirt. He grabbed at the wound on his stomach, looking down at the crimson fluid flowing between his fingers. Then he looked up at me, his confused expression asking, *What the fuck?*

There was another shot, then Kennedy hit the ground. I immediately began shooting toward the doorway, backing up as I fired the gun. I saw a man lying in the doorway, taking his last breath. In his hand was the gun that had fired the last two rounds that took Kennedy out.

"Son of a bitch," I murmured. Then I looked down at Kennedy's blood-soaked body, and it came out as a scream. "Son of a bitch!"

Kneeling down beside him, I lifted his head into my hands. "Kennedy, man. You okay? You're going to be all right."

Gurgling through blood-stained lips, he gathered the strength to tell me, "Go. Go to Vegas, now."

I shook my head. "I can't leave you like this. I'm going to call for help."

"No! You're a Duncan. You're too valuable. Just go. Go to your brother. Lincoln is on the way."

"I'm not leaving you. No way, not going to happen. I refuse."

Barely able to move his lips anymore, he mumbled, "Rio, I would have come out for you. Please go. Please." He closed his eyes, and I knew it was only a matter of time before he would drown in his own blood.

Gently resting his head on the floor, I got up and ran to the car. It was unlocked, and the keys were still in it. Clearly Kennedy had known there was a chance we would have to make a quick getaway. I looked back toward the house and silently thanked him for looking out for me.

I had no idea if more of X's men were on the way, so I jumped in the car and wasted no time getting out of there. Fumbling for my phone as I drove, I dialed Orlando's number.

"Kennedy is dead!" I cried out. "Fucking sons of bitches killed him. O, man, we need to get that motherfuckin' Brother X."

Sasha

16

After we left Lojack in his hood, Paris and I switched cars and changed into black jeans and yuppie T-shirts to head over to Brooklyn Heights. Montague Street, the main drag, might as well have been on the other side of the planet, with its high-end clothing shops, quaint cafes, and overpriced juice bars. As you can imagine, locating Samuel's six-foot-tall Puerto Rican tranny sidepiece in a gentrified neighborhood like this was not hard at all.

It turned out that Darlene worked in a chi-chi salon called Beauty, which could conveniently be watched through the window of a coffee shop across the street. Two lattes and a corn muffin later, a flaming ball of Puerto Rican attitude exited the salon, scurrying down the street. We got in our car and followed those five-inch heels until Darlene ducked into an apartment building two blocks away. Shortly afterward, we watched a six-foot-something, bald-headed brotha wearing a black bow tie get out of a sedan and enter the building. The assumption was that we had just unofficially been introduced to Brother Samuel.

"You think gay men really give the best head?" Paris asked, her eyes on the building as if she could imagine what was going on behind the closed door.

"Maybe better than you, but my dick-sucking skills are world class," I said with a laugh, waiting for my competitive cousin to weigh in.

"Please. I was sucking dick when you were in diapers," she boasted.

"That is so foul. You just can't stand to not win."

She laughed with me, which was a relief. She had been so wound up ever since Lasalle mentioned Niles Monroe that I was beginning to worry about her.

Twenty-two minutes later, girlfriend came switching her hot-to-trot ass out of the building in a new outfit and wig. Guess old boy had made a mess of the last one. Darlene headed back in the direction of the salon, and not long after that, Samuel came through the door and out to his car with a big grin on his face. When he pulled off, we stayed on him.

"You're tailing him too close," I snapped, worried that Paris would blow our cover and lose the one opportunity we had to find X.

"Hey, I got this, okay?" She gave me the side-eye, although she did drop back a little.

We'd been tailing Samuel for forty minutes when he finally pulled over at a small store. Paris parked half a block away. I already had the binoculars out and was adjusting the focus to see what was going on. I laughed out loud when I saw what he was putting on the counter in the store.

"Ha! He's buying mints," I told Paris. "I guess he doesn't want to be around the brothers smelling like Darlene's nuts."

"Whoa . . ." Paris muttered, but it wasn't because of my comment. "Check it out," she said, and I looked in the direction of the store again.

Samuel was coming out of the store, but now he had two other bow tie–wearing brothers with him. From the bulges in their jackets, I knew they were all strapped.

"Looks like Samuel stopped here to get more than just breath mints," I said.

"Yeah," Paris agreed. "This just got real interesting."

We watched as one man got into the passenger seat of Samuel's car, and the other followed in a separate car. Paris, who was always ready for action, reached for her piece. She opened the glove box to retrieve some more ammo.

I would never admit it to her, but I was glad to have Paris with me. She was a true bad-ass, and that's who I would want to have my back—even if she was also a pain in the ass who reminded me often that she was the older cousin, and therefore superior at everything.

We followed Samuel and his partners onto the Grand Central Parkway, where they exited at LaGuardia Airport, confusing the hell outta me. If they were getting on a flight, that could mean that Brother X was somewhere outside of New York, which would make it much harder to get at him.

I breathed a sigh of relief as they passed by the airport and drove down Ditmars Boulevard to the Marriot hotel. In the parking lot, they pulled in next to a black van. It looked like the driver of that van had been waiting for them, because they all got out and spoke to him.

"What do you think they're up to?" I asked Paris.

"I don't know, but it can't be good. I think we need to get in that hotel lobby before they do." We grabbed our baseball caps and headed for the hotel entrance.

"Oh, shit!" I grabbed her arm, stopping her twenty feet from the entrance.

"What?"

I directed her attention to a souped-up 1975 Plymouth Duster. "Isn't that one of Junior's cars?" This was really bad.

"Shit. Junior must be in there with Sonya."

We rushed to the lobby and posted up in a couple of chairs that gave us a great view of the front desk, lobby, and elevators just in time to see Samuel and his two henchmen enter. They headed straight for the front desk, where they were greeted by a smiling reservations clerk. She wasn't smiling for long, though, because Samuel started getting agitated. We weren't close enough to hear the conversation, but it looked like it was easily solved once he pulled out a wad of cash and slid it across the counter to her. Her smile returned as she typed something into her computer then handed Samuel a key card. Samuel snatched up the card, and he and his men turned toward the elevators.

Paris shot me a look, and we got our asses over to the elevator bank in a hurry. Just as the door was about to close, Paris reached her arm in to stop it.

"Hello." She smiled flirtatiously as we entered the elevator, joining the men. She got a big smile in return from one of Samuel's henchmen. Not to be outdone, I pushed my breasts out until they were straining against the fabric of my tight top.

"How are you gentlemen?" I purred. There was nothing like playing oversexed bimbos looking for dates. I had to admit it was my favorite act.

"We're great," the shortest one answered quickly. He was clearly the one least accustomed to two hot sistahs giving him the time of day. Yeah, he was definitely the one to focus on. The taller, skinny one, who looked to be all about business, barely cracked a smile. I would have to step up my game, but I didn't mind. I always enjoyed a challenge.

"You ladies might want to familiarize yourself with the Koran." Samuel sound disgusted, staring at us as if we were gum on the bottom of his shoe.

Paris ignored him, turning all her attention to the short one, the easiest target. "Mmmm. Big feet," she said. "Is it true what they say about big feet?"

I had to hand it to Paris; she definitely had some game. She was so seductive that I swear dude was reaching for his zipper like he was about to show her just how true it was. Samuel was having none of it, though.

"You two really need to get right with Allah," he barked at us.

"Oh, you not into women?" Paris poked at Samuel with a straight face. I swear if that brother was white he would have gone bright red. "A'ight. Guess that means two for two instead of three for two."

"I'm just not into nasty, dirty whores," he snarled.

She brushed him off with a shrug. "I guess you're not into these, then," she said, shocking even me as she pulled down the V-neck on her shirt, exposing her damn near perfect tits. I say *damn near* because since her pregnancy, they hung just a little lower than mine. "You gotta be a pussy who is just not into pussy to not be inspired by these."

Samuel refused to even look in the direction of her bare chest, but the other two dudes, their eyes were damn near bugging out of their heads. Seeing where she was going with this little act, I joined right in, flipping my tits out too.

One of the guys groaned like he was about to explode in his pants. I knew he wanted to reach out and touch them, but Samuel's stone face made him retreat.

"Don't act like you don't like them," Paris prodded. "Go ahead. You can touch them."

"Not interested," Samuel spoke for them all.

"She wasn't talking to you," I said, turning full frontal to his associates. "What about you boys? You interested?" I jumped a little to make my breasts jiggle.

The two other brothers looked at each other like they were wondering which one was going to defy Samuel first, and that was the moment of distraction Paris and I needed. We pulled out our silenced guns. The two horny ones never even touched their weapons before we made kill shots. Samuel, on the other hand, was a whole lot more experienced and closer to his weapon.

He aimed his gun at Paris. I leaped for his hand, spoiling any kind of shot he might have. I saved her life, but he was strong as hell and threw me across the elevator like a rag doll. By the time, I looked up, he had his gun pointed at me. I braced myself, twisting my body to make myself a smaller target like I'd been trained in school. I heard the sound of two silenced shots, and the back of Samuel's head exploded against the elevator wall.

I turned to Paris.

She shrugged, the smoking gun still in her hands. "What? You saved my life, so I had to save yours. You know I don't like to owe nobody, and knowing you, your ghost would haunt me the rest of my life."

"Whatever. Bitch, you know you love me," I said as she helped me up.

She bent down to search Samuels's pockets, pulling out the key card the reservation clerk had given him. "Come on. It's time to find Junior."

Junior

17

Two hours earlier

"You ready? Because this is it," I whispered into Sonya's ear as we entered the LaGuardia Airport Marriott. Her face lit up as she rolled her suitcase, which was a whole hell of a lot bigger than mine, into the lobby. I glanced over at the black van that had parked in a handicap space, probably so that the driver could get the best view of the lobby. So far, so good.

"You sure this is going to work?" she asked nervously.

"It's going to work. Trust me," I replied, heading for the desk.

"I do trust you, honey. I'm just scared."

The desk clerk glanced up, and seeing us approach, he handed me my room key, just like I had instructed him earlier. Who said you needed to be at a five-star hotel to get first class service? This place was about to meet all of my expectations and more.

Taking a quick visual inventory of the lobby, I spotted a few obvious tourists: Asians with expensive cameras hanging around their necks; badly-dressed, pale Europeans; a few Africans; and some locals, no doubt doing their dirty business where they wouldn't get caught. The coast was basically clear of interference, at least inside.

"Is it working?" Sonya asked, and I nodded in response, letting her know that I planned to honor my word to keep her safe. This woman was my life, and that meant protecting her the same way I would myself.

As we walked to the elevator bank, I turned to smile at Sonya. What I was really doing was looking through the large windows to make sure Brother X's man in the van hadn't followed us inside yet. He may have thought that he was slick, staying a few car lengths behind us, but he didn't know that by following us, he was simply following my plan.

We traveled up the elevator to the seventh floor and hustled into our room. Once inside, we threw open the suitcases and quickly changed clothing. In fact, the clothes we were changing into were the only outfits in the nearly empty suitcases. Even Sonya's big-ass suitcase was just for show, because we needed X and his men to think that we were leaving town. The best way to make them believe that was to check in to the largest hotel near the airport. I was sure X figured we'd be easy targets, but he would be surprised, and pissed, when he found out what we had planned.

Seeing Sonya half naked as she changed into muted colors, I had to take a deep breath and try to control my urges.

"Stop," she warned, catching me leering at her. "If you're really, really good and get us out of here safe, I may have something a little extra for you later, though," she teased.

"I'm going to hold you to that," I crooned, patting her on the ass. Damn, I loved all that ass in my hands, but it would have to wait. Timing was everything tonight. "Girl, you are distracting as hell."

"Good." She laughed as she finished dressing and picked up her purse.

"Wait." I stopped her at the door. "Give me your phone." I held out my hand.

"But all of my numbers are in there," she said with a pout.

"If we're going to do this, we have to leave our pasts behind. They can track us with our phones." I took out mine, waited a few more seconds until she reluctantly handed hers over, and tossed them both onto the bed. "Now, let's go start our lives anew."

I grabbed her hand and led her down the hallway in the opposite direction from the elevators. We'd just gotten into the stairwell when I heard the elevator ping. Damn, we were cutting it close. When we reached the main floor, we turned left and slipped into the kitchen, where a full staff hurried about, handling the needs of the large clientele. We were greeted by José, a professional waiter who used to work at one of my favorite spots in Queens before it shut down a year ago. I'd helped him get this job at the hotel, so he was repaying the favor.

"Junior, this way." He led us through a maze of activity, past a whole bunch of people too busy doing their jobs to care what the hell we were doing. When we got to the end of a long hallway, he opened the door to an alley outside.

Before we left him, I reached into my pocket and handed him a nice little bundle of cash.

"Nah, I can't take this," he insisted.

"You earned it. Just keep your mouth shut and we're good," I said, reminding him of my cardinal rule.

"You got it. Good luck." He pocketed the cash.

A yellow cab sat waiting outside the door. As José left us to go back to work, I opened the back door and let Sonya slide into the cab first.

"Where to, Mr. Sutton?" the driver asked.

"Corner of Patchen and Jefferson in Brooklyn," I answered. We weren't actually staying in Brooklyn, but I'd stashed a car near there a couple of days ago.

We were actually staying in a safe house that I kept at the residences at the Ritz Carlton hotel in Battery Park. By the time I'd parked the car in the garage and led Sonya into the private elevator, I could see the stress on her face. It had been a long and difficult day as we made moves to throw X off our trail. I could see that she was in serious need of some stress relief, which was why I'd had room service deliver food and champagne.

"I've never stayed anyplace this nice," Sonya said as we sat down to eat. She was staring out the window at the Statue of Liberty across the water.

"Yeah, it's beautiful. Just like you," I said, reaching for her hand.

We ate in silence for a while, lost in our own thoughts about the ordeal we were enduring. I, for one, felt confident that X and his men were still scratching their heads, wondering when we were coming out of our hotel room. Even if they'd figured out that we were gone, there was no way for them to pick up our trail again. I'd had the cab driver drop us off in front of a small bodega, and we didn't get into my car until long after he was gone. If anything, they might guess that we were hiding in one of the apartments above the store.

"I'm just glad we got away from X and his men," I said, but Sonya still looked uncertain.

"Babe, don't worry," I told her. "There's no way anyone could know where we are right now."

"What about your family? Don't they know you'd come here?"

I shook my head. "Even they don't know about this place. When I bought it, I didn't tell anyone."

She looked surprised. "You own this place?"

"Yeah," I said with a smile. "I might not spend lavishly like Paris or Rio, but once in a while I like to buy nice things."

"Okay, but, I mean, why would you buy a fancy place like this and then not live in it? And why would you keep it a secret?"

"For a situation like this," I explained. "I didn't buy this place to live in it. My brother Orlando came up with the idea years ago, that each one of us needed a safe place we could go to if things ever got dangerous, and this place was perfect for me. No one would ever come looking for a simple guy like me in this kind of luxury. "

She nodded like it all made sense to her now. "So, this is basically a hideout?"

I laughed. "Yeah, I guess you could call it that. And since not even my family knows where it is, you can relax and consider yourself completely safe tonight."

I saw some of the tension leave her shoulders. "Feel a little better now?" I asked, and she nodded. "Good. Now, about what you said earlier . . ."

"What did I say?" she asked.

"You said if I got you out of the hotel safely you'd have a little something for me tonight," I said, raising my eyebrows suggestively.

A sultry grin emerged on her face as she reached for the buttons on her blouse. "Let's get busy christening this secret hideaway."

Paris

18

The elevator stopped on the seventh floor. Good thing that Samuel had pushed the button before we took care of him, or else we would have had to search every floor to find Junior. Even so, I still had no clue which room on the seventh floor was his, so I did the only thing I could think of: I started putting the key card into doors to see if one would open. Sasha stayed in the elevator, holding the door open so it wouldn't travel back down to the lobby. The last thing we needed was for an elevator full of dead bodies to arrive down there. I moved as fast as I could, knowing that she could only hold it for so long before someone started to wonder why it was stuck on this floor.

"Hurry up!" Sasha hissed, as if I didn't understand how serious this was. I flipped her the bird at the same time I slid the key into a lock and the light turned green.

"Junior! It's me, Paris," I called into the room before entering so that my brother wouldn't greet me with a gun in his hand. We Duncans had been known to shoot first and ask questions later— or at least some of us had. As I stepped into the room, however, I realized that there had been no reason for me to announce myself. The room was empty except for a couple of suitcases.

"Dammit!" I stuck my head out of the room and called down the hall to Sasha. "Yo, push all the buttons to the top floor and then get down here."

When she got into the room, I gave her instructions. "I need you to go find the surveillance room and destroy the video of what just happened in that elevator—along with the one of us entering the elevator and the lobby." I didn't need to explain to her how bad things would be for our whole family if we were identified. It wasn't like we were in L.A. or Miami, where nobody knew us. This was New York. We lived here.

"You better pray to God that there is a man guarding those tapes. I'll meet you at the car." She took off, leaving me in the hotel room alone.

I opened the first suitcase to discover that it was completely empty, devoid of clothes, so it was no surprise when I found the second one held only a pair of Junior's jeans and a sweatshirt. A woman's outfit that must have been Sonya's was draped over a chair. I turned around and spotted two cell phones on the bed. Things were going from bad to worse. Ditching cell phones was the first thing someone did when they were getting ready to go off the grid.

With no valuable information to be found, it was time for me to get the hell out of there. By now someone could have spotted the bodies, and it wouldn't be long before I was hearing sirens. Grabbing the phones on my way out, I headed for the stairwell. Less than three minutes later, I was in the car, feeling jittery as I waited for Sasha.

She slid into the car a few minutes later. "Mission accomplished," she said proudly, always ready to brag about her skill for getting whatever she wanted out of a man. "But our handiwork has been discovered. Five-O should be here any minute."

Just as I drove away from the parking lot, two NYPD cruisers arrived in front of the hotel.

"Any clue where Junior and Sonya are?" Sasha asked as we headed down Ditmars to the entrance of the Van Wyck Expressway.

"No fucking idea. Probably in the wind." I showed her their phones. "They left these behind."

She shook her head. "Damn. This is bad, cuz."

"No shit."

I picked up my phone and dialed Orlando's number. "Hey, O, it's me. Tell Daddy that it looks like Junior and ol' girl have gone ghost for good."

"Are you sure?" Orlando asked.

"Yeah, I'm sure. We had to take out three of X's men to protect an empty hotel room. Only thing we found was their cell phones," I told him.

Orlando let out a frustrated sigh. "Well, he's a big boy. He can take care of himself. Right now I want you two to get outta there and go to one of our safe houses," he barked into the phone. "I got a feeling it's about to get real hot once X finds out about his three dead soldiers."

Brother X

19

I was feeding Lenny and Squiggy while I waited for word from our men at the Marriott. Those rats were the only thing that kept me from punching holes in the walls as I paced the room. Samuel and his men had been over by the hotel for almost two hours, so I was expecting that no-good heifer I called a wife and her punk-ass lover to be groveling at my feet at any minute. I couldn't wait to get my hands on both of those adulterous infidels.

I'd just sliced off a piece of pear and tossed it to Lenny when Elijah walked in the room looking very uncomfortable. I didn't have to ask to know that he was bringing me bad news. He stood there staring at me, his eyes looking everywhere but right at me.

"Tell me you have my wife." I slid a peanut across the table to Squiggy. "Tell me she's tied up alongside that homewrecker Junior Duncan so she can watch me peel his skin from his body inch by inch with this knife."

"I wish I could, Xavier, but—" He stopped, screwing up his face as if he couldn't figure out which words to say next.

"Just tell me what the fuck happened."

"As you know, we had Junior and your wife under surveillance at the Marriott. I sent three of our men, including my cousin Samuel, to retrieve them."

"And?" I said impatiently. "Do not tell me they lost them."

Elijah looked like he was in pain as he told me, "Worse. I just got word that all three of them were killed, including Samuel."

I pounded my fist on the table, sending Lenny and Squiggy scurrying away. "That's impossible. How did this happen?"

"I'm not a hundred percent sure . . ." he started weakly. He knew damn well that I wouldn't accept anything less than a full report. "All I know right now is that our men were ambushed in the hotel elevator, killed like fish in a barrel."

"Dammit! You don't just sneak up on a man like Samuel, Elijah. He was as good as we got. I trained him myself." I was up in his face now, furiously pointing a finger at his nose. "This is why I wanted to go there myself. If I was there, this wouldn't have happened."

Elijah stood his ground. "You know why you couldn't go there. Your face is plastered all over the news. The cops are blaming you for killing Nugent and Jefferson. Right now, you're the most wanted man in New York. You've got to keep a low profile."

I fell back into a chair, gripping the arms tightly as I tried to contain my rage. "You're right." As much as I needed someone to blame, I couldn't fault Elijah. He was always looking out for my best interests. "So you're telling me that Junior Duncan did this?"

"He's the prime suspect. I'm pretty sure it wasn't your wife. No woman could do this type of thing to Samuel."

I had to agree. "Who are these people, Elijah? Have you found out who they are?"

"The Jew was right. They're not who they seem to be, that is for sure. I've reached out to some of our Russian and Italian friends, but no one wants to talk about them. I'm working on something now to get us all the information we need."

A knock on the door interrupted our conversation. Elijah went to answer it, and when he returned, it appeared as if life had been pumped into him again. "We managed to capture one of their men during a shootout over at your wife's place. They've been working him over the past hour. I thought you might want to see if you can loosen his tongue. He's just a few blocks away."

"Let's go!" I barked, already headed to the door.

"Yo, X," Elijah called out, stopping me. I turned around to see him holding out a pair of sunglasses and a kufi cap for me to put on. "We're not going far, but you still can't risk being recognized."

It only took us five minutes to arrive at the garage where my men had stashed this guy. Ahmed rode along with us, ready with his M16 to take out anyone I directed him to.

"Is he talking?" I asked as we approached Barack, one of our most loyal soldiers, who was posted up outside the building.

"Nothing, except that his name is Lincoln. No idea if that's true or not."

Ahmed opened the door, and we entered the room where Lincoln was tied up. His face was covered in bruises, and blood leaked from his mouth. He had clearly been worked over. Two of my men stood over him, and both appeared sweaty and frustrated.

"Anything?" I asked.

"Not a thing," another soldier named Kori answered. "I mean, he's a straight-up soldier. I think the guy has a death wish."

"Let me be the judge of that." I approached Lincoln and took the seat right in front of him, removing my sunglasses. "Do you know who I am?"

His eyes widened, letting me know his answer, but I wanted to hear it from him. I waited silently, staring him down until he admitted, "Yes."

"I hear you're a real trooper. Do you want me to kill you?" I asked, leaving no question in my tone that I could do that swiftly and mercilessly. "Are you ready to die?"

"I'm not afraid of death, if that's what you're asking. Besides, we both know you're going to kill me anyway, so you might as well get it over with." He locked his eyes on mine. This guy was devoid of fear, or at least he desperately wanted me to believe that he was, but the one thing I'd learned was that every man has an Achilles' heel. I just had to find his.

"I probably am," I told him, "but there are just so many different ways to die. And who knows? I might be feeling generous today."

"Fuck you," he spat as he sat back, waiting for the abuse to begin. "You can't do any worse than your boys."

"Just tell us something. You do not want this man putting it on you," Ahmed said, sounding as if he was genuinely trying to spare Lincoln some pain.

Lincoln stubbornly shook his head, refusing.

I moved closer to him, pulling my secret weapons out of my pocket. Lincoln's eyes grew fearful as I placed Lenny and Squiggy on the ground. I squeaked, and they ran up under his pants legs, making their way up to his thighs. He started squirming, trying to move them, but with his arms tied behind his back, there wasn't much that he could do. They were having a field day on his legs.

"Aagghhhh!" Lincoln screamed. I looked around and saw some of my men grimacing as they witnessed this.

"They like dick, but they especially like nuts," I said, laughing.

"What the hell is this? What type of sick fuck are you? Stop!" He was pleading, but I wasn't ready to give in just yet. I was enjoying the effect my pets were having on this hard-ass. I always enjoyed it. I'd seen these two take down sadistic motherfuckers who were doing consecutive life sentences, guys so tough that they made Lincoln look like a little bitch.

I leaned in close to him, speaking calmly. "Tell me about the Duncans or I will let them devour your dick. If you think you're in pain now, can you imagine how much pain they can inflict on something as sensitive as your balls?"

"That's a whole lot of pain," Elijah commented. "If it were me?" He threw his hands up, admitting he would have surrendered by now.

"They will chew your nuts into tiny bits," I said.

"I've seen it. It's not very pretty," Elijah added.

"All right! All right! Please! I'll tell you what you want to know," Lincoln cried out.

I squeaked twice, and Lenny and Squiggy came scurrying out of his pants legs. I reached down and retrieved them, giving each a kiss.

"Tell me what you know about the Duncans, and don't leave out anything."

Lincoln couldn't take his eyes off of Lenny and Squiggy squirming in my hands.

It took him a minute to compose himself enough to speak. He finally said, "Honestly, man, I don't know much. The Duncans are like that. They keep things compartmentalized so that nobody outside of the family has that much information about them."

"But they're not just car dealers," I said, expecting him to confirm what I already suspected.

He hesitated, and I lifted Lenny and Squiggy closer to his face. That was all it took to get him talking again. "They're probably the largest distributors on the East Coast. I hear their business expands all the way from Canada down to the islands. I think they even do business in Europe."

"You *hear*? You *think*? How come nobody seems to know about them?" I asked angrily.

"Mainly because they are so good at what they do. Word is LC's not greedy, always makes his partners money, doesn't do business with street level people or folks he doesn't know, and most importantly, he doesn't trust anyone other than family. Men like that don't grow on trees. Shit, some say he was Ollie North's partner in Iran-contra."

I saw the look Elijah gave me. These people were seriously connected.

"And Junior, is he the most dangerous son?" It made sense to me that he would be the bad-ass because of the way he took out Samuel in that elevator.

"Junior is no joke, but the one I wouldn't want to meet in a dark alley is his younger brother, Vegas. You wouldn't know from looking at him, but dude's supposed to be some kind of Jason Bourne type one-man army. He had motherfuckers scared from his jail cell."

Ahmed jumped in. "Wait, I heard of a guy named Vegas on the inside. That cat had Sing-Sing on lock. He might as well have been the warden. Even the COs answered to him. That shit was crazy. But he wasn't a bully; he was calm and deadly."

"Yeah, that's him. He just got out." Lincoln shook his head. "He can be the nicest person, and in a second he turns into a cold-blooded killer. You do not want to get on his bad side." Lincoln smiled at me, looking like a devil as he revealed his bloodied teeth.

"He's the one the Jew warned us about," Elijah said. "Who else they got worth talking about?"

Half a squeak from me and he was talking up a storm this time. For someone who claimed not to know much about the Duncans, he suddenly had information on every member of the family. Lenny and Squiggy had really done their job getting what I needed out of this guy.

"Orlando, but he's more of a businessman than a gangster. He runs Duncan Motors, but he's not afraid to get dirty if that's what the situation calls for. The youngest son, Rio, is a straight up homo, but he stays strapped too. There's also a son-in-law, Harris. He's the family attorney, and he knows his shit. He's basically in charge of cleaning up their money and keeping them out of jail. Then there's the girls—"

"I don't want to hear about any useless women," I told him dismissively. He smirked at me and shut up.

"So, what's your detail? What do you do for the Duncans?" He was so busy watching me stroke my pets that it appeared he didn't even hear me. "Hello? What is your normal detail?"

"I'm in charge of one of the warehouses. I work for Kennedy, the guy y'all killed."

"One of the warehouses? How many do they have?"

"I don't know. Depends on the product. The one I work at houses weed. But I'm sure there are others that house different contraband. They got them all over the country, but I only know that the one I work at just got a shipment." He had finally gotten my attention again.

I peppered this snitch with questions until I was convinced that I knew everything he knew, and that was just enough to help us make our next move.

I pulled Elijah aside to talk to him. "Interesting. Very fuckin' interesting. It would seem that Bernie may have been right. Taking out LC Duncan is the key to destroying the Duncans from within."

"One thing I still don't understand," Elijah commented. "With LC Duncan dead and the Duncans crippled, what does the Jew get out of all of this?"

"I don't know. You'd think the way they have their fingers in everything that they'd lose money if the Duncans went under." I dropped Lenny and Squiggy to the floor to let them run around. After all, they'd done a great job.

"Fuck!" Lincoln yelled, kicking Lenny across the room.

I raced over and grabbed him by the throat. "You kicked him?"

"I should have stomped his ass. It bit me. I hate rats."

"Do you have any idea how much I love those rats?" I screamed. "After my wife, they are everything to me. Everything!" I grabbed my blade and drove it into his heart. Lincoln's head slumped onto his chest, and I looked up at Elijah. "Now that that's done, let's go kill some Duncans."

LC

20

"Gentlemen, you've given us a lot to think about. We'll be in touch." Orlando and I rose, shaking hands with Popeye Wilson and Tony Williams, two of the most powerful black gangsters in the world. Popeye, a short and stout, well-dressed man, ran his operations out of Washington, D.C., and Tony was a skinny-as-a-rail know-it-all from Atlanta. We'd distributed narcotics to both of their organizations for years, which technically made them beholden to us, but with everything going on with Brother X, they were suggesting a merger, so to speak. Our recent problems were putting us in a precarious situation, as far as the power structure was concerned. People who were once reliant on us were now looking to become partners.

"Well, LC, you know we're here for you if you need us," Popeye said.

"Yeah, man. We Blacks need to stick together like the Koreans, the Italians, and the Jews," Tony commented as they headed out the door.

"I know we need soldiers, Pop," Orlando's voiced under his breath as we watched them leave, "but are we really going to do this?"

"It's something to consider. Besides, it's better than the offer we got this afternoon, don't you think?" Truthfully, it was starting to look like we didn't have a whole lot of options. At least none that I liked.

"I don't know, Pop. I'm afraid that if we let them in, we're never going to get them out." Orlando's tone was serious. He'd been that way ever since he was a kid, always thinking things through and imagining every possible outcome. It was the reason I had chosen him to take over the family business when I retired—if I ever got the chance. It seemed every time I thought things were falling back into place, another crisis hit the family and I was forced to delay my plans. Still, I appreciated Orlando working side by side with me through it all.

"You know as well as I do that Popeye and Tony will sell us down the river first chance they get."

"I know that, Orlando, but blood has already been spilled on both sides. With Junior MIA and Kennedy dead, we're going to need all the help we can get. Those men have small armies—armies we may need to use to take X and his people out."

"Maybe, but I'm starting to think that the offer we got this afternoon might be the way to go. It's a win-win for us all."

"Everything that glitters isn't gold, Orlando," I replied, pulling a crisp Cohiba cigar from my breast pocket. "Let's just hope Vegas has good news."

"Okay, if you say so, Pop." I patted him on the back.

"Look I'm gonna step out back and smoke this stogie." I ran the cigar across my nose, inhaling the scent. "And don't tell your mother I was smoking." I loved my wife, but the older we got, the more she started to act like my mother. That was the reason I only smoked after hours at the dealership, when no one else was around.

"Wouldn't think of it, Pop. I know how much it relaxes you. Look, I'm going to see if I can get a hold of Junior. I'll be in my office if you need me," he said.

"Sure thing," I replied as I headed for the rear entrance and the new car prepping lot. I sat on a bench, cutting the tip off my cigar and lighting up. There used to be a time at the end of the day when my brother Lou and I would go out there, light up, and look at the cars. Lou used to call it "enjoying the fruits of our labor," but I'd been so busy lately that I hadn't taken advantage of one of my simpler pleasures.

A dark blue Range Rover caught my eye. She was a real beauty. I had a mind to go inside, grab the keys, and take it for a ride. That's when I felt a buzzing in my pocket and reached for my phone. It was the call I'd been waiting for the past three days.

"Did you hear about Kennedy?" I said as soon as I answered the call.

"Yeah," Vegas said sadly. "Rio told me when he picked me up at the airport. What's up with Junior? What's his status?"

"He's been MIA since this morning. I told your mother he's working on something for me so she wouldn't worry, but we need to locate him before X does." I took another pull off of my cigar. The sweetness of the smoke did little to counteract the bitterness of this conversation. "How'd your trip go?"

"Not as well as I expected." I heard a heaviness in Vegas's voice that hadn't been there when he left town. It damn near broke my heart, especially since I had a good idea why he sounded like that.

"So it wasn't him?" I felt bad for my son. Somebody had to be playing a nasty trick on him, but what choice had he had other than to check it out? It must have felt like he had lost his best friend twice. I'd had my doubts about the outcome of his little trip to begin with, but even I didn't question Vegas when he set his mind to something.

"No, it was Daryl in the flesh," he said.

"Are you sure?" I found this hard to believe, considering the fact that after his death I'd had some of my people break into the morgue and take pictures of his burnt-up body for my own peace of mind.

"Yeah, it was him. I spent almost five hours talking to him. Felt like we'd seen each other last week," Vegas reminisced.

"That's all nice and dandy, but then why do you still sound like you have bad news? Was he on the plane with you, son?" I couldn't hide the desperation in my voice. We needed all the help we could get at the moment.

"No, Pop. He wasn't."

"Did you tell him what's going on? That we need him. That the family needs him." I felt myself getting worked up. Daryl was like another son to me, so I was happy to hear he was still alive, but it was hard to understand how he could have ignored the call to come help. He and Vegas together were as formidable a team as there ever was. Throw in the girls, hopefully Junior, a couple of Daryl's Israelite buddies, and favors from a few business associates, and we actually had a chance of surviving this whole mess.

"Of course I told him. He has his own issues, Pop," Vegas assured me.

"Well, obviously I don't know the whole story, but I have to say I'm a more than a little frustrated that he's putting something else before family. I did not raise my kids that way, and I treated that boy like one of my own."

"His wife is dying."

"I see," I finished, knowing that I had to let it rest.

Vegas changed the subject. "What's this Ma's telling me about you meeting with Popeye and Tony the pimp?" Vegas had never really liked Tony; something about some woman they both messed with a few years back. But of course, there was always a woman involved where Vegas was concerned.

"They're suggesting we all pool our resources. Merge together so we have a united front against our enemies and a stronghold on the black drug trade."

"They're looking for weakness, Pop. They don't give a damn about any united front. If we weren't up against X, they'd never come to us with this crap."

"You sound like your brother Orlando."

"Can't fault a man when he's right," Vegas replied.

"One thing's for sure," I said. "We need to get our soldiers together because like it or not, we're at war." I sighed, suddenly feeling too damn old for this shit.

"Sure sounds like it. I just wish we had more options. I can't believe that with all the money we make for these people, no one is coming to our aid." Vegas sounded as frustrated as I felt.

"We did have the same visitor from Williamsburg who offered not just to help, but to solve our problems. As far as I'm concerned, that's a route of last resort."

"I agree. We take that deal, we might as well close up shop."

"Tell that to your brother when you see him," I said.

"Let me make some calls. I already pulled together some guys from the old days that were always dependable," he suggested, but neither of us finished that sentence with the words I was sure we were both thinking: "Not as dependable as Daryl Graham."

"You do that. I'll see you back at the house." I hung up the phone.

I heard a sound coming from behind me and turned toward the back of the lot. A slight movement caused me to pull out my .38 as I went over to investigate. Halfway there, I saw a figure appear from the shadows.

I raised my gun, pointing it dead center, until the person was close enough for me to see his face. "What the hell are you doing here?" In that instant, I saw a flash from the corner of my eye and felt a strange warm sensation on my chest. It took me a second to realize what had just happened.

"You—you shot me?" I put a hand on my chest and felt the warm, sticky blood oozing through my shirt just before I collapsed and everything went black.

Vegas

21

I rode in the middle car of a small caravan of vehicles, wearing all black from head to toe, with Bonnie strapped to my hip. From the moment Orlando had called and said the old man was shot, I'd taken over security at the house, orchestrating things to get my family to the hospital safely.

Despite my cool demeanor, I was feeling overwhelmed. The stagnant silence in the car seemed to be sucking all the oxygen out of the atmosphere, but it didn't matter, since I could hardly breathe anyway. Ever since I got Orlando's call, I'd felt like I was suffocating, and being in the confined space of the car made it even worse.

We couldn't have pulled up in front of the hospital soon enough. I needed out. I think I jumped out of the car before it had even come to a complete stop. I exhaled and began issuing orders.

"I need two men on the front entrance and two men around back. Richie, case the place for any side entrances, and make sure that wherever there's an entrance and an exit, it's covered with one of our people."

Once my men affirmed their understanding of my orders, I made my way back toward the rear of the car, checking the perimeter. When I was sure the coast was clear, I opened the door and allowed my mother to exit. I had to give it to her: She took "Never let them see you sweat" to the next level. She got out of the car looking as unruffled as if I were just taking her on a Sunday afternoon drive. There I was trying my best to be strong for her, but like always, she was the one holding me down.

We were joined by Harris and London, who'd traveled in the car behind us. I led the family to the automatic sliding doors at the hospital's entrance.

I turned to give one last order to my men, who would be staying outside. "If you see anyone who looks like they might have so much as a fingernail clipper, stop and frisk them."

"What about the police?" one of them asked me.

"What about them? You all have carry permits. Tell them to call Captain Marks of the hundred and third if they have any problems. Harris has already spoken to him."

He nodded his understanding, and I ushered my family into the reception area.

"Duncan," I said to the woman behind the intake desk. "I need to know which room LC—"

"Fourth floor, surgery," the woman responded, cutting me off. Apparently she'd been asked this question already. We dashed off to the elevator bank without even saying thank you. I pressed the button to go up.

As I paced back and forth in front of the doors, I felt a hand on my shoulder and heard my mother's soothing voice. "Calm down, honey."

"I'm all right, Ma," I replied, although we both knew that wasn't true.

The elevator chimed and the doors opened. I raced in and hit the button for the fourth floor, pacing inside as we rode up. When the elevator arrived on the fourth floor, I darted out in front of the others, looking around until I spotted Orlando staring out a window overlooking the parking lot. He looked as bad as I felt.

I called out to him, and when he turned to me, I gasped at the sight of his shirt covered in blood. I'd seen plenty of blood in my life, but knowing that it was my father's blood that stained my brother's shirt was almost more than I could process.

"He's in surgery, Ma, but it doesn't look good," Orlando said to us as we approached. He was obviously trying to hold back tears.

Despite everything, my mother was still stronger than all of us. I watched as she embraced Orlando. London lingered close by, touching his back, not quite sure what to do.

"Vegas, can I talk to you for a second?" Harris tugged on my arm and then led me a short way down the corridor. This did not sit well with me. I already didn't like the guy, and now he was pulling me away from family at the worst possible moment.

"What?" I asked bluntly, looking back to where Ma and Orlando were still embracing.

"So what are you going to do?"

I looked back at Harris to see him standing there with his arms folded like he was scolding one of his kids. If I didn't already have bigger things to worry about, I would have laid his ass out for this arrogant disrespect.

"In reference to what?" I asked, swallowing the urge to punch him in the throat.

"Everything," he huffed. "LC's on his death bed, the girls barely escaped three Muslim hit men at the Marriott, and I just heard Kennedy's dead. You're the Duncan messiah. With LC dead, how the hell do you plan on stopping them from killing the rest of us?"

I flexed my fists, still contemplating how good it would feel to break his jaw. "First of all, you arrogant son of a bitch, my old man's not dead yet. This isn't the first time he's been shot," I growled under my breath, glancing back at my mother, who was engrossed in conversation with Orlando and unaware of me and Harris. London, however, was trying to ear hustle. At least she was smart enough to keep her distance. "And second of all, I'm nobody's messiah, but if you don't get the fuck out my face with this bullshit, I'm gonna nail your yellow ass to a cross like Jesus Christ himself and use you as bait to catch whoever did this to my father. So I suggest you step the fuck off."

I was reminded of why the little part of me that did like Harris could tolerate him. He was so damn good at following Duncan orders. He backed right the fuck up.

I walked back over to Orlando, who was now by himself, staring up at a television. My mother had released him, and she was now consoling Paris, who'd just arrived with Sasha.

"You see this shit?" Orlando said.

I looked up at the screen to see a breaking news story about the shooting at the Marriott. Thank God it was being reported as a gang-related event.

"O, what happened?" I asked, pulling him over to a row of chairs where we could talk alone.

"I . . . don't know." He dropped his head in his hands, rubbing his eyes as if it could erase the images of all that he had seen. "We had just finished our meeting with Popeye and Tony. Pop went outside to smoke a cigar, and I went to my office to see if I could reach Junior. Ten minutes later . . . *Bam!*" He looked up at me, his eyes wet with tears. "He was just lying there, Vegas. I didn't even know if he was still alive."

"You think it was X and his people?"

A look of fury passed over his face. "Who else? Vegas, I'm gonna kill that son of—"

"Excuse me." A deep-voiced doctor interrupted us as he stepped into the room and announced, "I'm Doctor Hondo." He was scanning the notes on the chart in his hand.

Everyone raced over to the doctor. "How is he?" my mother asked, revealing her desperation for the first time. "How is my husband?"

"Not much has changed. He's still in surgery. We're doing all we can. There was a lot of blood loss," the doctor said.

"Doc, come on," I said, urging him to keep it straight with us. "Truthfully, is he going to make it?"

He removed his glasses and looked me dead in the eye. "We've got our best people in there, but if you believe in prayer, now would be the time to pray," he said with no emotion whatsoever, then he turned and left the room.

I rubbed my hands over my face, trying to wipe away any expression that would give away the true fear I felt. I had to remain strong for my family.

Orlando and I went back over to the chairs to continue our conversation, but my mother was right behind us.

"How are my boys doing?" she said, sitting down next to me and putting an arm around my shoulder.

"Never mind us. How are you?" I said.

She looked to me then Orlando. "I'll be better when this is taken care of. Do you understand?" Even with the doctor's news, she was standing strong as ever. The fight in her overpowered her pain—a true Duncan trait.

"I got this, Ma," I said. "I promise I'll take care of it."

"I know you will, Vegas. Orlando, give him whatever help he needs. I don't care what it costs or who has to die. I want this taken care of sooner rather than later." She walked away, leaving me and O to take in her words.

"You heard, her little brother. It's time to make some moves. X has his way of fighting, and so do we." Orlando didn't say anything. Technically my little brother was in charge of the family business, but as the older and more experienced brother, it was my job to bring down our father's shooter.

Chippy

22

I had no idea how long I'd been sitting in a chair in the corner of LC's hospital room, willing him to open his eyes. At one point, I'd approached his bed and pulled the bottom of the sheets up to watch his feet, hoping he'd just wiggle a toe. Exasperated and feeling defeated, I went back to the chair and squeezed my eyes shut. It was the only way I knew to keep the tears from falling. Once they started, there would be no stopping them, but with the children coming in and out to check on LC, I needed to keep my poker face. I had to be strong for them, to let them know that everything was going to be all right—although the poor prognosis made that so hard to do. The doctors didn't sound hopeful, so no matter what I portrayed for my kids, inside I was breaking into a million little pieces.

When the door opened, I figured it was the nurse coming in to check his vitals for the thousandth time that day. I'd spent every waking moment at my husband's side in the ICU, so I'd witnessed for myself the sad reality that there were no changes, no signs of improvement. I didn't even bother to open my eyes to greet the nurse; instead, I started praying for a miracle.

When I heard the sound of a chair scraping gently across the floor, I opened my eyes to see Rio taking a seat next to the bedside. I started to say something to him, but then he started talking to LC, and I knew it was best to let my son have his moment alone with his father.

Rio and LC had a tough relationship. LC loved Rio, but he came up in a time when it was wholly unacceptable for a man to be homosexual, so he'd had a very hard time regaining his footing when Rio came out to us. It probably didn't help that his first three sons were alpha males, mirroring their father in so many ways. They played sports, shot guns, and were hyper competitive. Our oldest three boys were homing pigeons for beautiful women, which accounted for this mess we were in right now.

Rio, on the other hand, was quite unlike his father, and it made it so difficult for them to communicate. Often it seemed like Rio didn't feel brave enough to open up to LC, so if he wanted to talk now, I would keep my eyes closed and let him have his moment with LC. After all, none of us knew when it might be the last time we could speak to him.

"You can't die on me," I heard him say, choking back tears as he spoke. "We were just starting to get along. At least I felt like you were beginning to see me as more than the son who disappointed you."

He was silent for a moment, and it took all my strength not to go over and take him into my arms, comforting him like I did when he was a little boy.

"I know we've had our problems in the past," Rio continued, "and I also know that you will never be able to fully accept that you have a gay son. I wanted so much to be like my brothers, but I'm not. I'm gay, and that's my normal. But I know you were doing what you thought was right, and I want you to know that I forgive you, Pop."

LC and I had fought over that very thing so many times in the past. I couldn't understand why, even after some time passed, my husband couldn't accept Rio for who he was. LC liked to be in control, and I couldn't make him understand that Rio's sexuality was something neither one of us could ever change. He didn't have to like it, I told him, but at least he could try to accept it. What Rio said next made me think that in his own way, perhaps LC had been coming around to see things differently.

"You sending me on those missions recently with Paris and Sasha helped me to see that you really do consider me a valuable part of this family business—and that you weren't going to punish me forever for being the flaming gay son. You sending me off with Kennedy lately has meant so much. It tells me that in spite of everything, I *am* LC Duncan's son. So, Pop, thank you, because I know that I'm hard for you to fully accept."

He seemed to relax a bit now, as he went on. "I mean, I'm not just gay; I'm super gay, unable to slide under the radar. People see me coming a mile away in my Barney's fashionista clothing and my swishy walk. Yes, I probably exaggerate it in front of you to piss you off, but that's because I need you to know that I'm never going to change. Not for you, and not for anyone."

Listening to my baby pour out his heart made me so proud of him. He'd probably never say any of this if his dad were awake, but it was obvious that he had been needing to get this off his hairless, waxed chest. Yes, I could have a sense of humor about this too.

"Pop, I love you, and I need you to get up so that maybe one day I can actually tell you all of this to your face."

He sighed, and then I heard him stand. He dragged the chair back to its original position, and a few seconds later, I could feel him standing over me. I kept my eyes closed as he placed a kiss on the top of my head. A few seconds after that I heard the sound of the door closing.

As I opened my eyes, a lone tear escaped and dripped down my face. I brushed it away and exhaled hard to release my pent-up emotions before more tears could begin cascading. I heard the door open again, and I turned, expecting to see Rio returning, or maybe one of the other kids. They were coming and going so often lately that they might as well have installed a revolving door.

The person who walked in was definitely not who I was expecting.

"Donna. What are you doing here?" I was sure my face revealed my feelings about her presence. I'd been caught too off guard to slip my mask of calm back on.

She closed the door behind her. "I came to see LC, of course. How's he doing?"

"Of course," I echoed then got up and went to stand protectively beside my husband. "I'm sure LC would appreciate you coming to see him."

"Please," Donna said, waving her hand. "You and LC, you're like family."

"Yes, family." I pulled the sheets up to LC's chin.

"I came as soon as I heard."

"I'm sure you did."

She walked over and stood next to me. "How's he doing?" she asked again.

I shook my head. "Not good. He's in an induced coma. They have him on a respirator for now."

Donna looked down at him. "Oh, no. I can't imagine what it would be like . . . for you . . . if LC were to—"

I put my hand up. "I don't even want to think about that right now."

Donna respected my wishes. "How are the kids holding up? I saw Vegas in the hallway, and the rest of them in the waiting area."

"As well as to be expected, considering their father's in the hospital in a coma."

"I didn't see Junior," she said. "Is he okay?"

I stared at her for a moment, unsure how much I wanted to say. My feelings about Donna were complicated, and I didn't know if I really wanted her to know all the details about our situation with Brother X just yet.

"He'll be around shortly," I lied. Truth was we hadn't seen or heard from Junior in days.

Fortunately, a knock on the door prevented her from probing any further.

"Knock, knock," London said, sticking her head in the room. She saw who was with me and walked in the room to give her a hug. "Aunt Donna!"

"London, how are you?" Donna asked.

London pulled out of the embrace but kept one arm around Donna. She looked at her father. "About as well as can be expected, considering."

"I know, I know," Donna consoled London. "But just hang in there. Your father is a strong man."

"Yes, he is," London agreed through her tears. She looked over at me as I struggled to hold back tears of my own. Reaching her hand out to take mine, she said, "And so is his wife."

When she squeezed my hand, I quickly turned away. This time the tears fell freely, and there was nothing I could do about it.

Vegas

23

"You ready for another game, O.G.?" one of the young bucks on the handball court boldly challenged. There was nothing like being out in the fresh air, playing a little handball. I loved watching basketball, baseball, and football, but when it came to actually playing a sport, I'd take handball any day. I guess it was a New York thing, or perhaps the lone wolf in me.

"I'd love to stay and kick your ass, young brother, but I'm late for an appointment. You brothers be strong." I gave each one of them some dap before walking to my car to retrieve Bonnie and Clyde. Once I had them holstered in, I put on a jacket and headed into the brownstone across from the park. Hopefully I hadn't taken too long or moved too quickly. Neither would be a good option.

The building had three floors, with two apartments on each floor. Surveying the doors for a telltale sign, I kept moving from the first floor. Running up the stairs, I spotted what I'd been looking for: an apartment with an Italian flag sticker on it. I definitely had the right place.

Reaching into my holster, I pulled out Clyde. It wasn't always the case, but sometimes bigger was better, and I was most definitely looking to make an impression. Taking a deep breath, I ran at that door and slammed my right foot into it, knocking the door right off the hinges.

"Damn, they just don't make doors like they used to, do they?" I said, stepping into the studio apartment.

"What the fuck?" The big, hairy naked bastard on the bed jumped up, reaching for his pants, which probably contained a gun. He froze when he saw Clyde aimed at his head. I took a few steps closer to the bed, watching his eyes light up with terror as he recognized my face. "Oh, shit. Vegas! You're out!"

"That's right, Johnny. I'm out." I grabbed a chair, pulling it up next to the bed, then motioned to the cocaine on the table. "You still fucking with that shit, I see."

"Just a little here and there." Johnny Calzone was a mid-level Mafioso for the Genovese crime family. He specialized in street level gun sales. Rumor had it that a quarter of the guns on New York City's streets came through his hands at one time or another.

"Where's my money, Johnny?" I eased his pants closer to me with my foot, just in case.

"What m—money, Vegas?" he stuttered.

I glanced over at Terri Russo, the bleach blonde wife of Genovese capo "No-Nose" Frank Russo. She pulled the sheet up above her breasts. Johnny had a bad cocaine habit, and an even worse habit of fucking his boss's wife and daughter. He'd been doing both since before I went away. How the hell he'd kept this secret from his boss for all these years was a mystery to me.

I took out my phone and snapped a quick series of pictures of the happy couple. Terri, a feisty, big-titty woman, looked like she wanted to jump up and snatch the phone out of my hands, but her obvious fear of Clyde kept her at bay.

"The money for the key of coke I gave you before I got locked up." I snapped a couple more pictures, this time pulling back the sheets so their naked bodies were exposed. Terri tried to cover herself again, but when I pointed Clyde at her head, she backed the fuck up.

"Man, Vegas, I paid you for that dope. Don't you remember?"

"No, I don't remember shit, but that's okay." I lowered Clyde, placing him back in his holster, then took a good look at my phone. "You know, these iPhones really do take great pictures." I turned the phone so they could see a full-screen shot of their naked bodies, side by side.

"You motherfucker!" Mrs. Russo grabbed the lamp off the nightstand and raised it up like she was about to throw it at me.

"No, Terri!" Johnny screamed, wrestling the lamp out of her hands.

"Smart move, Johnny. Now, about my money . . . I guess I'll just take the matter up with her husband. He still has the same cell number, right? Maybe I should just text him."

Terri looked at Johnny with fear in her eyes. "Do something! Give him his money or kick his ass, but do something."

"Well, he's not gonna kick my ass," I said with a laugh.

"I don't have that kind of money, Terri," Johnny said, on the verge of whining. She looked totally disgusted with him.

"Hmm, now, that's a problem, because I need my money. Maybe I should just send these pictures to Frank. I'm sure he'll pay me to find out where these pictures came from." I lifted my thumb to start writing a text, and before I could press the first letter, Johnny was begging.

"Come on, Vegas. How long we known each other? You know I'm good for it. Matter of fact, I'm more valuable to you alive than dead. You know that."

I scratched my head. "Look, I'm not a totally unreasonable guy. Maybe we can make a trade."

"A trade? A trade sounds good. What kind of trade?" He turned to Terri, looking hopeful. She rolled her eyes and turned away from him.

"An informational trade," I said. "Rumor has it that you supply the Islamic Black Panther Party with guns."

"Well, you know you shouldn't believe everything you hear," he replied, but his face told the truth. Johnny did way too much coke to be able to hide his thoughts.

"I don't, but I believe *that* shit. Now, are you going to tell me what I want to know or what?" I started to type a text.

"I'm not messing with IBPP," he insisted. "Those dudes are crazy. They'll kill me."

"And you think her husband won't kill you? Have you met Frank Russo? I used to play cards with him in prison. He's not a very nice guy when he's upset."

"Come on, Vegas. Anything but that." Sweat beads had started forming on his forehead.

"Johnny, all I want to know is where they're held up. I'm not asking you to mess with them. It'll be our little secret." I looked down at my phone then glanced up at Terri. "Unless you want me to send these pictures to Frank."

"Johnny, tell him what he wants to know." Terri sounded even more scared of her husband than she was of my gun. "If Frank sees these pictures, he's going kill us both."

Johnny still wasn't giving in. "Vegas, you don't understand."

"No, John, you don't understand. I want that information. Now, you have about five seconds before I hit send." I started a countdown with my fingers.

When I was down to two, I started waving my thumb over the screen like I was preparing to hit the button, and Johnny finally relented.

"Okay! Okay! They spend most of their time at a safehouse in Rosedale. Two-seventeen Wilshire Road. Jesus Christ, don't send those pictures."

Paris

24

"Daddy, the others, they're not like you and me. I'm the only one who understands that you should never appear weak in this business, because it makes you an even bigger target. If somebody hurts one person in your family, then it's your job to make sure their entire lineage is dead.

"That's what's pissing me off right now. To our enemies—hell, even to our supporters—we're coming off like some scared-ass little pussies instead of the powerful Duncan family that you raised us to be. To them it'll look like we're impotent without you here to guide us.

"I feel like I'm the only one who knows what to do. Now, I'm trying to be patient, I am, Daddy, but you and I both know that's just not how I was made. I will not be patient, especially when it comes to killing the bastard who put you in this bed."

I stared down at my father, holding onto his hand for dear life and willing him to answer me. I needed him to say something, anything that would help me at that moment, because I wasn't getting a whole hell of a lot of comfort from waiting. "You hurt my family, you die," had always been the Duncan motto, which was why I couldn't believe that my brothers hadn't waged an all-out war to avenge this.

Only thing I hated more than waiting was being helpless, so to have to experience the two together felt like my own personal hell. Hospitals were cesspools of incompetence, if you ask me. You can walk into the hospital with a small issue and come out worse than when you walked in—if you come out at all. As far as I was concerned, these inept fools who worked here were half the reason Daddy didn't seem to be getting any better. I swear, if he didn't make it, I would come back here with my guns blazing, right after I killed the motherfucker who shot Daddy in the first place.

"Honey, we all just need to remain positive," my mother said as she walked in and joined me at the bedside.

I shook my head in amazement. I didn't understand how my mother, of all people, was not raging mad. Hell, I hadn't even heard her complain once, even though I knew it had to be eating her up, watching her husband lying comatose in this bed. Those two had a deep connection. Not only did my parents have a strong partnership, but they were still, even after all these years, madly in love.

"Mom, I am positive. I'm positive that the person who did this should burn in hell, and I should be the one to light the match."

She put a hand on my shoulder, but didn't stop me from continuing my rant. "I don't care how Junior feels about Sonya. He's wrong. I would never choose another person over this family, and you know I've been in that position," I said, reminding her of the sacrifice I'd made when I had to kill Niles Monroe. "And I have never regretted my choice, Mom. I loved Niles, but family comes first." I looked down to Daddy, the man who had instilled that valuable lesson in me ever since I was a child. "So I don't understand how Junior can betray us for some girl he didn't even know a year ago. I mean, am I the only one who thinks he needs to give that damn crazy man his wife back and move on? How the hell can he choose her over us?"

She sighed. "I don't know what to tell you, Paris. I don't know what your brother is thinking at the moment. I swear that woman must have some kind of voodoo or something, the hold she has over him." She looked down and put her hand on Daddy's arm, giving him a sad smile. "Then again, there was a time your father felt the same way when other people were telling him to stay away from me. I guess there's no telling what a man will do when he's in love."

"It's not the same thing," I said, refusing to ignore what was right in front of our faces. "If it weren't for my pussy-whipped brother, Daddy would not be in here fighting for his life."

She shot me an angry look. "Paris, you will not talk about my son that way!"

Oh, Lord, I thought, rolling my eyes. *There's nothing more fierce than a mother protecting her son.*

She went on, insisting, "Your father would want you to keep a cool head right now."

"No, he wouldn't." I stood up. "I'm gonna go get some air. I'm sure you want to spend some time alone with Daddy." I left, knowing I was incapable of saying what she wanted to hear.

Entering the waiting area, I found Orlando, Vegas, and Sasha. Orlando and Vegas were deep in conversation, but Sasha spoke up when she saw me enter the room.

"Paris, how's Uncle LC?" she asked loudly, glancing at my brothers. They stopped their conversation as soon as they heard my name.

"How do you think he's doing?" I snapped. "While y'all are sitting here talking about nothing, my father is in there fighting for his life, and there is not a damn thing any of you are willing to do about it."

"It's not that simple," Vegas jumped in. As happy as I'd been to see him when he first came home from prison, I was growing sick of his "Let's wait and see" attitude. It seemed like instead of prison making him hard, it had turned him into a punk. Even Rio would have been tougher than this.

"Yes, it is that simple. We should just kill these motherfuckers. Not like we don't know who they are or why they're doing this," I reminded them.

"Why I got to be the motherfucking voice of reason?" he said, sounding thoroughly fed up with me. "You need to calm the fuck down, Paris. Don't nobody know where Junior is."

"And?" I challenged. "Who gives a fuck where he is? This is all his fault anyway."

"And what if they got him?" Vegas asked. "If we act without thinking this through, they will not hesitate to kill him. And if you think Ma is upset about Dad, just imagine what Junior's death would do to her."

I was struck speechless for a second. I hadn't thought about that possibility.

"Vegas is right." Sasha had the nerve to open her big fat mouth.

"If I were you, I'd shut the fuck up. This don't have nothing to do with you. That's our father in there, not yours," I snapped.

"Fuck you, Paris," she shot back. "Did you forget that I already lost my father to the family business? So don't try and tell me this has nothing to do with me. I have as much right to be here and to give my opinion as any of you," she shouted before storming out of the room.

"See, you always got to say something stupid. I thought that motherhood would have calmed you the fuck down and given you some maturity, but I see I was wrong," Vegas said.

To hear him coming to annoying-ass Sasha's defense like that had me seeing red. What the fuck was wrong with my family these days?

"Oh, please!" I yelled. "You the one who got your ass sent to prison, so don't call me stupid unless you looking in a mirror."

Orlando finally stepped in to the fray. "Well, I agree with Paris." He stood up and moved closer to me. You could have knocked me down with a feather. Orlando and I were never—and I mean never—on the same side.

"Then you're both stupid asses." Vegas stood his ground.

Orlando reminded him what was up. "Look, I'm the head of this family, and at the end of the day, it's going to be my call what course of action we take. Not yours."

"Yeah, okay, little brother. We'll take your course of action—if you want to get all of us killed. If you haven't noticed, they're cherry-picking our top soldiers. As fast as I'm training them, they're getting killed or injured. This is not some half-ass game, in case you've forgotten." Vegas got up in Orlando's face.

"Man, fuck you!" Orlando balled up his fists. My brothers were about two seconds away from tearing each other apart.

"Stop it! Stop it right now! You two are supposed to be our leaders and you're fighting like dogs in heat. What would your father say?" Mom stood in the doorway, dropping the ultimate bomb and silencing us all.

Vegas

25

There was a time when Uncle Lou was alive that I would have turned to him for advice, but with Pop out of commission and Uncle Lou dead, I had to turn to another elder outside of the family. I sought out Minister Farah to ask for his opinion about how best to utilize Johnny's information. While we both wanted the same thing, Orlando was letting his need for revenge overrule common sense about our predicament. He wanted us to go in guns blazing, like a bunch of street corner thugs, and take out X and his people. Not that I didn't want to put Bonnie and Clyde to use myself, but we weren't built for that type of warfare. The Duncans were more like ninjas than samurai. That was why we'd survived when others couldn't.

"So you think my plan is solid?" I glanced over at Minister Farah, who was sitting on about five pillows so that he could see over the dashboard of his SUV as he drove. We'd just come from staking out X's little hideaway in Rosedale.

"Very solid. It'll keep the body count down and give you some breathing room to negotiate. I'm proud of you. It's a well thought out plan," he said as he maneuvered the car to the curb. "You know, Vegas, this may not be coming at the most ideal time, with your father being in the hospital, but I have always considered you to be the son I never had," he said sincerely.

"Minister, I don't think anyone has ever given me a greater compliment. Thank you." I leaned over and offered my hand, but he pulled me in for a quick guy-hug. Truth be told, if anything did happen to LC, I knew Minister Farah would be there for me. Other than my family and Marie, he and Daryl had been the only constants in my life.

"Be safe, my son. I will keep you in my prayers," he said to me as I exited the car.

After he drove off, I headed down the street and cut through a hidden passageway to get to my next stop. When I arrived at a pink metal door, I rapped on it quickly and waited until I was let in by Dexter, the burly bodyguard I'd been considering hiring away from this joint.

"What's up, Vegas?" He offered his huge knuckles for a fist bump.

I tapped my fist against his. "Nothing much, Dex. She still here?"

"She's waiting for you."

I disappeared down the long brick hallway, opening another door and stepping into an elegantly decorated fifties-style brothel, where there was so much scantily clad pussy that even in my current state of distress over Pop I couldn't help but notice. There were a couple of leggy white girls, including one whose ass gave Iggy Azalea a run for her money, and a sister or two that made a brother homesick. In spite of all the beauty that surrounded me, however, Marie was still the hottest woman in that place, and she knew it.

"Hey, sexy." Marie's face broke into a wide smile the second she saw me from a couch across the room. She came over and wrapped her arms around me, leaning in for a deep, passionate kiss. Even as her hands found their way to my crotch to properly welcome me, she let me know that she had noticed and didn't appreciate my wandering eyes. She said, "You have the best in the house, so there is no need to be breaking your neck looking at the help."

Shit, I was no fool. I knew better than to argue with her, but that didn't mean I was going along with her agenda. No matter what she said, I'd have to be six feet under before I stopped appreciating beautiful women.

Taking my hand in hers, she led me to her own personal room, where I knew she occasionally saw super high–priced customers. Behind the closed door, she moved in and threw her arms around my neck, obviously ready to get busy.

"Hey." I untwined her arms and pulled away.

"What? Baby, it's been two days. I miss you," she whined, rubbing her breasts against me. "Come on. Let's make a baby."

"Look, I missed you too, but I'm here for business, not pleasure." She gave me a sexy pout and reached her hand out to grip my manhood again, but I shot her a look that caused her to step back.

"Is Conrad here?" I asked.

"Yeah, he's here. And you owe me big time," she said with a frown. "For hooking him up and for not fucking me."

"Don't you know by now I'm a man who always pays his debts?" I kissed her gently. "Now, stop frowning, I'm going to make it up to you."

"And you're going to pay me back with interest," she snapped with attitude.

"Looking forward to it." I smirked, leading her back out of the room. "Where's Conrad?" We stepped into the hallway, and she knocked on the door next to her room.

Inside the room, a very happy Captain Conrad Marks of the NYPD sat on the bed as two hot, naked black-and-Asian biracial twins flanked him, buttoning his shirt. Captain Marks and I had been friends since he was a lonely white beat cop back on Jamaica Avenue, and I was in my late teens. Junior and I helped him quite a bit with his career—with the help of Pop and Uncle Lou, of course. To say he was a dirty cop was an understatement, but he was *our* dirty cop.

"Vegas, I have to tell you that I haven't been fucked like that since I was a sergeant and we used to go to your friend Majestic's strip club in Long Island City." He was grinning like a twelve-year-old boy as he offered me his hand.

"It's good to have you back," he said. "I'm sorry about that trouble you had a while ago. Wish I could have been more help, but it wasn't in my borough, so it was off limits."

"Nah, it's all good. Your loyalty was never at question."

Marie directed the girls, "Lia and Mia, you can go now."

Conrad and I watched as they skipped their perfect asses out of there. I knew Marie was watching me like a hawk, but I couldn't help myself. There was something about that combination of an Asian girl with a little chocolate in her that just got me every time.

Marie closed the door behind them. "I'm glad you enjoyed our services, Captain. I'm sure I can arrange for you to have a weekly visit." She handed him a gold VIP card.

"Why, thank you, young lady. After that little treat you provided for me today, I think I'll be taking you up on that." Marie smiled graciously and then stepped out of the room, leaving Conrad and me to talk.

"So, Vegas, today I get laid by two of the most beautiful women I've ever seen. I get a free pussy card, and on the seat of my car this morning, I find twenty thousand dollars cash." He stood up and started looping his belt through his pants. "What am I supposed to make of that?"

"Conrad," I said with a huge smile, "if I were you, I'd just go with it, because today must be your lucky day. Now, come let me buy you a drink so I can tell you why it's going to be even luckier."

Brother X

26

The brothers and I finished our evening prayers then sat down to eat a fantastic meal prepared by a handful of the brothers' wives. I'm not sure if it was that the food was so good or that I hadn't eaten all day, but I was on my third plate of food. Elijah had been constantly prodding me to eat during the day, but we'd done an arson job on one of the Duncan car dealerships in Long Island earlier, and I always found it hard to eat until after a job was successfully completed.

"Xavier," Elijah called to me as he hung up his phone. I glanced his way to acknowledge I was listening, but I didn't stop devouring the chicken leg in my hand. "Most of the Duncans are still at the hospital, except for Vegas, who is impossible to follow, and Junior, who has fallen off the grid with your wife. I'm not quite sure if they know about the fire yet."

A satisfied smile emerged as I imagined the shock on their faces when they found out one of their precious dealerships had gone up in flames. This was the message I wanted to make sure everyone heard loud and clear: You fuck my wife, I fuck your entire family and everyone associated with you. They had no idea what we had planned for them next.

"What about tonight? Have we gotten the call? Is everything in place?"

"Everything is in place, and the men have all been issued weapons. We're just waiting on you."

I dropped the chicken back on my plate, my mind back on business. "Well, then let's move out."

***

An hour later, everything was in place, and we arrived at the Staten Island warehouse where Lincoln had told us he worked. From the outside, the building appeared abandoned, but upon closer inspection we could see the infrared surveillance system. We sat in our cars at a safe enough distance to go undetected as we watched the Uzi-carrying sentries who circled the building just like Lincoln had described it to us.

"Let's take 'em out," I told Elijah. He gave the signal, and within seconds our sniper hit the sentries. We watched them fall one by one, and then our men, almost forty strong, stormed the building.

"We've been compromised!" A Duncan guard hollered into his walkie-talkie when he spotted us. He lifted his gun at an unsuspecting Elijah and was about to pull the trigger.

"Drop it," I commanded, pointing my Desert Eagle handgun at him. Four of our men were standing nearby with their weapons trained on him also.

He didn't pull the trigger, but he didn't drop his weapon, either. Lincoln had said the Duncan employees were loyal, and that was proving to be an understatement. Most men would have dropped the weapon on command when faced with multiple firearms pointed at them.

"I can't do that," he answered, which came as no surprise to me.

"That's too bad," I replied right before I unloaded two shots into his chest. His body flew backward before he landed dead on the concrete.

Elijah turned and gave me a grateful nod.

I looked down at the man on the ground and shook my head. "You're incredibly loyal—for a dead man." The laughter of my men broke some of the tension, if only for a moment.

"Fan out," I ordered. "And bring me the person in charge—alive."

They spread out like a swarm of roaches, covering every exit and entrance. For the next five minutes, all I heard was automatic gunfire and screaming. The Duncans' employees were putting up a good fight, but they were outnumbered five to one, so it didn't take long for me to hear the echo of "Clear . . . Clear . . . Clear . . . " on my earpiece.

Elijah came running to report, "We've got ten Duncan men down and one captive."

"Good. Losses on our side?"

"Two men dead, one injured."

"May Allah bless their souls on their journey to the kingdom," I said.

"May Allah bless their souls," the men repeated in unison.

"Brother Xavier, I think we might have something here," Ahmed shouted from across the warehouse.

Elijah and I walked side by side to where Ahmed was struggling to open a large, heavy door. Elijah stepped over to help him, and when they managed to pry it open, we saw something we definitely hadn't expected. I think we had all been surprised by the Duncans' power on some level, but this took it to new heights, because piled almost to the ceiling in that room was enough of marijuana to fill four tractor trailers.

"What do we do with this?" Elijah asked.

It took me a moment to wrap my head around just how much dope in dollars and cents was piled up in front of us. It had to be millions. Sensing that something was up, a group of our men had gathered near the doorway, and turning to look at them, I swear I could see dollar signs in their eyes.

"Burn it!" I barked at Elijah. "Burn every drop of this poison."

Elijah, as always, didn't hesitate. He shouted to his men, "You heard the man! Burn it!"

I was sure some of the less devout among our men were silently questioning my judgment, no doubt tempted by the money that could be made selling this weed on the streets, but no one was stupid enough to protest out loud. Wisely, they scrambled to set the Duncans' weed aflame.

I stepped outside as the smoke started filling the room, and one of my soldiers brought the lone Duncan survivor out to me. As they approached, I could see that he was terrified.

"My name is Brother Xavier, and I want you to deliver a message to the Duncans. Can you do that?"

The man nodded his head. "As long as I'm alive."

I laughed. "Tell the Duncans that we're going to keep making these little field trips until they give us Junior. Now, can you do that?"

"Yeah, I can do that," he said, looking like he was about to piss his pants.

"Good." I turned to Ahmed. "Drop him off near that hospital once we get this all wrapped up." As Ahmed escorted our guest toward the cars, Elijah approached me with his phone to his ear and a frown on his face.

"It's the Jew," he said, handing me the phone. "He says it's important."

"Bernie, this really isn't a good time," I said into the phone. He ignored me and began spelling out the reason for his call.

"Oh, really?" I replied when he was finally finished. "Well, thanks for the heads up, Bernie. I'll make the necessary arrangements on our part." I hung up and handed Elijah his phone.

"What'd the Jew have to say?" he asked.

Several of our men had started spilling out of the building as the smoke inside grew thicker. They were loitering around, close enough to hear anything I might say to Elijah. "Come on," I said. "Let's get out of here before we all get contact highs. I'll explain it to you on the way back to Rosedale."

Junior

27

After a week of the most unbelievable sex with not a care in the world, Sonya and I had finally come up for air. We traveled down to Camden, New Jersey, in a Zipcar, had a little lunch at Joe's Crab Shack, then left the Zipcar in the parking lot and headed down the street to an old tenement. We went around to the unmarked entrance in the seedy-looking alley in the back. It was a place where you had to be either desperate or brave to enter. At the moment, I was a little of both. There was nothing I wanted more in life than to be with Sonya, and I was willing to do anything to make that happen.

"Hey, man," Damon greeted me as we slipped into his office, a twenty by twenty room jam-packed with computers and printers.

Damon was one of the East Coast's best counterfeiters, and quite possibly the most successful in the world because of his approach. Most U.S. counterfeiters concentrated on making fake $20 and $100 dollar bills, but Damon's specialty was foreign currency. He'd pretty much cornered the market on people looking for non-U.S. money. Our fathers had done business together for years before his pops died, but this was the first time I'd come to him for my own needs. Because of our personal history, he was willing to expand his services beyond counterfeit bills for me.

"My man." We slapped our palms together in greeting. "You got everything we need?" I asked.

"Yeah. New identities, with passports and credit cards to match." He held them up for me to see, but his eyes kind of glazed over and he looked away, which made me think he had something else on his mind. Damon had always been a little odd—a genius at what he did, but seriously lacking in social skills. I figured he was just uncomfortable about asking for his payment.

"Don't worry. I got your money," I said, motioning to Sonya. She opened her purse and handed over the large envelope containing his six-figure fee. Sure, it was a hell of a lot of money, but like I said, I was willing to do anything to be with my woman.

He looked down at the envelope and scrunched up his face. "It's not that," he said. "I just . . ." His voice faded away and he got that glazed-over look again. Dude was acting truly weird, and it was starting to piss me off.

"What, Damon? Just spit it out."

"Just, well, I just didn't think you'd go through with jumping town with what's going on with your family."

Damon usually stayed holed up in this dark room with all his computer equipment, so it hadn't occurred to me that he would have heard any talk about our beef with Brother X and his crew.

"Shit, to be honest, that's why we're leaving," I offered as an explanation. "With us gone, X should lose interest and back off my family."

Damon didn't say anything as he walked over to one of his desks and picked up a newspaper. I looked at Sonya, who was still holding the envelope full of cash, and shrugged. I probably should have prepared her for how weird this guy was before we came over here. When Damon brought the newspaper back to me, however, I realized that he wasn't acting strange for no reason.

"This was five days ago, man. You didn't know?"

"What the fuck!" I dropped the newspaper to the ground after I saw the headline: CAR DEALER SHOT IN LOT AMONGST LUXURY CARS. The room started spinning, and I had to lean against a nearby table to keep myself from falling over. How could I have misjudged the situation so badly? I thought that me and Sonya disappearing would stop the war from escalating, but it seemed to have done the opposite. And now Pop had been shot. Guilt ran through me like a knife to my heart.

Sonya came running to my side. She screamed when she saw what had set me off.

"Oh my God! He did it." She started to cry.

I don't know how we got out of there and into the car, but Sonya was behind the wheel as I started working the phone.

"O," I shouted as Orlando picked up. "Is it true?"

"It's bad. I ain't gonna lie. It's real bad." He sounded as broken as I'd ever heard him, even more than when his baby mama took off with his son.

"Where is everyone?"

"We're at the hospital," he answered.

"So, he's not dead?" I asked, sending up a split-second prayer that my father was still alive.

"Nah, but it's not looking good," he admitted.

"What hospital are you at? I'm coming."

Sonya placed her hand on top of mine as she drove, offering me some of her strength.

"We're at Long Island Jewish, but you can't just show up here. There's a bounty on your head."

"Man, fuck that. I'm coming."

"Look, go home through the tunnel and let me figure out how to sneak you in here."

"No, I'm on my way!" I was screaming at him now.

"Don't." It was Vegas's voice on the phone now. "We need you to be smart, because if anything happened to you, Mom would not make it. Just give us an hour, that's all. Plus, you need to get Sonya to the house so that she's safe. We'll figure something out."

Where Orlando had sounded broken, Vegas sounded calm and in charge. I realized that he was talking sense. "Fine," I said. "We'll go to the house, but if I don't hear from you in an hour, know that I will be on my way."

"Of course. You're a Duncan. And, Junior, this isn't your fault. This is the life we live, and it was only going to be a matter of time."

I hung up, hoping that one day I would come to believe, like Vegas did, that I wasn't to blame for all of this.

Sonya and I drove in silence. Finally, as we approached the family compound, she asked, "Should I be here? I mean, this is all my fault."

I reached out and touched her face. "You're a part of me. You're my family, so you need to be where I can keep you safe."

"But your mother hates me," she protested, unable to contain her worry. "She'll blame me for what happened to your father. For going back on my word to stay away from you and setting this all in motion. And she won't be wrong."

I shook my head. "You tried to stay away, but I wouldn't let you. I wouldn't give you up."

She still looked uncertain, so I tried again to convince her. "Sonya, here is something you don't know: When my father met my mother, they were not supposed to be together. They were on two very different paths, but they fell in love, and sometimes love forces you to make a choice. They went through a whole lot of challenges because of their choice, but that's just what you do when you love someone. Trust me. No matter what she said to you, my mother understands this, and one day she'll admit that to you."

"I can't stop loving you," she said.

I squeezed her hand. "Good, because I don't want you to. Ever."

Sonya fell silent again, and my mind traveled to the image of my father lying in a hospital bed, fighting for his life. I would find the person who gave the order and the one who had carried it out. There was no place on this entire planet where they would be safe from me. The only way I could free myself from guilt would be to kill the bastards who did this.

When we got to the safe house, I directed Sonya to drive the car into the garage. As soon as the garage door lowered, I hit a button and the floor slid open, revealing a rig that lowered the car into a sub-basement. Once we were down below, the floor closed again, so that there was no trace of our car ever having been there.

Sonya looked surprised, but of course she was. This was some James Bond type shit that allowed us to come and go like ghosts if we needed. I led her through a maze until we arrived at an underground bank vault, where I put in the combination. We stepped through into a stairwell that led us upstairs to another solid steel door with another combination, and then through one more door that opened into a back room. I touched my thumb on a keypad that validated who I was, and then we were safe.

As we entered the main house, I spotted Harris seated at the kitchen counter. He didn't even bother to let us get all the way inside before he went at me.

"Where the hell have you been?" he snapped without acknowledging Sonya at all. "Do you know what happened to LC?"

"Yes, I know, and that's why we're here," I answered, working to steady my voice because I probably had a five second window before I jumped all over his ass. Sonya, sensing my mood, reached out and grabbed my arm.

"Well, it's a little late considering whose fault all this is." He glared at me.

"Fuck you, Harris. And unless you want the next blood that's shed to be yours, you'd better step the hell back," I threatened.

"Well, I'm the one here helping your mom and your family as you run around with another man's wife," he continued boldly. If it hadn't been for London rushing into the room, he would have wound up face down on the floor.

"Harris!" she shouted, getting her husband in line. "You okay?" She came toward me, wrapping her arms around me. "I've never been so happy to see anyone."

We held each other tight for a minute, until she noticed that I wasn't alone.

"Sonya." She smiled, acknowledging my woman in an appropriate way. "We were worried about you too."

"We're good. Sorry to hear about your father," Sonya offered as the two of them hugged.

"He's strong, and I don't care what anybody says; it's gonna take way more than this to kill LC Duncan." I hoped like hell that my sister was right.

"Well, clearly I'm the only one around here dealing with reality," Harris chirped, sounding like he was still itching to get his face smashed in.

"Honey, can you go check on the girls?" she asked, with anger simmering just beneath the surface in her tone.

"Marisol is with them," he said, still not understanding how unwelcome his presence had become. The look that passed between them must have clarified it, because he stood up and left the room.

"Yes, I know he's being a jerk," she said in defense of her husband, "but we all deal with our fear differently."

My phone rang, and Orlando's number showed up on the screen.

"In ten minutes, a bulletproof car is going to meet you on Dixon and Third. Three of our men will be there, along with a second vehicle. Two blocks from the hospital, a paramedic vehicle will meet you, and they will transport you into the emergency wing, where you will be placed onto the back elevator and brought to Dad's floor. We have guards at every entrance to the floor. You will be safe."

"What about Sonya?" I asked.

"It's probably best she stay with me," London announced.

I looked at Sonya, who nodded in agreement. "I'm not ready to see your momma, Junior."

"Okay. See you soon." I hung up, kissed my woman, and then I was on the way to see the man who had given me life, hoping that somehow my presence would help him hang on to his life now.

Paris

28

It had been two weeks since I'd seen my son Jordan, so I was on my way outside to call his grandmother, Consuela, and check up on my little rug rat—or at least I was, until Orlando spotted me as he got off the elevator. I could see from his serious expression that something big had gone down. He took my arm and pulled me down the hall in the opposite direction of Daddy's hospital room, where the rest of the family was loitering around the door.

"Hey, I was just coming to find you." He looked like he couldn't decide whether he wanted to kick somebody's ass or cry. Talk about having the weight of the world on your shoulders. My brother had always been an intense man, but I'd never seen him look like this before.

"What's wrong?"

It took him a long time to answer, and while I waited, I could see a storm brewing behind his eyes. He blew out an angry breath and finally told me, "X and his people took out our Long Island dealership. Torched it to the ground."

"What the fuck!" I stomped my foot against the wall, leaving a permanent mark with my stiletto heel. "This motherfucker is getting on my last nerve."

"That's not the worst of it. They also took out warehouse number nine and killed everyone but Victor."

I was stunned silent. I could not believe what I was hearing. How the hell did X know how to find one of our illegal warehouses? I wasn't so worried about the dealership; we were insured for that, but the loss of that warehouse and its contents was going to cost us millions, and that came under my job description as the family's troubleshooter.

Orlando peeked around the corner to make sure no one was listening. "Don't worry. I got Popeye Wilson's people on their way from DC. I need you and Sasha to get down there and meet them so you can lead the charge. I'm sick of waiting around. We're taking out Brother X at his Rosedale hideaway tonight."

I threw my hand up in the air and he high-fived me, "Now, that's what I'm talking about, Orlando!"

He placed his finger over his lips. "Keep it down. I'm not trying to have the world hear our plans."

"Oh, sorry. I'm just a little excited," I whispered back, grinning. "How did you find out where he was?"

He leaned in closer and said quietly, "Vegas told me."

"Damn, that Vegas is a beast. Is he going with us to take this motherfucker down?"

"No, and I don't want him to know what we've got planned until X is dead. Can you do that?"

"Wait. Is Vegas cool with this?"

His irritated expression gave me my answer, which his words confirmed. "He doesn't know."

"He's not going to be happy," I warned him. We both knew that making Vegas unhappy was something to be avoided.

"I don't give a shit whether he's happy or not. Protecting this family is my job," Orlando said, "and him walking in here trying to run shit stops right now. We are at war, Paris. As big and bad as Vegas seems, he's not ready for war, so I need you and Sasha to let these motherfuckers know that they can't just mess with the Duncans."

"Done!" I whooped, already heading to the elevator to get Sasha from the cafeteria. I turned to Orlando after I pushed the down button. "O, you need to tell Vegas what you're up to. You owe him that much, just for the information he gave you."

Orlando nodded his understanding, but didn't reply as I disappeared into the elevator.

Chippy

29

"Honey, you know that I consider myself the luckiest woman in the world to have a man like you love me for as long and as well as you have. We could have each made different choices back then that would have led us away from each other, but we didn't. We were smart enough to choose to be together, and neither of us has ever regretted that decision. We just kept moving closer together, and our love has helped us to withstand a lot of crises that would tear apart most couples.

"I can't imagine my life without you, but I know that I need to honor your wishes and do what you would want, even if it's the last thing I want to do. What I want is to have my husband back . . . for you to wake up the great LC Duncan, and for us continue loving each other for the next thirty years. That's what I've been praying for all these days, as I watch you lying here hooked up to all these machines.

"But I know it's selfish, because you have made it clear to me in the past that if anything ever happened to you, you didn't want to suffer. I don't want to see you suffer, either, my love. That is not fair, and I know it's not what you would want.

"So, I've come to the conclusion that I am giving you twenty-four hours to decide if you want to wake up and to rejoin your family. I know you're in there listening, and I know it won't be easy, but we are all here fighting for you. All I'm asking is for you to fight too. You have twenty-four hours to get up and get the hell out of this bed, or I'm going to have no choice but to let the doctors pull the plug." I leaned close, peppering his face with kisses, giving this man all the love I had in my whole body, praying that it would be enough to help him to come back to us.

"We love you, and now this is your time to decide what you really want, LC. You have six children, four grandchildren, and a wife that wants more time with you. Baby, I need you to do this. Come back to us." I got up from my chair beside the bed, watching him closely to see if my words had had any impact, but there was no change. His heart rate monitor still beeped at the same steady pace, and his eyes were still closed and motionless.

The sound of someone clearing her throat let me know that I was no longer alone. I wiped away a tear and turned to see Donna standing in the doorway.

"Excuse me. I didn't mean to interrupt such a beautiful moment."

"How long have you been standing there?" I asked, feeling a little uncomfortable that she had witnessed my private moment with my husband.

"Long enough," she answered, moving closer to LC. "You really think this stubborn man is going to just give up?"

"Lord, I hope not," I answered with all my heart as she reached her arm around me. Donna and I had come a long way.

"Speaking of the Lord, I went to church yesterday. Not the fancy First Jamaica Ministries I attend for image and photo ops," she said. "I found me a little place. Reminded me of the one I attended as a girl. I got down on my knees and I prayed like I hadn't since I was young, back when I believed that God would grant my every wish and I would never, ever suffer. That all I had to do was love the Lord and my life would be perfect." She shook her head as if to laugh at the naïve child she had once been.

"Well, I went back to that God, and I begged and pleaded for him to let LC live. To let this family continue with the patriarch that so many black families don't have."

I took her hands in mine. I knew why she'd had that crisis of faith years ago, and in spite of our past differences, I also knew that she truly loved my husband.

"Now, all we can do is wait." I said, and I felt strangely calmed by the depth of that truth. LC had really passed into God's hands, and I just prayed that God wasn't done with him on earth and would give him back to us.

Pulling me away from the bed and speaking in a quiet voice, as if LC might overhear our conversation, Donna said, "Chippy, I've been here a while and seen all of the children. Everyone except for Junior. You want to tell me what's going on?" She stared at me unflinchingly so I got the message that she wasn't giving up without getting the truth out of me.

"He's good. He's just taking care of something." I knew it wasn't the answer that she wanted, but as far as I was concerned, it was the only part of the truth that she was going to get out of me.

"Then why is everybody saying that the reason LC is lying up in this bed is because of Junior?"

escape. Then someone yelled, "Check every room!" and I
pped back down behind the boxes in a panic. It was only a
tter of time before one of them kicked in the right door and
nd my cousin. I had to get to her somehow.

Paris

30

Sasha sat in front of me in one of our warehouses, along with about a dozen of Popeye Wilson's best soldiers and another six from our camp. They didn't have to say what was on their minds, because their expressions said it for them: they wanted to know why this hot-ass woman was standing in front of them, giving orders. Well, maybe that's not what Sasha was thinking about. Hers eyes were glued on Popeye Wilson's son, Larry, who she'd been flirting with for the past twenty minutes. Besides, she knew exactly what I was trying to convey. She'd been my sounding board during the ride over from the hospital, and she was one hundred percent on board. Now I had to convince the other eighteen to hop on the bandwagon as well.

One of Popeye's men spoke up. "Can I ask a question?" He was a big, burly guy who was almost the same size as Junior.

"Sure. What's on your mind?"

He stood up and made his way closer to me, carrying an assault rifle. "I mean, other than the fact that we get to look at that phat ass of yours from behind as we go in the door, why should we follow you? What qualifies you to lead us?" He was now close enough for me to smell his body odor.

"Shut the fuck up and sit down," I ordered.

"Aw, what, did I hurt your feelings?" He laughed, and the other men joined in.

I glanced over at Sasha, who very casually nodded her head.

"You wanna know what qualifies me?" Before anyone could blink, I hit the funky-smelling dude with a quick chop to his throat that damn near crushed his larynx. I followed it with a swift kick to his gonads, which sent him keeling over like a fallen tree. By the time he hit the ground, I had his rifle in my hand, cocked and aimed at his face.

As he lay groaning on the floor, I asked, "You still want to know my qualifications?" He shook his head. "Good. Now, you can either follow my phat ass into battle and enjoy the view, or take your smelly ass back to DC. I don't need any more distraction." I turned to the men, who all looked stunned. "And that goes for any of the rest of you too."

"You don't have to worry, Paris. We're with you," Larry said. He had a sympathetic tone to his voice. Despite the hard exterior I was displaying, he must have been able to catch just a glimpse of the pain I was feeling for my father. I was working hard to suppress those feelings because now was not the time for weakness. There was serious work that needed to be done, in spite of LC being out of commission at the moment. After all, the war was just beginning.

Now that I had everyone's undivided attention, I went back to explaining my plan.

"As you all know, we're going after the man who put my father in a hospital bed and has killed more than a dozen of our men. This dude Brother X ain't no joke, and he and his people have killed more men than I have sitting here in front of me, so if any of you wanna back out, let me know now."

"Ain't nobody backing out," Larry announced. I looked over at him and saw the way his chest was rising and falling, his fists were balled up, and the veins were damn near popping out of his neck. He was ready for battle.

"Yeah, like Larry said," Sasha added, gazing over at him.

Larry noticed the way she was devouring him with her eyes, and he smiled at her, letting her know the attraction was mutual.

"Okay, so if everyone understands, I want you to check your weapons and make sure you have plenty of ammo. We roll in twenty." I tossed the burly man his assault rifle.

Sasha stood up and announced loudly, "I have to run to the bathroom real quick." She glanced in Larry's direction as she left the room.

In my peripheral vision, I saw her stop in the hallway, turn back toward our group, and make a beckoning gesture to Larry.

Like clockwork, Larry waited five seconds a[nd] say he was going to use the bathroom too. I [ ] Leave it to my cousin to make a damn love [ ] hour before we went into battle. Part of me wa[ ] fools they weren't as slick as they thought, [ ] the time for lighthearted jokes. Their horny a[ ] minutes before I went looking for them.

"Before I continue," I said, planting my hand "Does anyone else have to go to the little boys' room

Suddenly, there was a huge crash, and the floo[r] there was an earthquake occurring. Everyone started and I instinctively ran up the stairway behind me, w[ ] a catwalk piled high with storage boxes. Crouching [ ] boxes, I drew my gun, then watched in horror as anot[her] happened and a portion of the brick wall crumbled. [ ] truck was now sitting in the spot where my men had just least four of them were laid on the ground, killed by the of the dump truck and the wall falling on them. Than[k] everyone had scattered after the first crash or there woul[d] been more casualties.

I began firing my weapon when two men jumped o[ut] the cabin of the truck. My soldiers, who were now disper[sed] throughout the room, starting shooting also. The men from [the] truck began firing back, and bullets were flying like firewor[ks] from both sides. A swarm of at least twenty of X's soldiers cam[e] out of the back of the truck with their guns blazing.

Ducking down behind the boxes, I peeked through them at the scene taking place below me, and watched as my men were taken out, one by one. I leaned back, trying to think strategically about my next move. If I stood up and started shooting, I was sure to end up dead, so as much as I wanted to blow those fuckers away, I stayed put behind the boxes for the time being. It wasn't long before the gunfire ceased.

"This way!" one of the invading men yelled, and they fanned out, stepping over the bloody bodies of my dead soldiers as they headed down the hallway. For a second, I was relieved that no one seemed to be headed up the steps, so I prepared to make

Sasha

31

"That's it, baby. Give Momma that dick! Give Momma that big dick!"

I was bent over the desk in the office where Larry and I had ended up after our "convenient" trip to the bathroom at the same time. Larry was pounding me like it was the last pussy he'd ever have, when suddenly the building started rumbling. That shit was shaking so bad it damn near knocked me over. At first I was impressed. I'd done my share of fucking, but Larry was definitely the first man who had made the world shake like that. Then that fantasy died about a second later when I heard gunshots and knew that there was more to my earth-shaking experience than the skills of my well-hung lover.

"Did you hear that?"

Larry pulled his dick out and reached for his assault rifle, pulling up his pants. He was about to run out the door when I grabbed his arm.

"Hold up. Let's evaluate this first. I don't know if you want to go out there."

My training told me that, according to the variety of sounds I was hearing, there were at least thirty guns being fired out there, and most of them sounded like Uzis. That was bad news for us, because our men were strapped with Tech-9s and assault rifles, not Uzis, which meant that someone was firing on them pretty hard.

"Evaluate my ass. Our people are in a firefight. I'm going to help my men." I had to give it to Larry. He was about his business.

He pulled his arm out of my grip, but by the time he reached the door, the shooting had suddenly stopped. Whatever had happened, it had gone down that quick. I was just praying they hadn't killed everyone. And by everyone I meant Paris.

"That's not a good sign," I whispered to him.

I heard someone yell, "This way!" and then the sound of doors slamming as they checked every room in the hallway. Larry and I shared a worried glance. It was only a matter of time before they reached us.

"Hide," he said as he locked the door.

I squatted underneath a desk, while Larry stood by a filing cabinet, ready to blast the minute X's men burst through that door. The doorknob jiggled, and he gave me a nod to assure me that he was ready to handle it. I wasn't the least bit worried. Hell, so what if it was only two of us against twenty or thirty of them?

The knob jiggled again, and this time a man's voice said, "There's someone in there."

Automatic gunfire left a trail of holes in the door, but it remained closed.

Larry let loose a spurt of gunfire, and we heard someone drop outside the door. He'd hit at least one of them, but it was clear that there were more right behind him to pick up the fight.

I watched as another volley of bullets tore through the door. When there was a brief pause, I let off some rounds myself. Another thud and a loud "Fuck!" and I knew someone else was down.

Their return fire gained in intensity, and the windows in the room were blown out. The sound of shattering glass was accompanied by a large *Crack!* as the door splintered and one of X's men tried to Rambo his way into the office. Knowing it would only be a matter of seconds before the others came charging in, I raised my gun and pulled the trigger, expecting to see a hail of bullets coming out of the muzzle. My heart dropped when all I heard was a clicking sound.

I heard Larry cry out in agony.

I looked over to see him lying on the ground. The Rambo dude was lying dead next to him, but Larry had obviously been shot in the process of taking him out.

Acting purely on instinct, I threw my useless gun in Larry's direction and dove back under the desk just before two more soldiers burst into the room, weapons drawn.

I placed my hands over my ears and began crying. "Please, don't shoot me! Oh, God! Please!" I forced tears out of my eyes.

One of the men turned sharply in my direction, his finger on the trigger of his weapon.

"Wait! Hold up." Had his partner spoken up one second later, I would have had a bullet through my head. Even as the shooter lowered his weapon, he looked disappointed, like a shark who'd just missed a bloody feeding frenzy.

"Who are you?" the man who'd saved my life asked.

"I'm Sasha," I answered quietly. The fear in my voice was only partially an act at this point.

"Sasha who?" he asked.

"Duncan. Please, what's going on? Don't hurt me."

The men eyed each other, and the one with his gun on me smiled like he'd caught the big fish of the day.

That's when a man in fatigues wearing schoolboy glasses appeared. "What's going on?"

"She's a Duncan," the shooter said with a sinister grin, raising his weapon and aiming it at me. "Elijah, man, you gotta let me do her."

"A Duncan, huh?" Elijah said. "Go check her out."

The shooter walked over and snatched me up off the ground. "You got anything on you?"

I sniffed and choked back my tears, willing myself to keep up with the damsel in distress act. My life depended on it.

"Woman, I said do you have anything on you?" He flung me around like a rag doll as he started patting me down to look for weapons. Out of the corner of my eye I saw my gun lying next to Larry, and I thanked God I'd had the impulse to throw it away before I hid.

"Yo, careful, man," Elijah said to him. "She's just a woman, not one of the Duncans' thugs. No need to manhandle her like that."

I looked over at Elijah and made eye contact with him, wanting him to understand my gratitude. Obviously my tears had an effect on him, so I knew he was the one I needed to play up to. He could keep me safe in the presence of this thug who was itching to shoot me.

"She's clean," the trigger-happy one told Elijah, backing up and pointing the gun at me again. "What now?"

Elijah stared at me for a minute, then pulled out his phone and hit a couple of buttons. He kept his eyes on me as he placed the phone to his ear and waited for whoever he was calling to answer.

I shivered for added effect.

"Hey, Xavier," he said into the receiver. "I have a Duncan." He paused briefly to listen, and then ended the call with "Okay."

"What did he say?" the gunman asked.

"Just what I thought he would," Elijah responded. "He said to bring her to him now."

Vegas

32

WE'VE GOT THE PLACE SURROUNDED AND WE'RE ABOUT TO GO IN. I'LL CALL YOU ONCE WE HAVE THIS WRAPPED UP.

I read the text from Captain Marks right before I entered Pop's hospital room, so I had a smile on my face as I walked in. God, I wished he was awake to hear the good news. It was only a matter of time before Brother X would be taken care of. I leaned in close, running my hands along Pop's arms to warm him. All the machines in the room required the temperature to stay cool, but it also meant that he was colder than he should have been.

"Hey, Pop, I just want you to know that I'm about to have this whole Brother X thing handled. Trust me, him and his people are gonna pay. You'd be proud. It's exactly the way you would have wanted it to go down."

Now that I felt some control over this big situation, the smaller one nagging at me reared its head. I was going to have to sit down with Orlando and work things out. We were going to have to find a happy medium, like Pop and Uncle Lou had when they were younger, because this infighting was not what we Duncans were about. I knew Orlando couldn't see it, but in the long run, it would ultimately tear us apart.

I took a seat next to the bed. "Pop, you know I don't ask for much, but I'm begging you, please come back to us. Come back to me. I know we're getting older and you trust us to run things—and Orlando is doing a good job, so you were right to give him the reins—but we all still need you. There is so much that we don't want you to miss. Hell, I haven't even had a kid yet."

"Hey, man. You see Junior?" Orlando entered the room looking exhausted. I guess we were all tired. None of us had had a decent night's rest since X escaped from prison.

"Yeah, he just left to get something to eat with Ma and Aunt Donna."

"How's he doing?" he asked.

"About what you'd expect. He blames himself." We both looked down at Pop. "I swear sometimes I think Pop's just testing us. Seeing if we can handle a crisis or if we'll fuck it up."

"Yeah, that would be just like him to put us all through this," Orlando said with a sad laugh.

"I just want him to come back," I said.

Orlando fist-bumped me, showing mad brotherly love. He obviously knew I needed it at the moment. Hell, who wouldn't need some comfort sitting beside Pop's bed? The closer you were to all those machines and tubes, the more you had to confront the possibilities.

"You and me should talk," I told Orlando. I wanted to fill him in on the solution I'd come up with involving Captain Marks.

After we left Marie's brothel, I had given Marks X's location. Obviously the NYPD would have some interest in taking out the most wanted man in New York. The cops could take the place of our muscle, so that we wouldn't have any losses on our side. It also meant we could avoid taking on partners like Tony the Pimp or Popeye Wilson, who would come looking for a piece of the pie when it was all said and done.

The real beauty of the plan was that X had basically given himself a death sentence when he took out the two corrections officers. I wouldn't bet against the possibility that some cop would find a way for X to be caught in the line of fire before he ever made it into handcuffs.

At least that was the way I expected the plan to fall into place now that I knew Captain Marks and his people were making their move—until my phone rang and that fantasy came crashing down.

I looked down at the caller ID and saw Marks's number. "Hey, O, you might want to hear this call. I might have just ended the war." I pressed the speaker on my iPhone.

We heard police sirens and lots of shouting in the background. I could picture the chaos, and a smile came across my face as I imagined Brother X laying in a pool of his own blood.

"Hey, Conrad! How'd it go, man?" I said.

"To fucking shit!" he yelled back. "That's how it went. I don't know what kind of fucking game you were playing, Vegas, but I fail to see the fucking humor in it!"

This was definitely not what I expected to hear. Two days ago he was singing my praises after getting laid. Now he should have been ready to name his firstborn after me, because he was probably going to be promoted to deputy chief after this bust.

"Conrad, what the hell are you talking about?"

"Twelve dead cops, that's what I'm talking about, and just as many injured, you motherfucker." He barely took a breath before he continued yelling into the phone. "I sent my men in that warehouse on your word, and those sons of bitches had the whole fucking place booby-trapped. We were fucking sitting ducks, and it's all your fucking fault!" He sounded like he was going to have a coronary.

"Get the fuck outta here!" I grabbed my head in frustration. Shit was not supposed to go down like this.

"Conrad, I don't know what to say. I checked that place out myself. I'm sorry, man. I swear I didn't know. We'll take care of each of those officers' families."

"I'm gonna hold you to that. Those were good fucking men."

"I'm sure they were."

"I've gotta go, Vegas, but before I hang up, I'm putting you on notice. I want the man who did this. I want that fucking Brother X, and I want him brought to me alive!"

"I understand."

I hung up the phone and looked up, expecting to see Orlando hovering over me with a million questions. Instead, he was sending a text. He hit send and looked at me with an expression somewhere between confusion and rage.

"What the fuck did you do without talking to me?" he asked.

I glanced over at my father. I didn't know if he could hear us, but if Orlando and I came to blows, I didn't want it to be in front of Pop. "Come on," I said. "Let's go out in the hall and I'll explain."

Outside the room, I gave him all the details about what I'd set in motion with Captain Marks. "So as you can see," I said as I finished up, "in theory it was a great plan. I just don't know what the fuck went wrong. Marks said the place was booby-trapped. I mean, how the fuck did X get wind that something was about to go down at his place?"

Orlando was about to say something, but we were interrupted by Paris, who came flying off the elevator looking like she had been taken through a meat grinder. Her clothes were torn, her hair disheveled. Paris would never be caught dead in public looking like that, but it was the haunted look on her face that caused me the most alarm.

"What?" Orlando shouted, getting to her first.

"They took her. We got separated and they took her. There was nothing I could do. They just took her!" she yelled.

"Who?" I didn't even know that she had left the hospital. "Who was taken?"

"Sasha! They took Sasha." She was crying, but underneath the tears I could see her fury, and worst of all, I could see fear in her eyes. The sister I knew was fearless—or at least she used to be. "Oh, God," Paris cried. "Momma's gonna kill me. We gotta get her back."

"Slow down. Who took Sasha?" I questioned.

"Brother X's men. The Muslims. They took her."

"Wait, this doesn't make any sense. What do you mean they took her? Took her from where?" In the corner of my eye, I noticed that Orlando had started pacing nearby.

"Yo, O," I said. "Any reason you're over there instead of over here asking questions to help me figure this out?" He stopped walking, but he couldn't look me in the eye. Bad sign.

I turned back to Paris. "Where were you?"

"We were just about to leave for Rosedale to raid Brother X's spot. Then his men showed up at our warehouse and took out all of our guys, plus Popeye Wilson's twelve men. Vegas, it was a fucking bloodbath!" She broke down sobbing, and I pulled her in close and held her as her tears soaked my shirt.

"Popeye's men . . ." I said, looking over Paris's head at Orlando. "And what were you going after X and his men for anyway?"

She didn't answer, but turned to look at Orlando, which told me everything I needed to know.

"What did you promise Popeye, Orlando?" I asked him.

He finally made eye contact, but remained silent.

"Answer me, dammit! What did you promise Popeye Wilson?"

Orlando's shoulders slumped as he admitted, "I gave him the distribution rights to Virginia, Maryland, and parts of PA."

"You did what?" I asked, seething. "Those weren't your rights to give away. They belong to the family." I was trying to remain calm because we were in a public place. Lucky for him, because my instinct at the moment was telling me to pump a bullet into my stupid, stupid brother. "How the hell could you do that?" I shouted at him.

"It was my call. Not yours," he yelled, matching my volume with his own. "I'm the one Pop left in charge, so I made an executive decision. It didn't go as well as I planned, but I had to do something."

"Paris, go check on Pop." I shooed her toward the room. When she was out of sight, I lit into him. "What the fuck were you thinking? Do you have any idea how long it took us to get those rights? How many people had to die? For you to just give them away."

"I did what I thought was right for the family," Orlando fumed, holding his ground in a martial arts stance. Just the idea of my little brother challenging me set me off. I snatched him up by the collar before he could blink.

"No, what you did was sell this family down the river. Same way you sold me out when you revealed X's location. You and I were the only ones who knew where he was holed up, O, and yet somehow X knew we were coming for him, and he had time to set a trap. Now we're gonna be beholden to twelve NYPD widows because of your fucking mouth. How many folks did you tell about his warehouse in Rosedale?"

Orlando remained tight-lipped.

"How many?" I asked again, tightening my grip on his collar.

"Just Paris . . . and Popeye and Tony."

I shoved him against the wall. "You stupid ass."

Orlando shook his head, still not putting the pieces together. "No, man, Popeye and Tony were helping us. It wasn't them."

"Did Tony send any of his men for this raid you had planned?" I asked slowly.

"No." He still wasn't making the connection, so I spelled it out for him.

"That's because he didn't want any of his men killed—after he told X you were coming. That booby-trap wasn't there for the cops; it was there for our men," I said, slamming my hand on the wall just inches from his head. "You better hope like hell that they don't kill my cousin, Orlando." I stormed off, leaving him to think about the shit storm he'd just created.

Junior

33

We'd had a consultation with the entire medical team in charge of Pop's care, including hospital executives who were probably there to make sure we didn't intend to sue. They were all pressing us to come to some kind of decision about his future treatment. The longer we listened, the more times we heard their fancy ways of saying the same damn thing: They didn't think our father would ever recover, and considering the alternative, they thought that he was better off dead. They hadn't put it in those direct words, but what they did talk about was atrophy. They said that he would gradually waste away from being bedridden. They presented charts and summaries of worst case scenarios, all offered to convince us that we really only had one decision.

Not one of the doctors could be one hundred percent certain about his brain activity. They may have been experts, but as far as I was concerned, they didn't know shit. Every time they did an MRI it came back differently, from no brain activity to slight activity and everything in between, which made it possible to believe that somewhere in there, the great LC Duncan was pulling some elaborate hoax.

"They're acting like they need Pop's bed or some shit," Orlando said. He had been relegated to the dog house since he screwed up Vegas's plan and got Sasha snatched, so he'd been pretty quiet up until now.

"Fuck them. We will buy that hospital and put those same doctors out of work. He's going to wake up, and right now that's all we need to be focused on," Paris fumed, pacing the length of the living room floor.

"You know what they're suggesting? There is no way I'm ready to do that," Vegas said, his voice cracking with emotion.

"Me neither," I jumped in, adding my vote. Of course, Pop's death wasn't what anyone wanted, but I felt like I had even more at stake than they did. If he died, everyone would blame it on me and Sonya. I didn't know if I could survive the guilt, and I definitely didn't think our relationship could survive that.

Sonya caught my eye, probably reading my mind. She was across the room laying out a feast for our family.

"I talked with a Dr. Lindquist in Stockholm," I told them. "He's one of the world's leading neurologists. According to him, there are all kinds of new treatments that aren't approved in America. He says we can't get caught up with the percentages that the doctors are giving us. His exact words were, 'For every terminal diagnosis, there are people who have long outlived them.'"

"I just want him to get up off that bed and prove all these motherfuckers wrong, 'cause no way are we pulling the plug," Paris added.

"That's not really up to you guys," Harris announced as he walked into the room holding up a manila envelope. Rio was following behind him. "At least not according to these."

"What the hell is that?" Orlando snapped.

"Hopefully nothing you can fuck up." Vegas dug in again, pushing all Orlando's buttons.

"It's a health care proxy form that LC signed two years ago," Harris answered, still holding on to the paperwork.

"What's a health care proxy?" Rio asked.

"It a legal document stating that in a situation like this, your father doesn't want to be kept alive artificially. He wants to be left to die."

"And you let him sign this?" Orlando snatched the envelope out of Harris's hand and pulled out the document. "What kind of lawyer are you?" he asked, perusing the legal paperwork. I went and stood over his shoulder to read it along with him.

"I didn't *let* him do anything. Can any of you imagine trying to stop LC from doing something he wants to do? Ain't a lawyer in hell can control that man."

I happened to believe what Harris was saying. LC was stubborn as hell. Orlando, on the other hand, wasn't convinced.

"Ma would have never let him sign that. Must have been you," he accused Harris.

"Well, to be honest, she signed one too," Harris explained, shocking us all. "I wish you guys would stop acting like I'm the bad guy all the time, especially when I'm as loyal, if not more, than people who should be."

I knew he was poking at me, but Pop would have wanted me to help keep the peace, and the way folks were acting, I needed to take that position seriously. So, I decided to give him that one.

"He ain't lying," Orlando announced, looking down at the paperwork. "Pop did sign this. It's his signature." He looked around the room, making eye contact with each of us. "Maybe we should give this some thought."

Vegas protested. "Oh, hell naw. You best believe Pop would not want to die with the mess you've made of things." He was glaring at Orlando, who jumped up, ready to go to blows. I stepped in between them.

"We need to respect this document. We need to respect LC's wishes," Harris insisted.

"Fuck you, Harris. And fuck you," Vegas yelled at Orlando.

"Stop it! Stop it right now!" We'd been too busy engaged in the drama to notice when our mother entered the room. Suddenly everyone snapped into line, like little children scolded by Mommy.

I glanced over at Sonya, who was still moving around cautiously, getting our food ready. I could tell she wished she was invisible at that moment. Clearly my mother had seen her, but she didn't say anything.

London walked in with a tight scowl on her face, like she couldn't understand how we had upset our mother at a time like this. This was just one more example of why we all referred to her as Little Chippy behind her back.

"Your father is in that hospital fighting for his life, and you, Harris—I told you not to show that paper to anyone."

"But we need to address this," Harris said. "What could be more important at a time like this than figuring out how to let LC go?"

"Is that why we're here? To make a decision about Daddy?" Paris's words squeaked out. She looked like she was about to break down as she flopped onto one of the chairs and buried her head in her hands.

"Initially, that's one of the things we were going to discuss, but right now we can't," Ma said calmly.

She went over to Orlando and stood behind him, gripping his chair. From my position it appeared like she was about to deliver one of her "Come to Jesus" speeches. We'd all experienced them.

"Orlando, you are supposed to be our leader, so I don't care what you have to do, but you boys have to do it together. You all are not only coworkers, but you are family. There are all different types of leaders. Orlando, you're the head of the family. Vegas, you are the heart and soul of our family, and we need both of those things. So you two need to work together.

"And Junior?" She turned her attention to me. "I'm not happy with your decisions lately, but you are grown, and I'm not so old that I've forgotten your father having to defy others when he chose me. But I need you to hear this: We are a family, and that means that you are not allowed to run off anymore. We're all in this together," she said, making a motion to include Sonya.

"But what are we going to do about Daddy?" London posed the question we'd all wanted to ask our mother.

"If that health care proxy is what he wants, then that's what he's going to get," Orlando said.

"Whoa, whoa!" Rio chimed in. "I don't give a damn what it says he wants. We all have to make this decision."

"No! None of you are making this decision. You may all have a part in the family business, but when it comes to my husband, I am his health care proxy, and I'll make the decision."

We looked at her expectantly. I don't know about the others, but I was praying she wasn't ready to pull the plug.

"I've listened to everything those experts have said and to all of your emotional pleas, but ultimately the final decision is mine and mine alone." Mom took the paperwork off the counter and tore it up, making certain that Harris was watching.

"I know your father better than anyone else in this room, and I'm telling you that LC would not want this happening, not now.

Not while Sasha is missing. She is a Duncan, and at one point or another she has saved every one of your lives, so bringing her home safe needs to be our priority. Only after Sasha is home will I sit you all down, and then I will tell you exactly what I am going to do about LC."

Chippy

34

"I know that this is difficult." Donna stood next to me as we watched LC lying helpless in his bed, tied to God knows how many different tubes and machines. It had been days with no real progress, and I felt like as hard as I was fighting to keep it together, I was slowly going out of my mind.

"You do? You know what it's like to watch your husband of over thirty years lie in a coma and there's not a damn thing you can do about it?" I snarled at her, tired of every damn body trying to tell me that they knew how I felt. As far as I was concerned, unless they were standing in my shoes, no one understood a damn thing. Hell, I couldn't be sure that I even knew how I felt sometimes. My feelings were coming like tiny hurricanes of emotion, catching me off guard. I should have felt bad that Donna was bearing the brunt of my frustration, but I was too damn tired to care.

"Chippy, you know that's not how I meant it," Donna apologized as best she could. "LC is important to me too."

"Yes, he's important to a lot of people," I replied, hearing the hostility in my voice. It wasn't her fault, but I just couldn't deal with people talking about LC as if he were public property, like some reality show star that everybody felt the need to spout opinions about all the time. Right now, my kids were about all I could handle outside of my husband, but I knew that didn't matter to Donna. She had appointed herself as LC's watchdog, and she wasn't going anywhere.

"I heard what the doctor said. Maybe it's time you let him go," she whispered, laying a comforting hand on my shoulder—except that it wasn't comforting in the least.

"So now you're trying to tell me to pull the plug too? To kill my husband?"

"Chippy, he just doesn't seem to be here anymore. Not in the way he would want to be. Do you think LC even hears us? Does he know that you've been here nonstop, pleading and praying for him to wake up?"

I stepped back to put some distance between me and Donna as I reached out and pushed the call button above LC's bed.

A nurse's voice came over the speaker. "Can I help you?"

"Yes, I need to see Dr. Whitmore as soon as possible."

"I'll let him know," she replied, hanging up.

"So, does this mean you're going to do it?" Donna asked. In spite of everything she'd just been advising, she seemed surprised. "Is that why you're requesting the doctor?"

I turned to face her, trying to calm myself down before I spoke. She had known LC a long time, but I was his wife, and I didn't see myself asking for her opinion. Before I went nuts on her, though, I reminded myself that she was a friend and we had already shared so much pain together.

"I'm not sure exactly what I plan to do, but if—and that's a big *if*—"

"Mrs. Duncan."

I stopped speaking when Dr. Whitmore entered the room with his clipboard in hand, ready to console me with his charming bedside manner.

"Thank you for coming." I spoke, my relaxed tone concealing the emotional storm raging inside of me.

He glanced from me to Donna, unsure if he should proceed.

"You can talk in front of her."

"Have you made a decision about what you're going to do? Like I said, after discussing your husband's condition with his team, we're not sure it's beneficial to keep him on the machines." He used that "doctor voice" that let you know that his opinion mattered more than yours, while pretending to leave room in case you thought differently.

"I have made one major decision." I waited for him to lift his eyes from whatever he was reading on his clipboard. I needed his full attention, not just the half-assed kind reserved for relatives of hopeless patients. He noticed that I had stopped speaking and looked up at me expectantly.

"If my husband is going to die, it's not going to be here," I said. "He will die with dignity at home, surrounded by his family in the beautiful house he built and provided."

Dr. Whitmore's eyes widened. This was clearly not what he had expected to hear me say, and it took him a moment to compose his thoughts before he spoke. "That is a great scenario," he finally said, "and one I am sure your husband would prefer. But do you have any idea how expensive it will be? Imagine the expense of transporting him to your home, and then add in the machines he would need. I'm sorry, but it's not cost effective, and no insurance will cover it." He wrapped up his little speech, looking like he was pleased with himself. Obviously this guy was used to families who blindly followed his advice, so I guess he thought it would be easy to make me see the error of my decision.

"Doctor, do I look like a woman who doesn't get what she wants? Have you noticed the armed bodyguards we have posted at every exit and entrance of this hospital? Do you also notice that not one person has made an issue of it?" I stopped, seeing the wheels turning in his brain. He clearly hadn't considered those things. I'm not sure if it had to do with us being black, but he sure had underestimated our power.

He forged ahead with his argument. "Even if you could get your husband home, it's not a normal situation where he will only need a nurse practitioner. Your husband will still need a full-time doctor," he stressed.

"Both my daughter and my son's girlfriend are Registered Nurses, so the nurse thing I have covered, and the doctor—well, you're going to be a great help."

"Mrs. Duncan, I don't know of any doctors who would leave their jobs to give your husband the kind of round-the-clock care that he needs," he insisted. This man may have graduated from Yale Medical School, but he truly didn't understand how the world works.

"Let me explain this to you, doctor. You are going to take a month's leave of absence from the hospital. Then you are going to care for my husband—"

He opened his mouth to interrupt, but I raised a finger to let him know that wasn't an option. He snapped his mouth shut again. Good. He was finally starting to understand.

"I figure after medical insurance and taxes, you take home under four hundred thousand dollars, and that's only if your college loans are paid off. I'm going to pay you three hundred thousand dollars in advance to care for my husband for the next month."

"Wait, what?" The great doctor was so stunned that he lost his ability to speak.

"Three hundred thousand dollars for one month, and no matter what happens with my husband, the money is yours. Now, I'm going to need you to order everything you require, including a night nurse." I opened my purse and pulled out one of my AMEX black cards. "You can charge all the hospital equipment and transportation to this card."

I held out the card to him, and he only hesitated for half a second before taking it from me.

"I will have my attorney call you to handle your salary. Does that work?"

"Yes, absolutely." By this point he was grinning from ear to ear like I was his fairy godmother. He was a greedy bastard, but he was also the best doctor in this place, and LC deserved nothing but the best.

"Damn! I underestimated you," Donna said after the doctor left the room. "Now, who is this girlfriend that's a nurse?"

"Sonya. She's Junior's girlfriend and the reason all this mess has happened."

Brother X

35

I'd tried praying and reading the Quran, but the more I attempted to find solace in prayer and meditation, the more agitated I found myself becoming. There was a time and a place for God, and then there was a time and place to seek vengeance for the harm others had done to you. There could only be so much turning the other cheek, and frankly, that was the one part of my religion that I refused to subscribe to. My personality lent itself more to the eye for an eye way of problem-solving.

"Come on. It's playtime." I pulled Lenny and Squiggy out of my pockets and set them down on the table in front of me. I enjoyed watching the two of them play together without a care in the world.

Usually seeing them play could calm me down, but this time, it only added to my frustration when Squiggy jumped on top of Lenny. Even though I'd named them after my favorite male television characters, Lenny wasn't a male rat. That's why Squiggy jumped on top of her and started pumping away. I might have found the whole thing funny if I wasn't so caught up in my own rage because my wife was screwing another man. Seeing my pets go at it only made me think about Sonya and Junior Duncan doing the same damn thing.

Along with my anger, I had to admit to myself that I was lonely. With every passing day I missed my wife more. She was my better half, and I missed what being married to her stood for, despite the fact we'd been separated by bars. I missed talking to her every day on the phone, receiving her care packages, and of course, I missed the intimacy I hadn't experienced since she stopped showing up for our conjugal visits.

"Damn you, woman!" I pounded my fist on the table, scaring the rats enough to make them stop screwing.

Yeah, sex with Sonya was definitely the best part of our relationship. As much as I loved her, I think the fact that she satisfied me more than any other woman was the real reason I'd made her my wife. I thought I'd have the pleasure of that passion forever, but here I was now, all alone. I was finally out of prison, but life wasn't all that different than it had been when I was locked away with a bunch of sweaty men. Being a wanted man meant I spent most of my time locked up in the safe house, and when I did go out on a mission, I had to watch my back constantly. Shit, at least if I had a soft, feminine body to lie down with once in a while I could relieve some stress.

At the thought of feminine bodies, I decided it was time to pay a visit to our little prisoner.

Sasha Duncan watched my every move as I entered the room. Handcuffed to a chair, she wasn't in any position to resist my advances, and I had to admit that right now, that appealed to me. Maybe she knew why I was there. It wasn't like I was trying to hide my lust as my eyes wandered all over her body, which she'd put on display in the shortest skirt and tiniest halter top. There was nothing modest at all about the way she dressed. No self-respecting Muslim woman would be caught dead in such a brazen outfit.

"You like what you see?" she asked boldly, arching her back so that her prominent breasts were on display, further fueling my already burning desire. It was as if she knew that it had been too long and I was in need of a woman.

"And what if I do?" I asked, playing her game—no, fuck it, this was my game.

I moved beside her and untied the strings that held up her top, letting her know that I could do whatever I wanted to her. Beautiful, juicy round breasts popped out, her nipples at attention. I heard myself gasp at the sight of her nakedness.

"You want me, don't you?" she asked in a sultry voice, like a snake charmer attempting to seduce me. She didn't seem to acknowledge that I could make her do whatever I wanted. I was the one in control here, not her.

"Why would I allow a dirty whore to tempt me?" I spoke sharply, trying to hide my desire.

"Because this whore can give you the best blow job you have ever had," she said, licking her tongue across her full lips. "Your dick would love to be in my mouth, letting me suck and suck," she said.

My mind began racing with vivid images of her on her knees, taking in all of me. I shook my head, trying to erase the thoughts. The temptation was there, but this harlot could be trying to bait me into a trap. I had to keep my head on straight.

"I don't trust you. You might bite me," I barked at her.

"I wouldn't. After the way Sonya has treated you, don't you deserve a woman that will put your needs first? A woman that will treat you like the leader you truly are?"

Giving in momentarily to my desire, I reached out and rubbed my hands all over her breasts. I felt my penis hardening.

"I will lick all of the juices out of you," she promised. "Let me make you happy."

"I'm a married man," I told her, pulling my hand back and forcing myself to resist.

"You're a Muslim man. Doesn't the Quran say you can take more than one wife?"

I was a little surprised that she knew anything about my religion, but that didn't mean I trusted her. She was a still a Duncan, after all.

"Take me as your wife, X. Let me show you what my lips and tongue can do." The sexual images were returning to my imagination, and it made me angry. I could not let her get the upper hand.

"No!" I lashed out. "I will do to you what I want. I am the man. If I take you, I take you my way." I rushed over to her, pushing her skirt up to her waist so that she was completely exposed.

Opening my pants and releasing my rock hard dick, I then reached down to spread her legs apart. I couldn't wait to plunge into her.

I heard a thud and turned around to see Elijah entering the room. He had dropped the takeout food containers he'd been carrying. "What the—What are you doing?" He pushed me away from Sasha.

"I'm taking her as my wife," I answered as I pulled myself together and zipped my pants. "The Duncans took Sonya from me. I will take her as a replacement."

"You are a man of God. If you touch her, then you are no better than your wife. Is that what you want? To go against Allah?" Elijah said, taking off his jacket and covering Sasha's naked body with it.

"I am a man of God, but I am also a man," I reminded him.

"No! You are supposed to be better. You are supposed to be a leader, one who lives as an example."

"I am an example."

"Are you all right?" Elijah questioned the whore.

"I'm fine," she said, trying to sound like a wounded bird rather than the temptress she had been a few minutes ago.

"Don't be fooled, Elijah. This girl is not some saint. She is a whore!" I warned him.

"It's not her I'm starting to feel fooled by," he snapped, glaring at me.

Vegas

36

With Pops coming home from the hospital, Ma wanted all of us at the house for Sunday dinner. I guess she was trying to make things as normal as possible, despite the fact that he was still in a coma and damn near brain dead.

After I met with my Asian friend Tommy Young, I confiscated one of the new red Ferrari Spiders that came into the shop, to pick up Marie in the Bronx. With everything going on, I hadn't seen Marie since that night at the brothel with Conrad. The two of us had a lot of catching up to do.

We'd just hit the Rockaway Freeway when I noticed that Marie seemed to be in her own world. Neither of us had spoken much during the hour-long drive, but I just assumed that it had something to do with the fact that I had barely let the car go under ninety miles per hour since we hit the highway. Now I wasn't so sure.

"You okay?" I asked.

She didn't respond. She just held my hand as her eyes welled up with tears.

"Marie, you okay, baby?" I repeated my concern, but she still didn't reply, unless the stream of tears sliding down her face counted. "You know I love you, right?"

"Yes, but for how long?" The waterworks just got worse.

"Marie, what's going on?" I pulled the car over at the beach about five blocks from the house.

She got out quickly and started walking toward the sand. I followed, trailing her by about ten feet. I didn't like the idea of us being out in the open like this, but for now it was a chance I had to take. "Marie, what the hell's going on?"

She finally stopped halfway to the water, taking off her sandals as she waited for me to catch up. I took her hand, deciding not to push the issue as we continued to the water.

"I never told you this, but it was love at first sight for me. When Orlando brought me to that jail, he had paid me to sleep with you, but I walked into that visiting room and that was all she wrote."

"And here I am thinking it was the dick." I laughed, and to my relief, she laughed too.

"Don't get me wrong. The dick was good, but it wasn't the dick I fell in love with that day. It was you. Matter of fact, I gave your brother his money back."

"I heard. It's probably the reason why we're together today."

She turned around, looking up at me. "I don't wanna lose you, Vegas, but there is something I have to tell you."

The way she said it gave me a little concern. "Tell me what? You know I'm not much for beating around the bush. Spit it out."

She sighed. "You know we haven't been intimate since we left Saint Martin last month, right?"

I nodded. "Yeah, I'm sorry about that, baby. With everything going on with my Pops and this Muslim threat, I know I haven't been taking care of business, but I promise, starting tonight things are going to be different."

She shook her head, tears welling up in her eyes again. "You only did what I allowed. I'm a madam, baby, and very good at what I do. If I wanted you, even in the middle of a war, I would have known what to do."

"What are you trying to say?" I asked, not liking the direction this felt like it was heading.

Again she sighed. "I avoided having sex with you."

"What?"

"One of my more wealthy clients insisted that he had to see me and no other girl. He was paying twenty-five grand. I couldn't say no to that." She was talking fast, as if she was desperate to make me understand.

"Marie, I know what you do for a living. It's okay. You're safe."

"Yes, I usually am, but . . ." There was a long pause, and a million things went through my mind. She ended my suspense by finishing with "The condom broke."

My stomach tightened into a knot.

"Baby, I went to the doctor and got myself checked out right away. They gave me all kinds of tests, and he didn't give me anything. The main reason I stayed away from you was because it took a few weeks to get all the test results back."

I stared at her, praying I wasn't about to get devastating news.

"I got them back today, and they were negative. I'm clean."

I wanted to throw my fists in the air and shout "Hallelujah!" but I played it cool. "Okay, so everything was good. Why were you just crying?"

"Because . . ." Tears welled up in her eyes again, and she couldn't continue.

Then it hit me like a ton of bricks. "You're pregnant, aren't you? And you don't know if it's his baby or mine."

She shook her head. "God, I wish it were that simple."

"What do you mean?"

She turned her tear-stained face toward me. "I'm not pregnant, Vegas. The doctor told me I can't have any kids."

There was silence between us for a few seconds. I hadn't processed my feelings yet, so I didn't want to say the wrong thing. But I realized that I had to do something, so I pulled her in close and held her tightly.

Paris

37

"Ain't nothing like the real thing, baby. Nothing like the real thing," Aretha's voice sang out over the sound system, while Mom was busy in a million different places: in the kitchen putting together a meal, fixing the room for Daddy, and worrying over all of us. She was working overtime to make things as normal as possible, even though that was absolutely impossible. Normally, when I felt this upset I could calm myself with a little retail therapy, but no amount of Lanvin or Louis would fix this feeling. The only thing that would mean a thing to me now would be Daddy waking up. However, hitting someone to cause them extraordinary amounts of pain might help my mood just a little. The more I thought about it, the more I knew exactly who should be on the receiving end of my rage.

"Yes?" Junior looked up from LC's desk when I entered the room. Seeing him making himself at home in Daddy's office did nothing to alter my pissed-off disposition.

"Why are you here?" I fumed, unleashing my fury on him.

"Paris, I don't have time for one of your little tantrums. I'm trying to find out where Sasha is," he snapped before turning back to his work—as if he could dismiss me like that.

"You fuckin' kidding me? You need to get your ass up out of Daddy's office and let one of the real men in this family sit in that chair. No one wants you here. And for the record, you're the reason Sasha got taken, so you *should* be looking for her." I don't think I had ever hated anyone so much in my entire life.

"Look, I know you're upset, but you are going to have to do something unique, and that is to pull it together. Ma doesn't need you acting like a crazy person right now." He spoke to me in the calm way people do when they want you to believe that you're insane and they're innocent.

I blew up at him. "Upset? Upset! It's because of you that our father might die and our cousin probably is going to die. Because you were so fuckin' selfish that you chose a woman, someone else's wife, over your own family." I spit the words out furiously.

He looked up at me, and sure, I could see that my words stung him, but I didn't care how he felt. Not one bit.

"You don't understand. You can't. You have never loved anyone in your whole spoiled little rich-girl life. Go away, Paris, before you really piss me off."

Instead of leaving, I reached across the desk, wanting to destroy him. He grabbed my hand before I could connect with his jaw. He was too damn strong for me.

"You're fuckin' lucky I'm not strapped," I yelled, pulling myself away from him.

"Oh, boo fuckin hoo, you brat. Your problem is you've been sheltered from ever having to think about anyone other than yourself. Even motherhood is mostly done for you. This is the first time in your entire life that you've had to think about someone else."

"Really? So I didn't have to end the life of the only man I have ever loved because it would have cost us our father?" As usual, no one in my family ever understood how hard it had been for me to kill Niles. It had damn near ripped my heart out, and they all acted like it was nothing. Yet here was Junior expecting me to accept that he couldn't sacrifice his relationship with Sonya in order to protect his own blood.

"Fuck you and all your selfish bullshit, Junior. You chose pussy over our family, and it will be your fault if Daddy and Sasha die."

"Hey, don't you ever talk about Sonya that way. You hear me? And don't you dare upset her." He had the nerve to threaten me, as if her crazy-ass husband wasn't trying to extinguish us all.

"Upset her? I don't give a fuck how she feels. She can drop dead for all I care. As a matter of fact, if she did, I would throw a motherfuckin' party," I promised.

Junior jumped up and snatched me up in his grasp. I shook myself loose, ready to attack him with my fists.

"Don't you dare talk that way about the mother of my child." His words silenced my rage.

"The what of your what?" I asked, praying that I had misunderstood him.

"Yes," he confirmed, "Sonya is pregnant, and you best not upset her."

"Yo, stop all this noise!" Orlando stomped into the room. He seemed to think that being named head of the family business meant he could act like our father. "What is going on?"

"Ask the newest baby daddy," I huffed, catching sight of Orlando's shocked expression as I stormed away.

How the hell could Junior have gotten Brother X's wife pregnant? I could only imagine the massive explosion this news would cause when X found out. I wouldn't put it past him to try to kill all of us now.

"Mommy!" a little voice squealed with delight. I looked up to see my favorite person in the world racing into the house toward me.

"Is that my baby?" I cooed, relieved and confused to see Jordan flying into my arms. If ever I needed to see my baby, this was the time. I couldn't get over how much he had grown in that short span, but at two and a half, he didn't look anything like he had even a month earlier.

When those little arms wrapped around me, I felt a calm I hadn't since this whole thing happened. What I didn't understand was why Consuela would have brought him home now, while we were still in the middle of a war. Why hadn't she told me this was her plan?

"Mommy, I missed you," Jordan whispered sweetly in my ear, just melting me.

"Did you have a good time in California with Grandma?" I looked up at Consuela, questioning her with my gaze.

"Yeah. We went to the beach every day," he said, excited with all the wonder I'd forgotten how to feel about the little things in life. God, I loved this kid.

"Jordan!" London's daughter Mariah raced down the stairs to greet her little cousin. The two of them ran off to some other adventure, the nanny quick on their heels.

"He's gotten big, hasn't he?" Consuela remarked as she approached with her arms outstretched to me.

"Wait. Why are you here?" I asked, though I couldn't be mad. As worried as I felt to have him home, I really needed to see my son.

"Your mother sent the plane for us. Didn't she tell you?"

"No. She didn't," I answered, ready to find my mother and ask her what the hell was going on and why I was the last to know. "Where is my mother anyway?"

"She's in the den talking to *my* son."

Vegas

38

To say Marie had given me something to think about is an understatement. The five minutes left in the drive over to the house were awkward. The only thing that interrupted the silence was me saying whatever I felt Marie wanted to hear. I said things that would at least make her feel like it wasn't the end of the world. Things like, "It's going to be okay. We can adopt. You never know, anything could happen. God has the final say."

She'd nod in response each time I offered up another platitude, but her nod only confirmed that she'd heard my words. The look in her eyes said that she didn't believe a damn thing I was saying. I couldn't fault her for doubting. Hell, I didn't even believe the words myself. Honestly, when Marie told me that she couldn't have children, the world stopped spinning. I wasn't sure that it would ever be okay. Coming from my world, where family is everything to the point where my siblings and I still lived under the same roof as our parents, I couldn't imagine not being able to add to the legacy.

We arrived at the house to find the kitchen empty. I heard voices in the back.

"Sounds like everybody is outside," I said to Marie.

She didn't answer, probably afraid that if she opened her mouth, she'd break down into tears. I walked over to her, put my hands on her shoulders, and kissed her on the forehead.

"If you don't believe anything else I've said to you, believe that I love you."

"But I can't give you children." She couldn't even look me in the eyes. "You can't possibly want me now."

"Listen here." I lifted her chin so I could look into her eyes. "I want you, and only you."

"I believe you want me—right now. Until another woman comes along who can give you what I can't," she said. "Give you a child to call you Daddy."

"Look, for right now, being called Uncle is enough," I said, although my heart told me that even if it were true now, it definitely wouldn't always be.

As if on cue, there was a splash from outside, and the sound of my niece Mariah laughing. I walked over to the sliding glass doors that opened onto the patio. Marie stayed a few steps behind me as we went outside to join everyone by the pool.

As we approached, I noticed that although everyone was sitting around eating barbecue and talking, no one had a smile on his or her face. No one looked particularly upset, but it just wasn't the type of expressions one might expect at a barbecue. Then again, what the hell did we have to happy about?

"Vegas," my mother called out. She stood up with my nephew Jordan in her arms.

To me, it sounded like she was saying my name as a warning to everyone else that was present—like she was announcing me, rather than greeting me. Everyone who had been chatting just seconds before now silenced themselves.

"What, did I break up the party or something?" I raised my hands in surrender. Was the dark cloud I now felt hanging over me visible to everyone?

"It would seem to me that the party has just begun now that you are here, Vegas."

This time it was Consuela who spoke my name. She was the grandmother of Paris's son—although there had yet to be a blood test to prove the relation. With everything going on in the family right now, Jordan had been away with her. I had no idea that he would be back in the midst of this war, or that Consuela would be staying around. I hadn't seen her since I got out of jail. It would have been nice to get a heads up, considering my past with her and my present with Marie. I couldn't wait to get Junior and Orlando alone. There was nothing more awkward than standing in the room with two women you've slept with—although I hoped my thing with Consuela was such a long time ago that there wouldn't be any kind of awkwardness left over between us.

"Consuela." I returned the greeting. She was everything I remembered and then some. I couldn't help but admire how tight her body was, even in her late forties. Whatever was in J-Lo's water was in hers too.

"Vegas, Vegas, Vegas," she said in a sensual, singsong voice. "You're looking as handsome as ever." Consuela started walking toward me. I stopped where I stood, as did Marie.

"You don't look so bad yourself. I didn't know you'd be in town." I was trying not to be obvious as I checked out her curves, but I must have failed, because I felt Marie's elbow jab my arm.

I turned to face Marie, looking at her like she was crazy. She was like a mirror, giving me the same look. She cleared her throat and nodded her head toward Consuela.

"Oh, yes." I turned back to Consuela, who still had her eyes glued on me. If I had to guess, she hadn't even looked Marie's way. Marie was invisible to her. "Consuela, this is Marie. Marie, this is Consuela."

"Hello, Marie," Consuela said, still not taking her eyes off of me.

Marie didn't respond. Consuela probably wouldn't have acknowledged a reply anyway.

"Well . . . it's good to see you," I muttered, once again finding myself trying to fill in an awkward silence.

"It's better to see you." The singsong was gone. Her tone was full-on sultry now.

I swallowed and tried not to fidget. How was I supposed to respond to that, especially with Marie burning a hole through me with her eyes? And it didn't help that my family was watching us like they were watching a movie on the big screen.

"I heard you were home for good," Consuela said, "so I brought you a present. Something I've been holding onto for quite a long time. Something I should have given you years ago."

"Really?" That was a surprise, considering she never wrote to me once while I was locked up.

"Really," she said with a mysterious grin on her face. "Nevada," she called out, turning her head to the side as if she was speaking to someone behind her.

That's when I looked over her shoulder and noticed a boy stepping out of the pool He wasn't a little kid like my niece and nephew. He was a teenager. He was a tall, wiry, athletic-looking kid, wearing a pair of USA swim trunks. What really made my heartbeats pause and my mouth drop open was what else he was wearing. The young man was wearing my face. He looked exactly like me. Not a younger image of me, but who I looked like at that given moment.

"Yes, Mother," the boy said as he went and stood by Consuela.

"Nevada," she said to him, "this is the man I've been telling you about all these years." She turned and looked in my eyes as she said to her son, "This is Vegas, your father."

"Well, there ain't no denying that one," Paris joked to Rio loud enough for all of us to hear.

She'd only verbalized what I felt, what I knew the moment I laid eyes on him.

"Poppa." A huge smile spread across his face. "It's so good to finally meet you." He came over to me, and we just stood there staring at each other, until he threw his arms around me.

I didn't know what to do. I slowly raised my own arms. Was I supposed to hug him back? I looked to my mother for answers. She was smiling just as hard as the boy was. My mother's hands were clasped together, as if a prayer had been answered and she was thanking God. I placed my arms around his back.

I looked to Consuela. She was smiling, too, as she placed her hand on her son's—*our* son's—shoulder. Then I looked over to Marie, who raced away from the patio with tears streaming down her face.

I watched London chase after her, thankful for the assist, because once I held him, I did not want to let my son go.

Sasha

39

"Fuck!" I shouted in frustration. Being tied up in a room for days, mostly by myself, had begun to wear on me. It didn't help matters that the only time I saw anyone it was one fine-ass man after the next. And those Muslim brothers had willpower, let me tell you. Every time they came in the room, they acted like they were immune to the power of the pussy, and that shit just turned me on even more.

Okay, so maybe the average girl in my situation wouldn't be thinking about sex, but I am no average woman. I might have gotten a late start at the age of nineteen, but once I'd gotten my first taste, I'd been addicted to dick. Now here I was in the presence of all these strong, red-blooded black men, and not one of them appeared to be thinking about sex in the least—with the exception of Brother X, and even he backed down at the last minute. It was enough to drive a nymphomaniac like me crazy.

I was busy conjuring up yet another gang-bang fantasy in my head when Elijah walked in with his fine self.

"I hope this is sufficient." He was carrying a bag of something that smelled so damn good my stomach started doing backflips. It also smelled familiar.

He opened the bag and laid the takeout containers on the table in front of me. When he popped the lid on the carton, I understood why it smelled so good.

"Wait, you got this for me?" My undisguised surprise brought a smile to his lips. "You know this is my favorite."

Whenever Elijah was the one in charge of watching me, we'd have conversations. It was mostly small talk, like the conversation we'd had about our favorite foods. I was impressed that he remembered, and also blown away by the gesture. I had no idea where we were, but I didn't imagine we were next door to a Bon Chon, the Korean fried chicken place that put the Colonel's stuff to shame. Elijah had gone out of his way to get this for me. "You are so nice," I said, feeling taken care of for once.

"I'm not as nice as you think. Besides, you need to eat." He sounded concerned and authoritarian at the same time, making me imagine all the naughty things he could do to me. I liked to be dominated from time to time.

I looked down to my hands, which were attached to the chair. "You can either feed me, or you can let me feed myself."

"If you promise not to try to escape, I will allow you one hand to eat."

"I promise," I said, and he uncuffed one hand.

"This is a lot of food. Are you going to join me? I promise you it's not cooked in pork fat." I was pleased to see him smirk at my little joke. He was letting his guard down a bit.

I have to admit that the way I attacked that food was not ladylike at all. Of course, he put a hurting on the chicken too.

When we finished, he took me into the bathroom and washed my hands for me. There was something so erotic about it, with the slippery soap bubbles and the way he massaged my hands between his. This was the kind of man who knew how to take care of a woman, not like some of the Peter Pan boys I had been with lately. Something about his manliness made me hold back on my usual forwardness. I didn't make some graphic statement or try to sexually overpower him with my words. Believe it or not, Elijah made me feel a little shy.

"Am I hurting you?" he asked as he cuffed me back to my chair.

"No."

After my restraints were secure, he headed for the door, stopping once more to double check, "You okay?"

"For someone locked to her chair and held against her will, you mean?"

"Yes. That is correct. My apologies." He actually seemed embarrassed, like this hostage business was new to him.

"I'm bored. And lonely," I admitted, because there was only so much staring at the walls one could do without going mad.

"What would you like? I mean, within your current circum-stance?"

I was so grateful and relieved that he was even asking, rather than just walking away. There were plenty of things I would have liked from him, but again, I steered clear of sex talk. After the way I'd heard him lecture X about Muslim respectability, I didn't want to offend him just when he was starting to soften up.

"Well," I said, "when you took me to the bathroom, I noticed a couple of the men playing chess. Is there any way one of them could come in and play with me?"

"You play chess?" He didn't hide his surprise.

"Yes, my father taught me."

"Very good," he said. "A father should spend time with his daughters."

"Yeah, I loved when he spent time with me—most of the time. He also made me learn Chinese so that I could read the original text of Sun Tzu, so it wasn't all fun and games." I couldn't help smile at the thought of my father and his many life lessons. God, I missed him terribly.

"*The Art of War.* I know it well, but only the English version," he admitted, staring at me like I was some strange creature. "You're not like any woman I've ever met."

"And you're not like most men."

That made him pause for a minute. I guess he was trying to figure out if I meant it as a compliment or an insult.

"I mean, here I am your captive, and yet you treat me with great respect. You even went out of your way to bring me my favorite food tonight," I explained.

He tried to brush it off as if the chicken hadn't been specially ordered for me. "Women are to be taken care of. The Quran tells me that."

"Oh, so you were only doing what your religion tells you to do?" I challenged.

He nodded.

"Okay, but here's something I don't understand about your religion: Why are women expected to be second-class citizens? You know, walking three feet behind the man, covered up completely . . . that kind of stuff. I mean, do you believe in all of that?" Oddly enough, I found myself hoping he would say no, that he believed a woman could be his equal. I was surprised by how much I cared.

"I would not call them second-class citizens, but I do think a respectable woman should be covered up."

I looked down at the baggy sweat pants and oversized T-shirt he'd given me after X had torn my other clothes. "So you'd rather see a woman in something like this than the outfit I was wearing when you brought me here?"

"Yes," he answered. "If you were my woman, I would never want another man to see the outline of your body. That would be for my eyes only." He stopped, turning away from me. I was stuck on the way he'd phrased his answer: *My woman.*

"You mean I couldn't even wear a bathing suit to the beach? Are you serious?"

"Yes. If you are my woman, then you are mine, and not to be gawked at by any man on the street."

My woman. There it was again. It sent a strange jolt through me to hear him say it, but I still didn't agree with his philosophy on the clothing issue.

"What I wear should be my choice," I argued, "and if you loved me, then you should want me to have those choices." I held his gaze waiting for his response, while knowing it wouldn't be what I wanted to hear.

When he spoke, his voice was soft and not as confident as it had been. "Do you think you could worship the Quran?" His question took my breath away, because I realized what he was asking.

"I read it, and yes, there are parts of it that speak to me, but I just don't know. . . ." Just saying it was painful, realizing we were on two separate paths that would likely never meet.

I think my answer bothered him, too, because he abruptly changed the subject. "Let me go and get the chessboard for that game."

As soon as the door closed, I let all the air out of my body. What the hell was going on? Whatever this feeling was, I knew it wasn't something that was supposed to happen. I shook my head, as if I could release all my confused thoughts that way. What if I was experiencing Stockholm syndrome, where you identify with your captors after a while? *Oh, Lord,* I thought, *Paris would never let me live that shit down.*

"You ready?" he asked when he returned with the chess set.

"You play?"

He pulled up a small table and set the board in front of me.

"So, how's this going to work?" I asked, staring down at the handcuffs.

"Guess I will be the one making all the moves," he informed me as he set up the pieces.

"I also assume that I will be the white pieces?" I said with a laugh. "I mean, with you being a Black Muslim and all, you probably don't want to have anything to do with white."

"It's not that deep." He smiled, showing the most beautiful straight teeth as he placed the black pieces in front of me.

"Check mate!" I said proudly about an hour later. We were evenly matched and the game had been close, but I wasn't about to lose, even to him.

"Wow. I'm impressed. But promise you won't tell my men. None of them can come close to beating me, and—"

"It would be so embarrassing if you were shown up by a female?" I said, flirting openly now. "I get it. Your secret is safe with me."

He looked like he was ready to play along, but then one of his men opened the door and he straightened up, all serious again.

"Brother X wants to see you," the man said. "Should I wait in here with her while you are gone?"

"No. She will be fine. In fact, unless she has to go to the restroom, I would like her undisturbed."

"Yes, sir." He ducked back out the door.

Elijah exited the room, leaving me alone to wonder what the hell was going on between the two of us.

Vegas

40

We stood out like a couple of purple giraffes in the zoo as I parked the car in the Brighton Beach section of Brooklyn, home to the largest Russian community outside of Russia. Dotted along the avenue were cafes, coffee shops, pastry shops, and stores selling authentic goods that made the locals feel like they had never stepped foot outside of the old country.

"Leave your piece in the car," I told Orlando, placing Bonnie and Clyde in the glove box.

I reached for the door, and he placed a hand on my arm to stop me. "You sure about this?" he questioned, no doubt wanting to turn the car around and drive back home. One glance outside the car at the hulking Russians watching us from the corner and I understood his concern, but we had bigger issues than them.

"Bro, you have to trust me. I know what I'm doing," I said in my best big-brother voice. "You walk in there strapped and you're as good as dead."

"I just don't know." He still hadn't moved his hand off my arm. "I mean, Pop always dealt with—"

"Look, Pop did things one way, and he dealt with all these cats his age who did things a certain way, but we're a new generation. That means our way of doing things is going to be different, and the cats we deal with are gonna be our contemporaries. You feel me? Sometimes you have to be willing to change things up."

"If you say so." A look of solidarity passed between us as we got out of the car and walked past the group of men staring at us.

I led Orlando a few doors down into the Baklava Bakery. Olga, the woman who had probably held court behind that counter for the past forty years, stared hard as we entered. An older Russian man who looked to be hiding a shotgun, with a scowl that said he was not afraid to use it, stood up from his rear corner seat, blocking the entrance to the back room and making sure we now saw the shotgun. He didn't hide his displeasure at seeing us. Neither did the customers who filled the small tables situated around the room.

I turned to Olga. "I need to speak to Boris."

"He is busy," the old man barked in a thick Russian accent, expecting that to send us scurrying back out the door.

I ignored him, reaching into my pocket and pulling out a crisp hundred-dollar bill. I placed it on the counter and looked directly at Olga. "You must be his mother, Olga. He speaks very highly of you and your meat pies."

"How do you know my son?" she asked as the hundred-dollar bill disappeared into her apron.

"We spent some time Upstate together. He said if I ever needed to speak to him, I should come here. Can you please tell him that Vegas Duncan is here to see him?"

"Wait here," she ordered and then turned and walked to the back of the shop. She whispered in the old man's ear, and he slipped into the back. Olga returned to the counter, and we ordered the sour cherry baklava and some caramel cakes, more to stay busy and not look like two pussies while we waited.

By the time we finished paying for our goods, the old man returned and directed us to the back. We left our pastries on the counter and followed him through the back door, into a room where there were at least five sets of tables filled with men playing cards.

The old man pointed at another door, where we found Boris. He was working in a converted storeroom barely big enough to fit all three of us. Orlando glanced at me, and I knew what he was thinking right away. Boris did not look like a person who could help us out of our current situation. He had no idea who Boris and his family were.

"Vegas Duncan." Boris spoke with a deep Brooklyn accent, his Russian almost non-existent, since he'd spent the majority of his youth in America. "To what do I owe the pleasure?"

"We've got a huge fucking problem, man. I need you to speak to your uncle and have him call off his dog."

"I've heard. Things have not been good for the Duncans," he remarked. "What I don't understand is how your problem with Brother X is our problem."

"Our families have known each other a long time. Your uncle and my father have done business for a long time. You and me have done business recently and made a lot of money," I reminded him. "That relationship could come to an end if things keep going the way they have been." I had to explain it in economic terms he would understand—and the only terms he would truly care about. His help was necessary to the future of my family's business, but he wouldn't care about that unless he understood how our future was intertwined with his.

He settled in behind his desk. "What are you asking, Vegas?"

"That you and your people align yourself with us."

"That's asking a lot." Of course I knew it was, which was why I had chosen to have this conversation in person in the first place.

"I was told this is an issue amongst Blacks," he continued.

I wasn't surprised by his comment. No one, no matter how gangster, is going to jump into someone else's battle unless he thinks it's going to benefit him in some way. The good thing, though, was that he hadn't come right out and said no. I just had to explain the stakes to him in terms he understood.

"X's men burned up three million dollars' worth of weed that was supposed to be allocated to you and your people. He burned your shipment to the ground, Boris."

His eyes narrowed to angry slits. Boris was one of the biggest marijuana wholesalers in the country. Clearly word had gotten back to him about our warehouse fire.

"Still think it's only amongst us Blacks?"

"Are you saying we will not receive a shipment this month?" He studied me closely, our history right there on the table. I could tell that he was weighing all his options in his mind. I needed to give him one more reason to see the advantage in siding with the Duncans.

"I'm saying that we're going to take care of our friends first—the people that are aligned with us, not those who are sitting on the sidelines while a psychopath tries to take down our family and our business."

"This is a big decision, not one that I can make on my own." It was not a definitive answer, but at least now I knew what side of the fence he was leaning on. "I just want to know what your terms are." It was always about money.

I breathed a sigh of relief.

By the time Orlando and I exited the bakery, things were a little better.

"That wasn't their shipment that burned in that warehouse. That was our reserve," Orlando said as we crossed the street.

"Oh, it wasn't? You should have told me that while we were in there." I laughed, patting him on the back. "I'm sure Boris would have wanted to know that."

Orlando looked at me with the same admiration he had for me as a kid. "I like your style, Vegas."

"Our style, little brother. *Our* style."

"Now what?" Orlando asked, showing me that he trusted me.

"Now we meet with the Italians. Tomorrow you're going to meet with the Jews, and I'm going to meet with the Asians," I answered as we got into the car and headed to our next destination.

Brother X

41

Elijah and I headed into the south entrance of Prospect Park around eleven o'clock in the morning, wearing dark glasses and baseball caps pulled low to avoid being recognized. Joggers, bikers, nannies pushing strollers, as well as older couples taking a morning walk, all parted like the Red Sea as Elijah and I came down the paved trail. We stopped for a hot dog at one of the vending carts, a treat I'd long missed being locked up. There was nothing like a good old-fashioned kosher hot dog, piled with sauerkraut, onions, and a good helping of spicy mustard, washed down with a grape soda.

We finished our hot dogs then continued down the path, finally stopping at a park bench with a view of the lake. Elijah stood behind the bench, his arms crossed in front of him. Looking at him, you might think he was standing guard, or you might think he was meditating by the water.

I sat down and finished off what was left of my soda, watching a dozen pigeons congregate in front of the bench. They raced to the seeds being tossed by the old man who had already been occupying the bench prior to our arrival.

"So you like feeding birds, huh?" I turned and asked Bernie, aka the Jew.

He threw another handful of seeds. The birds scurried about, chasing their late morning meal. "I love feeding these birds. It's one of the few comforts I have in life."

I couldn't imagine something like feeding nasty, useless birds being one of life's comforts, but then again, who was I to talk? My best friends were rats. So, I just nodded and watched him throw more food to the pigeons.

After a while, Bernie said, "I hear LC Duncan is as good as dead."

It was no surprise that this was why Bernie had asked me to meet him at the park. What else would he have wanted to discuss? It was becoming an obsession of his. I bet he even talked about the Duncans in his sleep.

"That's what I'm hearing," I replied. "I have to admit, though, it's going to be hard to finish the job. They have that hospital guarded like a fortress."

"Doesn't matter. From what I hear his days are numbered. We're still going to give you credit for that one," Bernie said, not taking his eyes off his little friends. "As long as you make sure you take out Vegas Duncan. He was part of the contract."

I didn't need reminding. A bad memory wasn't what was keeping us from handling Vegas.

"We're working on him," I said, thinking how funny it was that I had set out with my red light aimed at Junior Duncan's head, yet every other Duncan seemed to be on death's menu.

"Good," Bernie said, finally turning away from the birds to look me in the eye. "Because he's poking his nose around where he has no business."

"He's elusive," I said by way of explanation for the delay. "We've taken out two warehouses and burned a couple million dollars' worth of marijuana, hoping to smoke him out, but these Duncans . . . they keep staying in their fortress. We spot Vegas one minute, then the next minute he's gone. The guy's like a ninja."

"I don't care if he's the President of the United States. You better figure it out and get him soon," Bernie snapped. "He's dangerous. He's talking to people, aligning people against you. Against us." By now Bernie was seething. He'd turned a deep shade of red. He inhaled and exhaled slowly, as if he'd been to anger management and was following his therapist's instructions to control his temper. "I'm not having this conversation with you again, Xavier. Next time we meet face to face, you know who will be there—and we both know you don't want that." He threw one last handful of seeds and then shoved the bag into my hand before getting up and walking away.

Elijah sat down in the space Bernie had vacated, and we watched the pigeons finish off Bernie's offerings before Elijah spoke.

"Why are you always taking mess from that guy?"

I turned and looked at Elijah. "Bernie Goldman is just a puppet. I'm not afraid of him. It's the man he works for that scares the hell outta me. Trust me. We don't want to have to go before him." I shifted my gaze out to the lake.

"So what's our next move?" Elijah asked.

The answer to that was simple: "We kill Vegas Duncan."

Rio

42

"Yo, I need you to watch my back. Put on a suit and meet me downstairs in fifteen minutes."

That was all Orlando had said when he knocked on my bedroom door forty-five minutes ago. Now we were in his Audi R8, pulling into the parking lot at the Kings Plaza Mall, and he still hadn't given me any more information. He'd never asked me to watch his back before, so I didn't want to rock the boat by asking too many questions. I was just glad to be there, and I figured I would wait to see what happened next.

He maneuvered the car to a remote spot, away from any other cars, and reached for the glove compartment.

"Why are we stopping here? Please tell me you didn't bring me here just to go shopping with you, O."

"Patience," he replied. How the hell was I supposed to be patient, I wondered, when Kennedy was dead, Pop was nearly dead, and poor Sasha was being held captive by some crazy Muslim freak who was out to get our entire family? Shit, I had run out of patience a long time ago, and I was starting to lose faith that my family would ever do the things we should have done already—the things we *would have* already done if it was the old days. With Pop in the hospital, it was like everything had fallen apart and no one knew how to handle a damn thing.

"You strapped?" he asked as he took out his gun and made sure it was loaded.

I nodded. Not that I always carried a piece, but Orlando had said I was going to be watching his back, so I'd strapped on a holster when I got dressed, just in case.

We got out of the car and headed into the mall, and that's when I started to worry. It didn't make sense that we were packing heat in a mall this size, especially one with wall-to-wall people. "Stay close."

"You expecting trouble?" I was looking over my shoulder constantly, feeling totally paranoid now.

"Nope, but I'm ready if it comes my way," he replied, not stressed at all. He stopped in the food court to order some meat on a stick. "You hungry?"

"Yeah, order me some chicken and rice."

We took our food to the other side of the court and took a seat. Orlando dug into his meal, but I was too busy scanning the room, still trying to figure out what the hell we were really doing there. That's when a white man wearing a yarmulke and sporting a gray beard and Shirley Temple curls sat down across from us. Dude had to be at least eighty. He had two beefy bodyguard types sitting at a table next to us.

Orlando looked up from his plate and said, "Bernie. I got your message, so I'm here. What's so important?"

"Before we get to business, first let me give you my most sincere wish for your father's speedy recovery. He is doing better, I hope?"

"The same, but thank you for asking. We brought him home a few days ago in hopes that he might do better in familiar surroundings."

Bernie nodded. "Well, I will pray for him. He has been a good friend over the years. Which brings me to you. Are you going to be a good friend, Orlando?"

"I hope so. This apple hasn't fallen too far from the tree. I'm very much like my father." Orlando turned to me for confirmation.

"Uh-huh. He is," was all I could say. I was too busy trying to understand what the hell was going on at this point. Like I said, I wasn't used to being included in this part of the family's dealings, so I had no idea who this white dude was or why he seemed to know all our business.

"Good," he said to Orlando, "because we made you and your father a very reasonable offer before he was shot, and we haven't heard back. It's customary to at least get a reply, especially since I hear your brother Vegas is running all around town trying to recruit help when we offered our help from the start."

"To be honest, Bernie, all I can say is I'm sorry. We meant no disrespect to you or your people." A mother with three young kids had settled in at a nearby table, so Orlando leaned in and lowered his voice to keep our conversation private. "To be honest, I liked your offer. I liked it a year ago when you proposed it, and I liked it even more three weeks ago. I thought it was a win-win for all of us, especially with you offering to take care of our little Muslim problem in your most recent proposal. But as you know, Pop was against it." He paused for a minute then added, "The crazy thing is that if he had agreed, he'd probably be sitting here talking to you instead of me."

Bernie didn't disagree with Orlando's assessment of the situation. This really got me thinking. What was the proposal that this guy had made, and why had Pop not accepted it? And was this all somehow tied to him getting shot? Damn it, I hated being kept in the dark like this.

Bernie and Orlando kept right on talking as if I weren't there.

"Well," Bernie said, "with LC's health situation being what it is, that should give you even more reason to accept our offer."

"You would think so, but we have a saying in our family: A man has got to know his limitations. And me, I know mine—which is why, three nights ago with my blessing, Vegas was voted in by the family to run the . . . shall we say . . . *the less legitimate* side of our business. I am now second in command and CEO of our other businesses."

Bernie did not look pleased. "What does that mean for our proposal? Should I be talking to Vegas right now?"

"No, Vegas asked me to speak to you because we have already established a relationship. And I trust that we can continue our relationship, but our answer to your proposal is still no."

Forget "not pleased." Bernie had gone past that straight to "pissed the fuck off."

"We got a half billion on the table," he said, barely restraining his anger.

I almost choked when I heard the amount. Orlando, on the other hand, stayed totally cool, like we were talking about pennies, instead of millions of dollars.

"I realize that," Orlando said. "But I am only telling you what our family has decided."

Bernie still looked pissed, but incredibly, he upped the offer even more. "Let's say we add ten percent. Will that get us a deal?"

I had to do a hell of an acting job to contain myself. I could not believe my brother was sitting here turning down more money than the gross domestic product of some small countries. What the fuck was going on here?

"I'll bring your offer back to Vegas," Orlando said, "but no promises."

"Make sure you do," Bernie said with an edge to his tone, and then he got up. Before he left, he said, "And please make sure your brother knows we can help end this war and return your cousin."

When Bernie was out of sight, I grabbed Orlando's arm and said, "What the hell did you just do?"

"I just turned down half a billion dollars." His answer was matter-of-fact, but there was still some uncertainty in his tone. Then he expressed his true concern: "The real question is, at what price?"

Vegas

43

Minister Farah raised his glass of ice tea. "Congratulations are in order, my friend. To fatherhood."

I raised my wine in a gesture of thanks, and we toasted once again to my good news. I'd invited Minister Farah out to dinner at this Thai spot on the border of Queens and Long Island to catch him up on everything that was going on with Pop, Sasha, the war with X, and of course, with my new son. I'd also been hoping to surprise him with another visitor, but the visitor didn't show up.

"Thank you, Minister. I can barely believe it myself. Me, a father?"

"So, your son—will he be attending the academy like you?"

"I'm not sure. With everything going on, I haven't had a chance to find out what his mother's plans are."

"Well, Vegas, I've never met the boy, but you do realize he's in a very unique situation. With you as his father and Consuela as his mother, he is the legitimate heir to two very powerful families. A young, impressionable man like that should be trained for his responsibilities. If you don't send him to the school, I'd like offer my services."

"I understand, but right now I just want to be a dad," I told him as the waiter brought us the check. Of course, Minister Farah tried to reach for it, but I was just a little too fast for him.

"Thank you. It was a real pleasure," he said, rubbing his full stomach.

I settled the bill and we stood up from the table.

"I really appreciate you always making time for me," I said, shaking his hand.

"Any time," he replied.

I turned toward the exit, and he said, "I'm gonna take a trip to the men's room before I head uptown. I'll give you a call in a couple of days."

We shook hands again and I headed for the door.

The moment I stepped outside, I could tell that something wasn't right. Call it instinct, intuition, or just a plain gut feeling, but I sensed it. I glanced down the block and saw the lights flash on the first car of my security detail, which made me relax a little. I shook my head, thinking it was time to get my paranoia under control. Lately I felt like one of X's men was lurking around every corner.

I went around the corner of the building where my car was parked, again getting an uneasy feeling. I was starting to regret my decision to park back there. It was just so damn dark in that parking lot. I froze until I saw the other car in my security detail flash its lights.

I relaxed a little, which turned out to be my biggest mistake. As I got to my car and put Clyde away to unlock the door, I heard the sound of a round being chambered in a shotgun.

"I wouldn't make a move if I were you." I hadn't even noticed the black-clad man in the passenger seat of the SUV, with its windows rolled down, next to my car.

I glanced over at my security detail and watched as three men got out of the car carrying weapons. My heart started pounding when I realized they weren't my men.

"Vegas Duncan, I've been wanting to meet you. My men tell me that you have quite the reputation for being the Third Coming."

I turned in the direction of the deep voice and found myself face to face with Brother X. He had just climbed out of the back of my security car.

"Where are my men?" I growled.

"Your men are—how can I say this politely?—taking a little nap," he said with a sinister smile.

He needed to understand that I had been born ready for any and all challenges. I opened my coat, reaching for my weapon.

"Have you forgotten about me already?" This voice came from behind me. It was the dude with the shotgun in the SUV. "Hands in the air."

Suddenly the sound of bullets being chambered came from several different directions. Turning to my right, I saw two capable gunmen, their weapons pointed at me. To my left were another two, also ready to fill me with holes. Now, I had gotten out of a lot of dicey situations before, but this was scary, and at the moment, I was drawing a blank as to how I would survive this many shooters when my guns were still in their holsters.

"Dammit!" I sighed, preparing myself for the worst.

The man with the shotgun got out of the SUV. "Cover him," he ordered the others as he headed over toward X.

He hadn't taken more than two steps before all hell broke loose.

Thump! Thump! Thump! Thump!

I knew that sound. It was a silenced sniper rifle. When I turned around, I saw all four gunmen lying dead on the ground. Anyone who was left standing, including Brother X, headed for the hills. Not wasting any time trying to figure out what had just happened, I pulled out my guns and ran after X, but it was too late. They jumped into a car and were halfway down the block in no time.

Back over by my car, I checked to make sure the guys on the ground were dead. The sniper had hit his intended targets precisely, and no one was left breathing.

I heard footsteps emerging from the shadows, and I cocked my weapon, prepared to shoot. Then the person came into view, and I lowered my gun.

"Man, you scared the shit out of me!" I said. Standing there, brandishing a sniper rifle and wearing a shit-eating grin on his face was Daryl Graham.

I glanced at my watch. "Damn, bro, you're two hours late."

Daryl looked around at the dead bodies. "My plane was delayed. But from where I'm standing, looks like I got here right on time."

"Is everything all right?" We both turned to see Minister Farah coming toward us. Thank God he'd stayed behind in the restaurant, I thought with relief. That trip to the restroom had probably saved his life.

Daryl

44

With Connie gone, it was good to be around people I considered family. I needed to be surrounded by those who loved me to help me cope with Connie's passing. In her, I'd lost not only a lover but my best friend. Of course, nothing could completely erase the pain of her death, but being around the Duncans helped ease it just a little. Putting my foot in this Brother X's ass for what he did to LC was going to help me channel my emotions even more. I had stayed by Connie's side the same way I knew she would have done for me, and now it was time for me to be there for the Duncans when they needed me most. They'd done the same for me in the past.

Call me corny, but as I sat on a lounge chair by the pool, listening to the birds in the trees and feeling the soft breeze on my face, I felt like Connie's spirit was right there with me. It was really peaceful, until I felt a shadow over me. My eyes flew open, and I was instantly on high alert.

"What's up, stranger?" I relaxed when I realized it was just Paris standing over me. "I didn't even hear you come out," I said.

"Yeah, you looked like you were miles away. On an island in Paradise or something."

"Far from it. I was thinking about my deceased wife."

"That's a little morbid." She smiled and licked her lips. "You should be thinking about a hot body like mine, not a cold one."

Leave it to Paris to say something inappropriate. She had always been like a bratty little sister to me, though I will admit her comment was almost crossing the line. "Damn, girl. I see your mouth hasn't changed one bit, has it?"

She rolled her eyes. "Anyway, if everything goes down how it's supposed to, we're all going out to celebrate later on tonight. I just wanted to see if you wanted to go out and have a drink with us."

"Drink?" I said, looking her up and down. "Are you even old enough to drink?"

"Yeah," she said with her usual sassy attitude. "Daryl, I'm not a child. I have a baby."

It seemed like just yesterday she was running around in braces. "I must be getting old."

"Well, you wouldn't believe some of the things I'm old enough to do. I wouldn't mind telling you—or should I say showing you—after you buy me that drink." She was like a little girl trying to act grown.

I chuckled at her antics, imagining her as the young, pigtail-wearing girl I once knew. "P, I just lost my wife. I'm not even thinking about being with a woman, least of all one I consider to be a little sister."

She threw her hands on her hips and pulled down her dark sunglasses just enough to reveal her eyeballs. "Hmmm, we're going to have to do something about this 'little sister' thing, aren't we?"

"Not if I have anything to do with it." I laughed her off.

"We'll see about that," she said and then turned to leave.

I shook my head as I watched her switch her hips back into the house.

"Mommy, watch me on the swings!" I saw London's little girl come out of the house, skipping past Paris.

"Okay, honey. I see you," London replied, trailing behind the little girl as she hopped on the swing set. London stood there for a minute, watching her, then made her way over to me.

"Hey," she said.

"Hey yourself," I replied. "What's your little girl's name? She's cute."

"This one is Mariah. The other one is Maria," she told me.

I laughed. "You always said you were going to have a little girl one day, and here you have two."

There was a moment of awkward silence and tension between us. Thankfully, Mariah's little voice cut through. "Mommy, you see me?"

"I'm watching, baby," London shouted over to her. She stood there and stared at Mariah for a moment, but I knew she was only doing so to keep from looking at me.

I almost thought our conversation was over, but then, with her back still to me, she said, "You know, I was really broken up when I heard . . . when I thought that you had died. I can't remember the last time I cried that hard." She finally turned to look at me. "I'm glad you're alive."

"I appreciate that."

Again an awkward silence fell. There was so much unsaid between us, but maybe enough time had passed that we should just leave it all as water under the bridge.

"So, how's married life?" I asked in an attempt to steer the conversation to safer subjects.

"Um, it has its ups and downs, but for the most part it's good." She shrugged. Not exactly a glowing endorsement. "I heard Vegas tell Mommy you were married."

"I was. My wife passed away a few days ago. Cancer."

Her hand flew to her mouth. "Oh, Daryl. I'm so sorry to hear that. Are you all right? You must be torn apart."

"I am. But it's good to be around you guys. I don't think I could do this alone."

"I can imagine. For you to have gotten married, she must have been something really special." There was so much unspoken meaning behind her words, but I sensed genuine sympathy for my loss.

"She was very special," I answered.

She looked as though something was on the tip of her tongue, but it took her a while to speak up. Finally, she said, "Can I ask you something? And if it's inappropriate, just say so and I'll shut my mouth and walk away."

"Sure."

"You don't, like, hate me for marrying Harris or anything, do you?"

"Nah, I'm over it," I said. I knew she would get around to that eventually. "I waited four hours and then I got on the flight . . . without you. It wasn't like I was gonna come back here and go to the wedding."

Her expression told me she still felt guilty about that day. "You don't understand," she said.

"I didn't then, but I do now," I said. "You didn't want to take the chance."

"Daryl, I—"

I put my hand up to stop her. "It's okay. That was a long time ago. You don't have to explain. I know what it's like to be in love with somebody."

"But do you know how it feels to be in love with two people?"

We locked eyes for a minute, but neither of us spoke. Everything that happened between us was like a distant echo now, muffled by the current pain of losing my wife. I didn't have the energy to rehash old hurts with London.

I think she sensed that I was done. Without a good-bye, she went over to the swing set. "Come on, Mariah. Time to go inside."

"London," I called out to her. She turned around. "I don't blame you. If I were you, I would have chosen a lawyer over a thug too."

Brother X

45

After the botched hit on Vegas, Bernie wanted to meet with me once again. As far as I was concerned, we'd already talked one too many times. He was lucky I'd even agreed to meet in that park the last time, while his old ass fed some pigeons. And yet here he was, calling for another meeting. I was not used to being micromanaged when someone contracted my services, and the Jew was really starting to piss me off. I always finished my jobs successfully, but how the hell was I supposed to do that if Bernie kept wasting my time with these fucking meetings?

I had a good mind to raise my fee to a million and a half, I thought, as I followed one of his men to a conference room. The thought made me laugh. Nothing would get that cheap bastard's attention faster than charging him more money.

Our escort stepped to the side and directed me and Elijah to enter the conference room. Bernie sat scowling at the large table, a security guard standing on either side of him.

"How come Vegas Duncan is still alive?" Bernie spat before we had even stepped fully into the room.

"Aren't you at least going to offer me a seat first?" I said.

"Vegas Duncan!" He pounded his fist on the table. He seemed pretty fearless, coming at a man of my physical stature that way. I studied his eyes and decided that one of two things was going on in his head: either he was feeling a false sense of security because of the guards surrounding him, or a deeper fear about something else was causing him to be reckless with me. Whatever was going on in that brain of his, he didn't look like he was in the mood for any type of pleasantries, so the same way he'd gotten straight to the point, so would I.

"We almost got him the other night, but the guy's like a cat with nine lives," I told him as I settled in to a seat. "Be patient—and trust me. We know what we're doing. I guarantee that all the Duncan are as good as dead."

Bernie looked unsatisfied with my answer. "I called you here to find out when you plan on doing what you're being paid a very healthy sum of money to do. And what do you give me?" He raised his hands and then let them fall. "Excuses. Empty promises. You've reached men in prison who are surrounded by inmates, gang members, and guards, yet you can't get to a fucking guy driving a red Ferrari?"

My jaw tightened, but I was determined to keep my composure. Elijah, on the other hand, was having none of it.

"Why are we even standing here and listening to his ass?" Elijah always did dislike the Jew.

I replied to Elijah but kept a hard stare focused on Bernie. "I'm starting to feel the same way."

"I have a million reasons why you're standing here listening to me." Bernie reminded me of the payout that awaited us when the job was complete.

"I said we'd do it," I snapped, "and we will. In the meantime, not that I'm one to give status reports, but we do have a Duncan being held hostage." I lifted my head and poked my chest out slightly. I was quite proud of this feat.

The sound of weak applause came from behind me. Bernie's eyes surfed over my shoulders to look at whoever had entered the conference room.

"Very good. You captured a woman." Our new guest's voice was laced with sarcasm. "Tell us, Brother Xavier, are we supposed to be impressed?" I recognized the voice instantly.

"Sir," I said, turning around with a mixture of fear and dread. Bernie had threatened to bring him to our next meeting, but I had hoped he wasn't going to show up.

I stood up and bowed my head in a gesture of respect. Once upon a time, we had both followed the Nation of Islam, but when Minister Farah returned from teaching in Europe, his vision had changed. He taught me his new philosophy of black economic empowerment, which truly meant "by any means necessary." On that day, the Islamic Black Panther Party was born, with me as its figurehead leader. Minister Farah maintained the appearance of being part of the Nation of Islam. He kept his involvement in the IBPP so deep underground that even my top men didn't know who he was.

He walked up on me. We were face to face—well, not literally, as I towered over the man who was even smaller in stature than the Jew. He looked at me for a moment like a father welcoming his son home, but then, in a swift move, the palm of his hand connected with my check so forcefully that I thought my head might spin around. I would never have expected him to be able to throw such a powerful blow.

He looked down at my fists, which were balled up out of reflex.

"Oh, what? You want to get physical with me?" He hit me three times: once in the ribs, once on the thigh, and a kick to my knee, paralyzing my left side momentarily. He had to have hit pressure points. "Is that what you want?"

"No, no, no." I raised my open palms in a gesture of surrender.

He snickered, knowing I'd never lay hands on him.

"We gave you Vegas on a silver platter the other night. How the hell did you screw that up?" he asked.

"We?" I questioned, looking over at Bernie.

"Don't play stupid," Minister Farah said. "You know the information came from me."

He was right. If I'd thought about it, I would have known that. Seemed like I'd been slipping a lot these days, starting with the way I'd slipped up and underestimated the Duncans. When this whole thing started, I thought I was dealing with a bunch of car salesmen. Sonya's infidelity had really thrown me off my game.

"I'm sorry. But he had help."

"Of course he had help," Farah shot back. "Daryl Graham is back in town. But that doesn't change the fact that Vegas should be dead right now. I will not stand for failure, Xavier. Do you think I fed you all that information about your wife and Junior Duncan just so you could get revenge for a man sleeping with your wife?" he asked me.

"It has always been about LC Duncan. Junior, he's no threat. He's soft. He has a heart. LC Duncan and Vegas are ruthless, and neither of them want to give up H.E.A.T. Now, we've got Orlando ready to give us what we want, and with LC on his death bed, all we need is Vegas dead." He stared at me like he was a ten-foot tall giant looking down on me. "You got that?"

"Yes, sir." I bowed my head, reiterating the respect I had for him.

"Then get the hell out of here!" he shouted. "Leave us grown folks to talk, and close the door behind you . . . boy."

I turned toward the door and hurried out. It didn't go unnoticed that Elijah paused before following me—almost as if he didn't want to follow me anymore.

Sasha

46

The way he'd gripped the ends of that rope and tied my wrists together, I knew those were some strong hands that could do magic. I just never imagined they'd be cupping my breasts the way they were now.

Hell, who was I kidding? Sure I had. I had imagined that and more from the moment I saw Elijah—once I took my eyes off the gun that was being aimed at my head. Brother Elijah was one fine-looking man. He couldn't hide from me what I knew was under that bowtie and suit. Almost made a sistah want to convert.

"So soft," he moaned, caressing them, using his thumbs to fondle my nipples and make them hard. It didn't take much for my young, perky girls to stand at attention. Unlike Paris, I'd had no kids, so my breasts were just as tender and firm as they were when I was in high school. And these beauties were bringing out the dirty little boy in Elijah.

I wanted to reach down and grab his manhood so bad, but my hands were still restrained. Truth was, though, that I was getting off on being tied up while he had his way with me. I was looking forward to having one hell of an earth-shaking orgasm.

"Put 'em in your mouth." Always the assertive one, I was giving orders even while I was tied up.

I watched him lower his head to my breast, his mouth open, ready to inhale my areola. My head fell back in ecstasy.

I jerked my head up and my eyes flew open when I heard the heavy footsteps of someone entering the room.

"Elijah," I said, wondering how much he'd witnessed. That little fantasy I'd been having had me really worked up.

If he knew what I'd been doing, he didn't let on. He closed the door behind him and walked over toward me, looking every bit as serious as he always did. Whatever was on his mind, it definitely wasn't sex.

He grabbed a chair and pulled it up next to mine.

"You all right?" he asked me.

I nodded.

"Did they treat you okay while I was gone?"

I nodded again.

He sounded more like a father who had left a child home with the babysitter, rather than the man who was holding me captive. You'd think he'd be trying to clip off parts of my body to send back to the family, but instead, he'd been going out of his way to show me small acts of caring. Perhaps he was starting to feel a sense of protectiveness over me. Maybe there was some type of kidnappers' syndrome named for that behavior too. I'd never been held hostage before, but from what I'd seen so far, it was making both me and my captor behave in some pretty unexpected ways.

"Do you need to go to the bathroom?" he asked.

"No," I replied. "I'm good."

"I brought you something," he said.

I raised my eyebrows expectantly, waiting to see what he had.

Reaching into his jacket pocket, he pulled out a peach. "It's organic. I know how you care about what goes in your body."

There was something else I wanted inside my body at the moment, but I stopped myself from saying it out loud. Instead, I just said, "Thanks. You going to feed it to me?"

He looked down at the ropes that bound my hands. "Oh, yeah." He got up and untied one of my hands and then gave me the peach.

"Thank you." I took a bite of the peach, savoring the sweet juice. My tongue darted out of my mouth to keep the juice from dripping down my chin. Any other time, I could eat a piece of fruit and turn it into a whole sensual show, but Elijah barely even noticed. He clearly had something heavy on his mind.

We sat together in silence for a while, and I thought maybe he was about to get up and leave, but instead he exhaled hard and said, "I have something I need to ask you."

"Okay," I said, and then, because I didn't feel threatened by him, I added, "but before you even ask, you know I can't tell you much about my family." Whatever weird connection was developing between me and Elijah, my loyalty would always remain with the Duncans.

"What exactly is H.E.A.T?" he asked.

I was a little caught off guard by his question. H.E.A.T was old news as far as I was concerned. "Of all the questions you can ask me, why would you ask me about H.E.A.T.?"

He shrugged. "I just want to know."

"Nobody just wants to know about H.E.A.T. Where is this coming from?"

"Someone brought it up today in association with the Duncans."

I took another bite of the peach, contemplating how much I should tell him. I decided that since H.E.A.T. was a dead issue for the Duncans, I wasn't betraying anything by telling Elijah about it. "H.E.A.T. is a drug my family developed."

"Like crack?" he asked.

"No, it was way better than crack. It was on its way to being the most successful drug ever. H.E.A.T. makes Molly look like aspirin. It was the answer to every weekend partier's dreams. It would have made the Duncans much more than multi-millionaires. I'm talking billionaire status. We had the game on lock with H.E.A.T."

Elijah was hanging on my every word, and I was enjoying his attention, so I continued my story. "People all over the world have tried to buy the formula from us. You wouldn't believe how much money we've been offered—enough for generations to come to be set for life. But we turn them down every time."

He sat quietly for a while, probably trying to process the story. I didn't blame him. Sometimes it was still hard for me to believe the Duncans had turned down so much money, and it was *my* family I was talking about.

"So what happened to it?" he finally asked.

"Cancer," I said, taking another bite of the peach and wiping the juice off my chin. He wasn't noticing anyway, so no reason to keep up the sensual act. "We found out it causes liver cancer. We didn't want that shit out there because ultimately the powers that be would make sure it settled in the black community like every other drug." He frowned, and I couldn't tell why. Maybe if I knew how he'd heard about it, I'd understand his motives better. As it was, though, it was a mystery to me, so I wrapped up my story quickly. "Long story short, despite the money, we didn't want to be responsible for all those deaths."

Elijah sat quietly, marinating on what he'd just heard. "Wow. I just can't imagine shutting down a billion-dollar enterprise."

"Yeah, not a week goes by that someone doesn't offer to buy the formula, but hey, the Duncans are drug distributors. For us, this is just business. We're not trying to kill off our entire race—or any other race, for that matter."

He looked truly stunned. "So the Duncans aren't as bad as I thought they were."

"No, we're hardworking people, just like everybody else. Your camp included." I wanted him to see me as no different than him.

"Just one more question."

"This is about your fifth one, but who's counting?" I said with a flirtatious smile.

"Why would Junior sleep with another man's wife?"

Now, this was the first question I would have expected him to ask, considering that was what started this war anyway. "I don't know. Junior's not the type to do that kind of thing. Maybe he didn't know Sonya was married at first. But now he's in love." I leaned in and shot him a seductive look. "If you were in love, would you give up so easily?"

He opened his mouth to reply, but we were interrupted by a knock on the door. Another soldier poked his head into the room and said, "Brother Xavier wants to see you."

Elijah got up and retied the restraints around both of my hands. "Thanks for the conversation," he said then left the room.

"Thanks for the fantasy," was my reply.

Daryl

47

"We've spotted his men on Jamaica Ave, Merrick Boulevard, and over by both airports," I said. "My guess is he's still got Sasha in Queens somewhere."

With Vegas's security detail getting killed in the restaurant parking lot, Kennedy dead, and Junior walking around with a price on his head, I'd been asked by Ma Chippy to bring in some of my Israelite brothers and head up Duncan security. I told her I couldn't commit to the job long term, but I was there until this whole situation was resolved. Truthfully, I was thankful for the work, because the distraction helped to keep my mind off of Connie.

"Yo, Daryl! Daryl!" One of Vegas's guys, Kareem, came running into the kitchen. "Y'all need to come out front and see this right now." He darted right back out of the kitchen, and I followed, along with Orlando, Vegas, and Junior.

Outside in front of the house, we came face to face with a man in a bowtie and schoolboy glasses headed our way. He was surrounded by seven of our guys pointing their weapons at him.

"That's the same cat that came into the restaurant that day when I was about to propose to Sonya," Junior said. "He's the one who supposedly warned me about Brother X."

"Well, this fool say he got a message for y'all," Kareem said.

Junior took quick steps toward the man, and I stayed right behind him in case I needed to rein him in. I didn't want Junior killing this guy before we found out why he was there.

I could tell by the vein pulsing in his temple that Junior really wanted to strangle this dude, but to his credit, he remained cool. "What are you doing here?" he asked him. "Why are you at my home?"

"Yeah, why are you here?" Paris was now on the top step, gun in hand.

"My name is Brother Elijah. I'm here because I have a message to deliver from Brother Xavier," he said, looking past Junior and directly at Vegas. He was so intense and serious that you would have thought the message he was about to relay had been spoken to him by Allah Himself.

"Another message, huh?" Junior grunted. "Kind of like the one you delivered to me that night at the restaurant?"

Junior's shoulders tensed up, and I could tell he was about to start swinging. "Calm down, man," I whispered. "Let's hear him out."

Junior looked to Vegas then me. He nodded, and the raging bull was calmed. For now, anyway.

"No, my friend, this message is a little different," Elijah said.

"Friend?" This time it was Orlando who was about to snap.

Vegas held out his arm in front of Orlando to cut off anything before it could get started. Everyone was calm again as we gave Elijah our undivided attention. I hated the thought of him feeling as though the ball was in his court. Sadly enough, though, it was.

Elijah stepped past Junior toward Vegas, who came down off the porch.

"We're listening," Vegas said.

"As you know from the pictures we sent you, we have Sasha Duncan," Elijah started.

"Tell us something we don't know!" Paris shouted. "You got her . . . for now. But we're going to get her back!"

Elijah cleared his throat and continued. "You're going to get her back, huh? Well, not without my help."

This statement had us all confused. Had this man, one of the ones responsible for Sasha's capture, just suggested that he would help us get her back? If that was true, then why the hell didn't he just bring her with him in the first place and stop wasting time?

"What do you mean, not without your help?" Vegas asked.

"If I can get back to delivering my message, I think you will understand."

"Go ahead. Deliver your message," Vegas told him, remaining calm in the face of this bastard's arrogance.

"Brother Xavier wants to make an exchange: Sasha Duncan for you, Vegas Duncan," Elijah said.

"Hell no!" Paris yelled. There was no need to look at her to know what her expression was at that moment. From what Orlando and Vegas had told me, she wasn't known for negotiating. She was a shoot-first-and-ask-questions-later kind of girl. Orlando was closest to her. He'd have to handle her while I kept Junior in check.

"What kind of bullshit are you coming here with? You're lucky we don't—"

"Paris!" Vegas's voice boomed. "Let him finish."

Elijah continued as if he hadn't even heard Paris's threatening rant. "If you want to see Sasha alive again, then I say make the exchange." A solemn look passed across Elijah's face, and I swear I saw something like regret in his expression. "Because if we don't get Sasha away from X, I'm afraid he's going to do the unthinkable."

"You're *afraid*?" Vegas asked the question that was surely roaming through everyone's mind. Why did he care whether Sasha was killed? He seemed sincere, but then again, why would he want to help set free the very person he was holding captive? This had to be a trick.

"Why him and not me?" Junior snapped, pushing his way in front of Elijah. "I'm the one he should want. I'm the one with Sonya."

"If it was up to me, you'd be the one I chose, adulterer, but it's not my choice. I'm just a messenger, and Xavier wants Vegas."

"Vegas ain't going nowhere, so whatever you and your boss are up to, forget it," Paris said as if she were the one making the final decision. "You come here acting like you ain't got nothing to do with it. Why should we even trust you?"

Elijah cleared his throat. "Do you have a Quran?"

"What the—?" Orlando asked.

Elijah turned to Vegas. "Do you have a Quran?" he repeated.

"Yeah," Vegas said. "Upstairs. What does that have to do with anything?"

"I'll put my hand on the Holy Quran," Elijah said. He looked directly into the eyes of each of us before he announced, "I may be a killer, but I don't harm women—and I'm not a liar."

We all looked around, silently questioning each other about how we should respond. I don't know what it was about this guy, but something told me that he might be telling the truth.

Sasha

48

Two guards on either side lowered me, blindfolded, from the van and brought me into a building. Immediately I noticed that the temperature was much colder than the last place. They led me through the building, down some stairs, and then I heard a door opening. One of the guards pushed me inside a room and then ripped the black sack off of my head. The other guard left.

Nobody was saying anything, but I could tell something was going down. I hadn't seen or heard from Elijah since our conversation about H.E.A.T., and the few times I'd seen X, he looked tired and stressed. The fact that he hadn't killed me told a story of its own. My hopes were that my family was putting pressure on them from all directions.

The guard who stayed with me crossed to the center of the room, where he sat me down in a chair.

"Where is Elijah?" I asked. It sounds strange, but I was missing him. I felt like he had made it his job to take care of me, and if I had to be held captive, at least that had been some small comfort.

This guy looked right through me as if I hadn't spoken a word. Of course, being a woman I should have expected that. These Black Muslims weren't exactly known for their progressive ideas about women. Maybe that was why I was feeling a closeness to Elijah. He at least spoke to me like he thought I had a brain. The rest of them treated me like less than a second-class citizen.

"Hey, I'm talking to you. Where are we, and why did you bring me here?" Again he ignored me. "Tell me!" I screamed at him. He responded by walking out the door, leaving me alone.

I wanted to kick myself for actually admiring his rock-hard ass as he left. My body parts might be female, but my insatiable sexual appetite was all male. Even in this fucked-up situation, I couldn't help but think about sex. Still, I thought, those fantasies were the only thing keeping me sane as I waited for the Duncans to get their asses in gear and free me.

"Miss me?" The door opened and there stood Brother X, smiling like a freak in heat. Now, that was a damn good way to get me to stop thinking about sex.

He closed the door behind him and came over to me. His smile had transformed into a lecherous stare. This motherfucker was planning to undress me again, and I didn't hold out any hope that Elijah would rescue me this time. Maybe Brother X had sent him somewhere and then relocated me to get me away from Elijah. Had he sensed that there were feelings developing between us?

"Where is Elijah?" I asked in a demanding tone. "Does he even know you brought me here?"

He reached down and began to fondle my breasts through my blouse, grabbing handfuls and massaging.

"Where is he?"

"Busy. Your hero Elijah is indisposed, so I hope you know what that means. We are all alone. Just the two of us." He ran one hand between my legs. Luckily, this time my body and my mind were in complete agreement. Instead of being turned on, I was creeped out. He began to rub his dick through the fabric in his pants, and I could see it hardening.

"Stop touching me," I snarled, refusing to give him the satisfaction of my fear.

"Wanna know why I'm so turned on? So excited?" He leaned down and bit my left nipple before rising to meet me eye to eye. "Because I get to kill someone today. You have no idea how intoxicating it is to kill a person."

He had no idea how much I did know about it.

"Yep. I'm going to kill somebody, and his name is Vegas Duncan." He started laughing.

"Fuck you. Vegas will wipe the floor with you, and then each and every one of us will give you such a beat down that you'll be begging to return to the safety of a prison cell."

Instead of striking me, he began to sing like some kind of lunatic. "I'm going to kill a Duncan today. I'm going to kill a Duncan today, and nobody can stop me."

"You are one sick dude," I replied.

"Yes, I am." He straddled me, still singing in my ear. "I'm going to kill Vegas. I'm going to kill Vegas today."

"Get the fuck off of me!" I screamed as loud as I could, hoping someone would hear me. I wondered if any of these other Muslims would care enough to rescue me from this crazy asshole.

"But first I am going to fuck you good," he continued, ignoring my struggle. "I bet you like it in the ass." He yanked me from my seat, then leaned in and whispered to me, "Well, today is your lucky day." His hot breath against my face made me want to vomit.

I felt such relief when he suddenly stepped back and pulled his phone out of his pocket. He had received a text. I wiped his saliva off my face as he read it.

"Well, well, well," he said. "Your boy Elijah's on his way back, and he's brought us a present."

The thought of Elijah being there soon was like a heavy weight being lifted from my shoulders. X led me to the door and opened it so I could see what Elijah had brought. A minute later, Elijah appeared.

"Vegas!" I gasped, relieved to see my cousin—until I realized that he was in handcuffs. I looked from him to Elijah, not understanding how Vegas could have possibly been captured.

He sensed my panic and said, "Don't worry about it, baby girl. It's going to be all right. Trust me." I just didn't see how that would happen, and I started to say as much, but Vegas stopped me. "Just go with him and do as you're told. You'll be home in an hour."

That's when the reality hit me so hard that I felt my knees nearly give out. He'd exchanged himself for me.

"No!" I screamed. This was not what I wanted, but all I could do was watch helplessly as Elijah brought Vegas close enough to make the exchange.

Elijah attempted to pull me away, but I resisted, kicking and squirming. "You bastard. I thought you were a good guy. I trusted you!"

"I'm gonna be all right, cuz." Vegas was still attempting to reassure me. "Just go with him."

"She's not going anywhere," X sneered as he wrenched me away from a shocked Elijah.

"What are you doing? We agreed to an exchange, her for him." Elijah attempted to pull me back.

"I changed my mind. I've decided to take this one as a second wife." He leered at me, not bothering to disguise his lust.

"Let her go!" Vegas growled. God, I wished there was some way for him to get out of those handcuffs, because those assholes wouldn't stand a chance against my cousin.

"Xavier, I gave my word, and my word is my bond. Let her go!" Elijah's voice had a warning tone that I hadn't heard before. "I'm taking her home."

"No, you're not taking her anywhere," X growled at Elijah. He was clearly unaccustomed to having his orders questioned.

Brother X pushed Vegas into the room I'd just come from and shut the door, locking it from the outside. Then he turned to Elijah with anger in his eyes. "Have you forgotten who I am?"

"No, I think you've forgotten who you are. Now, I'm taking this girl." Elijah reached for me—and X reached for his gun.

"You just had to challenge me, didn't you? You couldn't just follow orders." He pointed the gun at me, but Elijah stepped in the way.

Xavier looked disgusted. "It was her, wasn't it?" he said. "It was her who changed you. You let this bitch come between us, Elijah."

"I didn't let anyone come between us, Xavier. It was you who strayed from the teachings. You who got in bed with that Jew, Bernie Goldman."

Bam! Bam! Bam!

X pulled the trigger and shot Elijah three times in the chest. Elijah crumpled to the ground, staring at X in disbelief. I felt paralyzed as X shouted to his men. This dude was out of fuckin' control.

Three men ran into the room. When they caught sight of Elijah lying bloody on the floor, they looked even more upset than I felt.

"Unless you three want to be next, get him out of here. And put her in the other room. When I am done with Mr. Duncan, I will deal with her myself."

The next thing I knew, they were pulling me away, leaving Elijah's body on the ground and Vegas alone to deal with X.

Vegas

49

The second Brother X threw me into that room, I hit the floor and the door slammed behind me. I scrambled to my feet, which wasn't the easiest thing to do with my hands cuffed behind my back, and started kicking the door in frustration. At this point things were out of my control, and I could only pray that Brother Elijah was truly a man of his word and would get Sasha back home safely.

Bam! Bam! Bam!

All faith went out the window a few moments later when I heard gunshots coming from the other side of the door and then I heard Brother X shouting orders.

"Fuck!" I cried out, stomping my foot. I leaned against a wall, slowly coming to terms with the reality that I'd probably lost my little cousin.

I took a deep breath, trying to get my shit together. If he killed Sasha, it was only a matter of time before he came for me.

As expected, the door opened a minute later, and X walked in, grinning. "Miss me, bitch?"

My first instinct was to rush at him, but I had to temper that and try to stick to the plan. "Did you kill my cousin, motherfucker?"

He laughed. "And what if I did?"

Wham! He hit me, his fist landing against my face. I couldn't worry about Sasha right now. I had to deal with this asshole in front of me. "I can't wait to do this to your brother."

"You wouldn't be doing this at all if I wasn't handcuffed," I challenged, staring angrily at him like the piece of shit he was.

"Yes, I would. It wouldn't be as easy, but I've made it my mission in life to destroy punks like you. Even without you handcuffed, I would still be more than capable of kicking your ass. This way is just more fun."

"No, fun is what my brother is doing to your wife. Did you know they're having a baby?" I knew my words would destroy him, so when the expression on his face darkened with rage, I knew I'd accomplished exactly what I needed to. Emotions made most people reactive and threw them off their game, and X was no different. I just had to keep pushing his buttons to distract him from what I was doing, all while making sure I didn't push so hard that he reached for his gun.

He swung his fist around, and it landed with force against my abdomen. I ain't gonna lie—that shit hurt like hell. I didn't plan on sitting here like his victim for long, though.

"You probably used to those pussies in prison you been fucking," I taunted, knowing that my words were making him even more angry. "Makes sense that your wife would go after Junior. He's a real man's man. Not like you. You're like the ultimate girly-boy."

He turned to me with eyes full of hostility. "She loved me!" he roared, and I swear the guy was close to tears. "Me and only me, until your brother came along with his swine-eating big promises. She was committed to me and to my movement." He kicked forward, aiming for my dick, but I raised my leg in time to block the impact. "And all of you Duncans will die for his arrogance."

My leg was throbbing, but I forced myself to stay standing. "I guess it's easy to be all brave when you got a man handcuffed and an entire army out there that can run in and help you." I shook my head from side to side like I was expressing pity for his sorry state. This was all to distract him from my hands, which were working behind my back with the key.

Bam! Bam! Bam! Bam! Bam!

The sound of automatic gunfire was like music to my ears.

"What the—?" He pushed me backward then went to investigate, reaching for his gun. He didn't like whatever he saw, because he slammed the door and locked it. "Time to die, Vegas."

"I doubt that," I said. I was now two feet behind him, and when he turned back toward me, I knocked the gun out of his hand, pummeling him. His expression of undisguised shock almost made me break out laughing, but I had work to do first.

I had to give him credit. This guy could take it as well as he dished it out. I had hit him with about fifteen punches and he was still standing.

"H–how the fuck did you get your handcuffs off?" he stuttered, backing away as he struggled to get his bearings. I showed him the key I'd used to free myself, hoping to throw him off.

"Elijah?" he said hoarsely. I could tell that the reality of this betrayal hurt him more than any of my punches had.

"I guess your men are only as loyal to you as you are to them. Or maybe it's because you're a real asshole. Your boy Elijah seemed to think so."

"That's why I just killed him." He rose up. Now that he had come to terms with my freedom, the fighter reemerged, ready to take me down.

I was not going to make it easy for him by any means. Whether he realized it or not, I wasn't just fighting for myself. I was taking him down for what he had done to my father, and what he kept threatening to do to the rest of my family.

X did a roundhouse kick and almost knocked me to the floor, but years of martial arts training had prepared me to respond with a back kick that made him drop with a thud. Like a jackrabbit, he jumped straight back up into a fighter's stance. The two of us were evenly matched and ready to do battle.

Unfortunately, X had other ideas that tipped the scale in his favor. He dove to the floor. It confused me for a second, until I saw that he was going after the gun he'd dropped. Now I was staring down the barrel as he aimed at my face.

Orlando

50

Rio and I stepped off the elevator on the top floor of 26 Court Street in Brooklyn with a purpose. If ever there was a need for desperate measures to save one of our own, this was it—and I was throwing that Hail Mary pass right to Bernie Goldman. I'd called Bernie, asking him to meet with me right after the decision had been made that Vegas would be exchanged for Sasha. I just hoped this meeting would be in time to save my brother's life.

"Hold up," Rio said, grabbing my wrist in order to stop me from knocking on the door. "You sure you want to do this, bruh?"

"I'm not sure about anything"—I looked down at my briefcase and squeezed the handle tightly—"I don't think I have a choice. Do you?"

Rio released my wrist, and I knocked on the door to Bernie's office.

I heard latches being moved, and then the door opened and we were greeted by one of Bernie's huge bodyguards. Another equally large and imposing guard was standing behind him in the distance. I had to give it to Bernie: He sure knew how to pick 'em. These dudes were bigger than Junior. One of them looked like he could be a relative of Andre the Giant.

"Orlando." I heard Bernie's voice, but I couldn't see him with King Kong standing in the way.

I eyeballed the giant, and he stepped aside, allowing us to enter. I looked around the oversized suite, which had some very expensive-looking paintings on the walls. Bernie was sitting behind a huge, cluttered desk that only emphasized his diminutive stature. I heard the door close behind us. The jumbo-sized guard slid the locks back into position.

"Gentlemen, please sit," Bernie said, nodding to two chairs in front of his desk.

"I'll stand, thank you. You go ahead and handle business." Rio looked to Bernie. "By the way, I love how you decorated the place." He picked up a vase from the table by the door and began to examine it, making it clear to everyone that he would rather be anywhere but at this meeting.

Bernie ignored Rio's dramatic show and spoke to me as I sat down. "Your call seemed rather urgent. How can I help you?" Bernie was always one to get straight to the point. He valued time as much as he did money. Truth is, I think he could sense some weakness on my part too.

"I—the Duncans need your help."

"What do you need?" He opened his arms as if to say, "I'm here for you."

"My cousin Sasha has been held captive by Brother X for almost two weeks. As we speak, my brother Vegas is in the process of exchanging himself for her. I need you to help insure that Vegas is not killed by X."

Bernie sat back in his chair with a distinct lack of surprise in his expression, which led me to believe that he had already heard about Sasha's kidnapping. We had been trying to keep the details of our situation with Brother X under wraps, but from Bernie's lackluster reaction, it appeared that some of our associates had been talking about it amongst themselves. Just because they were talking about it, though, didn't mean they gave a shit about us or our problems—or at least Bernie didn't seem to.

"You're asking a lot, Orlando. At this point you're asking me to put my nose where it doesn't belong. To do something like that would take pulling a lot of strings and using up a lot of political clout." This was exactly how I'd expected him to respond. Bernie didn't do anything unless there was something for him to gain. Well, I'd come prepared.

"I know that, Bernie, and that's why I'm willing to make it worth your while." I reached down into my briefcase and pulled out a folder. Bernie and I made eye contact as I slid the folder to him. "To save my brother's life, I'm willing to give you this. Of course, there is the matter of the half billion dollars to be paid, but we can work that out."

Snatching it up like a shark coming upon a school of fish, he opened the folder and his greedy eyes devoured the content. "Is this everything?" he asked me, not taking his eyes from the pages. "All that I need is right here?" This time he looked up at me. I imagine he wanted to gauge whether I was telling him the truth.

"Absolutely everything. Of course, I will have to sit down with your team of chemists and clarify a few details, but for the most part, that's all you need to make the miracle drug of the century."

Convinced, a huge smile lit up his face. "Yes," he hissed in victory, closing the folder and giving it two hard knocks. "I will go make a call." He stood and extended his hand to shake mine.

I looked down at his hand then back up at him. "Like I said, everything you need is in that folder. However, you do realize H.E.A.T. causes liver cancer?"

"Everything causes cancer these days, young man. People have to learn to use moderation." I gave him a disapproving look and he laughed. "I'm just kidding. Don't worry. We'll fix it. I have a team of scientists who can do just about anything."

"Everything but create H.E.A.T. or duplicate it," said Rio from across the room. Bernie looked over at Rio, who was still studying the décor as if he was trying to get decorating ideas. "This drug has been my brother's life work. What makes you think your people can do what he couldn't?"

"Fresh eyes," Bernie answered.

Rio shook his head. "Fresh eyes my ass. You don't plan on changing that drug. And the truth is, I don't really care right now, as long as my brother Vegas gets to sleep in his own bed tonight, so stop talking and start calling." He finally stopped looking around the room and turned to face Bernie, staring him down as he spoke. "And leave that file on your desk. This ain't a deal until my brother is home." Rio's tone had a commanding bass to it that I'd never heard coming from him. I was shocked by it, and Bernie was visibly annoyed.

"Very well. I'll be right back." Bernie placed the file on his desk then quickly glanced at his bodyguards before heading to a side room.

Rio didn't say anything while we waited for Bernie to come back, but the way he paced around the room I could tell he was agitated. He hadn't liked the idea of coming here to offer up the formula for H.E.A.T. in the first place, and was only doing it to save Vegas.

His phone chirped with a text just as Bernie came back into the room, all smiles.

Bernie picked up the folder from his desk. "It's all taken care of," he said. "Your brother is being released as we speak."

I looked over toward Rio, hoping that news would put a smile on his face, but he was busy typing a text, looking just as mad as before.

Bernie had walked over to the bar to prepare himself a drink. "Scotch?" he asked me, raising his own glass.

I shook my head to decline. I wasn't ready to celebrate yet. "What about the transfer?" I asked.

"Michael is going to take care of that right now." Bernie took a quick sip of his Scotch then set down the glass so he could write something on a piece of paper. "Michael, take these instructions and make the money transfer for Mr. Duncan," he said as he handed the paper to one of the guards.

Michael looked down to read the instructions then nodded his understanding to Bernie. He opened his jacket and started to reach for something, but then two shots rang out.

"What the hell—?" The blood drained from Bernie's face as he realized that both of his bodyguards were laid out on the floor.

I looked at Rio. A minute ago he was holding his phone, but now he had a gun in his hands, and he was aiming at Bernie.

"What is going on here?" Bernie asked in a shaky voice. "I said I would transfer the money within a few minutes. Hell, I'll do it now." He made a move.

"Don't even think about it." Rio stepped forward, pointing his gun directly at Bernie's face. I stared at my brother, unable to understand where this was coming from—especially since Rio was usually the least aggressive of all the Duncans.

Rio must have sensed my confusion, because as he kept his eyes on Bernie, he explained to me, "Those texts were from Paris. After we left the house, Elijah told them some shit you're not gonna believe. This motherfucker here has been playing us, O. He's been in cahoots with X from the beginning."

Bernie began waving his hands in protest. "It's not like that!" he shouted, sounding scared.

I reached for my gun. Those bodyguards might have been big, but they sure were stupid, I thought thankfully. They hadn't even attempted to search me or Rio for weapons when we got there. Probably didn't think we were a threat. This was one time I was glad that someone had underestimated me. "Oh, no? Then exactly how is it, Bernie? Did you or did you not make a call to free my brother?" Bernie didn't answer. "Hell, you weren't even going to wire the money, were you?" I bent over and picked up the paper Bernie had handed to Michael, expecting to see nothing but scribbles on it. Instead, it was something much worse.

"What's it say?" Rio asked when he saw me shaking my head.

"It says *Kill them*," I replied. "But thanks to you, that's not going to happen, little brother."

"You fucked up, Bernie," Rio said. "No offense."

In spite of his fear, Bernie tried to play tough with us. "Do you know who you are messing with?"

"Yes, I do. I mean *we* do." I looked to Rio, who cocked his weapon.

"Obviously you didn't know who you were dealing with," Rio spat. "This is for LC Duncan."

Bam!

I got out of my chair and turned to my brother to ask the million-dollar question: "So, is Vegas still alive, or what?"

Daryl

51

Thunk! Thunk!

Junior and I took down the two sentries standing guard in front of the small East New York brownstone with no resistance, thanks to a major distraction from Paris. Those two Muslim brothers didn't have a chance the way she sashayed down the street in that skirt that left nothing to the imagination. Hell, even I had to raise an eyebrow at how sexy she looked, and I didn't want any part of that little vixen.

The moment the sentries were down, Paris kicked off her six-inch heels, snatched up one of the fallen guards' automatic weapons, and ascended the stairs, holding position at the door. Junior and I posted up at the bottom of the stairway, guns drawn, sending four men scurrying into the backyard. Two were then stationed on either side, while another two were set up as lookouts.

I thought I'd gotten it out of my system, but I really did love this Jason Bourne type shit that Vegas was always dragging me into.

"Where the fuck are they?" Junior groaned, checking his watch for the fifth time in the last five minutes. He looked at me with a frown.

"I know," I said, trying to keep Junior calm while we contemplated our next move. So far, all the intel that Elijah had given us had panned out, except for one big thing: He should have been out that door by now with Sasha in tow.

Bam! Bam! Bam! Three gunshots rang out from inside, without return fire. I turned to Junior, whose worried expression said, *This is not good.* Paris looked like she was about to say fuck it and just go in, so Junior and I ran up the stairs. Three of our men took our place at the curb, pointing weapons at the front door. We had ten other men around the building, ready to go at a moment's notice.

I turned to Paris, who was holding the gun she'd confiscated from the dead guard like she really knew her shit.

"You ready for this?" I asked. She checked her gun, giving me this sensual look that made me feel very uncomfortable.

"Just keep up, handsome, and make sure you don't get your dick shot off. I might have use for it after this," she said, pushing the door open.

I glanced over at Junior, who shrugged his shoulders and said, "That's just my sister, Dee. She's off the wall. I don't know what else to tell you." We followed her inside, with six of our men trailing behind us.

Junior and Paris handled things with a military precision, using hand signals as they entered the foyer to communicate that they spotted some of X's men nearby. One of those men came to the foyer, and Paris took him down with a quick burst before we stormed the living room, killing all but one of the men in there. Junior snatched him up like a rag doll.

"Where are they? Where are my brother and my cousin?" Junior's voice would have sent chills down the spine of any normal person, but this man clamped his mouth shut, refusing to answer. Junior whacked the guy over the head with his gun, sending him slumping to the floor.

At the sound of a disturbance, another soldier came rushing in, gun raised. Before I could take the shot, Paris landed a cluster right in his midsection.

"Good shot," I called out just as I took out another one of X's men who appeared at the top of the staircase.

"Fan out," Paris told our men. They all did what they were told, moving from room to room in pairs, taking out X's men on the first floor. Junior headed up the stairs in front of Paris and me. Two quick shots later, we heard bodies falling.

At the top of the stairs, there were three doors, the first of which was locked. Paris and I stood with our guns pointed at the other doors, ready to shoot, while Junior slammed his size eighteens into the first door, spraying the two gun-toting men hiding inside. It turned out no one was in the second room, but like the first room, the third room was locked. Tiptoeing up to it, Junior placed his ear against the third door. He jumped back, signaling to us that he'd heard movement.

With Paris and Junior on either side of the door, weapons ready, I ran up to that door, slamming my foot against it as hard as I could. The frame shattered upon impact. Don't ask me how, but Paris's overzealous behind scooted right past me, killing two assailants in no time. Junior and I rushed in and finished off the third. As bad-ass as Paris was, she softened up, squealing like a girl when she spotted the woman tied up on the makeshift bed.

"Sasha!" I could see the relief on Paris's face. She and Sasha must have been close.

When Paris ripped the tape off Sasha's mouth, the first thing Sasha said was, "Vegas! He's in the basement with X."

Before she finished her sentence, I was out of the room and headed for stairs, with Junior on my heels.

"Anybody go into the basement yet?" Junior questioned the second we hit the first floor. Two of our guys led us to the kitchen, where Kareem and James were having a firefight with at least one of X's guys, who'd barricaded himself in the basement.

"Is it X?" I asked.

"I don't think so," Kareem replied. "But whoever it is, they've got themselves barricaded in, so we can't go down the stairs without taking a bullet."

"What the fuck's the hold up?" We all turned to see Paris and Sasha standing behind us, holding guns. Junior quickly explained the situation to them, and Paris glanced over at Sasha. Whatever she communicated in that look, Sasha understood it, because without a word the two of them stripped their shirts and bras off like they were about to go on stage. I watched as both tucked their guns behind their backs and forced their way past us to the basement door.

"Move," Paris said to a still-stunned Kareem and James, who did exactly what they were told.

I turned to Junior and said, "We really going to let them do this?"

"Dee, I've seen these two pull more rabbits out of their hats than Houdini himself. It's a damn shame us dudes are so weak."

"Hey, baby, please don't shoot. I just want to talk," Paris said sweetly before they headed downstairs.

I think I was holding my breath the whole time, until I heard a single shot. A few seconds later, Paris called up to us, "Y'all coming down or what? And someone bring us our tops. It's cold as shit down here."

I glanced at Junior, and he said with a smirk, "Told you."

We ran down the stairs. Sasha was standing in the middle of the room, pointing at a metal door. "They're in there. That's where X was keeping me." Her eyes traveled down to a pool of blood on the floor. There was no body, but whoever had been there had lost quite a bit of blood. I prayed it wasn't Vegas.

We all jumped back and aimed our weapons when we heard the sound of a bolt sliding on the other side of the metal door.

I felt all the tension leave my body when a battered Vegas sauntered out of the room carrying a gun. "What?" He laughed. "Y'all were expecting Brother X to be walking out of here, weren't you?"

Both girls screamed with joy, running to him, while I went inside the room Vegas had come out of. I was expecting to find X's dead body. Surprisingly, he was out cold, but he was very much alive, with two big-ass rats running in circles around him.

Chippy

52

"Lavernius, the war is over, and your boys won. They did you proud." I took my husband's hand between mine, desperate for it to be strong and solid, the way it had been all these years. But that didn't happen. It felt limp and absent of him, although I refused to give up hope that he was still in there somewhere.

"Sorry to interrupt, Mrs. Duncan. I need to change his IV," Sonya mumbled. She stood in the doorway, looking too afraid to enter.

"Go on then." I waved her in and waited as she tiptoed into the room and got to work, swapping out the empty bag of saline for a fresh one. As I watched her taking care of LC for the hundredth time since he'd been home, something deep inside me shifted.

"Sorry about that," she muttered as she finished, ready to dart out of the room and leave the two of us alone.

"Sonya?" That had to be the first time I'd spoken to her directly since LC had been shot, so the look of fear she gave me was well deserved.

"Yes, Mrs. Duncan?"

"I need to thank you for all that you are doing for my husband. You have gone above and beyond to help him, and I want you to know that I notice, and I'm grateful that you're here."

A look of embarrassment crossed her face before she responded.

"Please don't thank me. We all know that it's my fault he's in that bed in the first place. If I had just walked away when I gave you my word, then Mr. Duncan wouldn't be laying here." She lowered her head, refusing to meet my eyes.

I had been so busy blaming her and being angry that I hadn't accepted a hard truth, but now it was time to share it with her. "You know the business that my family is in?" I asked her.

"Yes, ma'am."

"So you realize that danger and retribution is a very real part of this job. You don't get all the rewards we have been given without a large degree of danger. There is a reason my son chose you. Most women couldn't deal with this life, but you and I, we're different. But that also means that we come with a history, one that makes this lifestyle an option. Yours just happens to include an angry husband. So yes, I needed to blame someone, but if I'm being honest, then I'm as responsible as you are for putting my husband in that bed."

"You?" She seemed confused by my statement, but I wasn't willing to explain the part I played in my husband entering this business in the first place. That was ancient history at this point, and it was between me and my husband. All she needed to know was that I understood why my son had chosen her.

"My son is very lucky to have you . . . and Sonya?" She glanced up at me, tears falling from her eyes. "So am I."

"Thank you." She closed her eyes and released a breath from deep within. When she opened her eyes again, I could see the relief, like a weight had been lifted off of her. "Can I bring you anything?" I shook my head, and she left the room, allowing me to be alone with LC again. There was so much I needed to say to him.

"Junior is going to be all right," I said. "He chose the right woman. I know you would agree. She has a lot of the same qualities you've told me you value in me over the years. She can handle this life, and she can make Junior feel that love we always wanted for him. He always put us and his siblings first, but this time he took care of himself.

"You told me he wasn't going to leave her, and you were right. You're always right," I said with a sad smile. "But if you wake up now 'cause you heard me say that, I'm going to deny it. Women like being right. We need it."

I walked over to the mantle to look at one of the photos displayed on top. The memory of that day made me smile. It was a picture of Vegas and Daryl before their high school prom. We had taken pictures of them with their dates, of course, but I figured those girls would be history too soon to take up permanent residency in our house, so LC had made the boys pose for a photo without them, one we could keep.

I turned back to LC. "Daryl is back, and that's really good for Vegas with everything going on. They work really well together and—get ready for this surprise—you know who else Vegas works well with? Orlando. The two of them were bumping heads, about to go to war, but now they're working as a team. Kind of reminds me of you and Lou. I miss those early days, when we were too young to know where we were headed," I said, wiping away a tear.

"And your grandson Nevada is the spitting image of Vegas. He's a smart, kind boy, but I can see that Duncan fire in him. If you were here, you'd help him to hone it, and you'd love him on sight. Of course, I have no idea what Consuela was thinking by keeping him from us. Now that she's single, I'm not sure what her intentions are for Vegas, and apparently neither does his girlfriend." It took everything I had not to burst out in laughter. "That son of ours has been like the Pied Piper with women since he was in grade school. Not like the studious Orlando, always thinking about work. That's why I'm still praying we'll be able to get Orlando's son back one day. I know it's hard for him not to have his son around. . . . Oh, LC, I just wish you were here to help him," I cried.

"Mom?" London came in and stood over me, hovering as usual.

I wiped away my tears. "Honey, I'm just having a chat with your father," I said in a tone that told her I didn't want to be interrupted.

"Well, I'll come back later." She turned and left me alone without any more fussing. That was odd for London.

"London just came to say hi to you," I told LC. "She and Harris and the girls are fine, but now that Daryl is back, I'm going to have to keep a close eye on things. Funny how our children always think they're doing things behind our backs—like we can't tell when they're having feelings for someone." Thoughts of London's wedding came rushing back to me, making me wonder if we had done our child a disservice. There were so many of them to worry about.

"Rio. He needs you even more than the others. He needs you to show him that you're proud of him. You should see what an important part of the family business he's been these weeks. He's really growing up.

"And speaking of growing up . . . Yes, we all know that Paris is your favorite. She's always going to be a handful, and without you here to control her, I'm not sure anything can be done with that girl. Now, Sasha has a lot of Lou in her, and she can temper herself, but that Paris is a lot harder to contain. If she had someone to really love her, soften those rough edges like you did for me, then I know she'd be okay. Guess that's why the whole Niles thing still bothers me."

"Hey." Donna's voice interrupted my thoughts. "You all right?" She came over and took my hand, looking down at LC.

"I just don't want to let him go," I said. "I know that probably sounds selfish, especially when he's lying here in this bed not able to do anything for himself, but when you have loved a man as long as we have been together, it's hard to do the right thing. Especially when the right thing is to let him die." Donna reached up and wiped the tears streaming down my face.

"He's always going to be in your heart." Her words were meant to comfort me, but I didn't want my husband in my heart. I wanted him in my bed, in my arms, in my life. Everywhere.

"What are you going to do?" Her question was one I hadn't wanted to answer out loud, and yet I had to, because I needed to hear myself say it.

"I'm going to let him go. I'm going to give his friends some time to pay their respects, and then I'll let the children know my decision."

Daryl

53

Vegas and I were sitting on the trunk of the BMW 750i his mother had just given me, eating Chinese food out of the container. We'd been parked under the Van Wyck Expressway overpass for about ten minutes when three police cars, two marked and one unmarked, pulled up on either side of us.

"Here comes the cavalry," Vegas announced as the police car doors flew open. A very familiar-looking police captain exited the unmarked car, followed by three uniformed officers. As they approached us, Vegas and I placed our Chinese food containers on the roof of the car and stepped forward.

"Vegas." The captain nodded, offering his hand, which Vegas took. He turned his attention to me. "Daryl Graham, I thought you were dead."

"Well, you never was that smart, were you Marks?" The two of us eyed each other, until I felt a jab in the ribs from Vegas. I hated cops, and I especially hated Marks' corrupt, greedy ass, but he had always been a Duncan ally, and they couldn't afford to lose that connection, so I backed down.

"Look, I was hoping after that mishap at the warehouse that this would somehow help." On that note, Vegas opened the rear car door and pulled out a half-filled green trash bag that he handed over to the captain. Marks looked in the bag, nodded his head, and handed the bag to another officer a few steps behind him.

"We good?" Vegas asked.

"I'm not going to say we're one hundred, but this will go a long way to making things right."

A long way to making it right? There was almost two million dollars in that garbage bag, and I doubted a quarter of it would find its way into the hands of the families of those fallen officers. Realizing this truth just made me hate this corrupt, dirty motherfucker even more.

"Okay, then maybe this will make it all the way right?" Vegas nodded at me, and I hit a button on my keys that released the trunk.

Vegas motioned for Marks to follow him to the trunk. I stood back and watched Marks' face light up like a Christmas tree.

"Get the fuck outta here. Is that—?"

"Sure as hell is."

Marks motioned for the other officers to check it out. I glanced over at Vegas, who smirked at me. He'd called it right. Turning Brother X over to the cops would be ten times worse than killing him. "We good now, Conrad?" Vegas asked.

"Better than good," Marks replied, turning to his men. "Get his ass outta there."

"He's got a broken jaw, so he might not do too much talking," Vegas said with a laugh as they dragged X out of my trunk and into one of the patrol cars.

Marks shook Vegas's hand.

"Conrad," Vegas whispered, "if he happens to end up dead, I need a body so my brother can get married without jumping through hoops."

"You got it," Marks said before he walked back to his car. The three cop cars rolled out, and Vegas and I went back to our Chinese food.

"So, what do you think the odds are that X will see the inside of a jail cell?" I asked.

"Not good. There's no doubt in my mind that he's going to end up dead somewhere. It just comes down to how many days he's going to have suffer," Vegas replied.

"Damn, that there is the definition of that old saying, *a fate worse than death*." We both laughed as I picked a shrimp out of my container.

"I guess this is all over now?" Vegas said.

"Yeah, I guess, but there's still something I can't wrap my head around."

"What's that?" he asked.

"This whole X and Bernie thing. It just doesn't make sense to me. X was a radical Muslim, right?" Vegas nodded. "Now, from everything we've been able to put together, and from what Elijah told us, X was taking orders from Bernie Goldman. Not just a Jew, but a Hassidic Jew. What radical Muslim is going to do that?"

Vegas shrugged. "Hey, maybe it was all money related. I mean, Elijah did say Bernie put a million dollars on the table to kill Pop, and X took it. Plus, don't forget Elijah said some other brother was at their last meeting, ordering X around, so maybe that's who was really in charge."

"Yeah, that's what worries me. Something tells me this whole thing is far from over."

Vegas

54

Once the war was over and word got out that Pop had returned home and may never recover from his coma, people he'd known for years began stopping by to pay their respects. Frankly, we were growing tired of the stream of visitors and wanted time alone just to be together with our family, but LC Duncan was a legend and deserved to be honored. They came from as far away as Australia and India, Europe and South America, and they all said the same thing: that our father was an honorable man who they knew they could count on. He had a reputation for saying what he meant and meaning what he said, and that alone made him stand out in our business.

People talked about their desire to continue working with him. No one mentioned him being on death's door, or discussed how long he was expected to live. In fact, all anyone wanted to talk about were the moments he had touched their lives. Pop was decidedly old school about the way he did business with a simple handshake, but once you took his hand, you were not going to mess things up.

"When your father shook someone's hand and looked them in the eye, they did whatever it took to make sure they stayed good on their word," Willie Hopkins, a good old boy from Texas, raved as I walked him out to his car with Junior, Orlando, and Daryl. He and Pop had worked together almost from the beginning, so Willie considered him more than an associate.

"Vegas," Willie said as he got in the back of his chauffeured Bentley, "if you turn out to be half the father that LC is, then your son is a lucky boy."

"Thank you, Willie," I said as I closed the door and waved good-bye.

Willie's comment got me thinking about Nevada. I hadn't had enough time to spend getting to know my son yet, although his cousins, and especially Ma, were already crazy about him. As the oldest grandchild, he seemed to have plenty of patience with his younger cousins, who wanted to monopolize all of his time. At first Paris was a little hostile because suddenly she wasn't the only one with a male heir in the house, but even she had been won over by Nevada's charm. That boy certainly reminded me a lot of myself. The whole thing happening the way it had was weird. Great, but weird. Now, if I could just get Consuela and Marie to make peace with each other.

"Hey, isn't that . . . ?" I turned to look at whatever had caught Daryl's attention. Our security team was directing a familiar black Mercedes truck to park in front next to London's Rover. Minister Farah got out of the car and came toward us, followed by a bodyguard.

Minister Farah greeted Daryl and me with a quick embrace. "Gentlemen, I'm here to pay my respects. I hope you don't mind. I also wouldn't mind meeting that son of yours, Vegas."

He reached over and shook Junior's hand. They hadn't seen each other since our first visit to Harlem, when we went to him for advice. With everything that had happened since then, it felt like a lifetime ago.

Orlando stepped up and introduced himself. "How are you, Minister Farah? Orlando Duncan. Nice to meet you."

"So how are you doing, Minister?" I asked.

"I'm surviving, thanks to the grace of Allah. How's your father?"

"He's the same." I took a deep breath and left it at that.

"Pops is a warrior. He may be down, but he's not out." Junior's words resounded through all of us, especially because we needed them to be true.

"He'd be proud of you boys and what you accomplished against Xavier. The odds were stacked against you, and you persevered." He gave us that wizened smile that said he was proud of us as well. The four of us shared a prideful look.

"Thank you, Minister. Come in." I led him inside, with Daryl following. Orlando and Junior stayed out in the driveway to get a break from all the sadness in the house.

We hadn't made it five feet into the house when we heard Ma's voice.

"Minister Farah, so good of you to come." She came down the stairs, always impeccably dressed and gracious, to greet our guest.

"I am so sorry this couldn't be a happier occasion. It's been years." He kissed my mother on both cheeks.

"Thank you so much for coming. I appreciate it."

"Is there anything I can do?" he asked, taking her hand.

"Just go on in and visit with him. It's been too long." She turned to me. "Vegas, you boys take Minister Farah in to see your father."

Ma gave him a kiss on the cheek and then left to greet some more visitors. Daryl and I led Minister Farah to Pop's room. Sonya was in there, changing the dressing on his wound. As soon as she finished, she scooted out to give us privacy.

Minister Farah moved close to LC, staring down at him for a while. I could tell that seeing Pop in this condition affected him. He seemed out of sorts, and for a man as buttoned up as him, that was saying a lot.

"Hey, let's go back outside," I offered, giving him an out.

"Is it that obvious?" He tried to keep his tone light, but his feet were almost at the door.

We followed him out of the room. Minister Farah seemed to be in a real hurry, so it didn't take long before we were at the front door and then back outside.

"You all right?" Daryl asked him. He nodded, but the expression on his face worried me. Minister Farah and Pop were acquaintances, but I guess I hadn't realized that they were so much closer than that.

"To see a man that powerful stuck in the in-between is jarring," Minister Farah said, reaching for his keys distractedly. Seeing a person in a medical crisis can affect people all kinds of ways.

He turned his attention to the basketball hoop at the side of the house. "Hey, is that your boy?"

"Yes, that's him." Nevada was shooting hoops with Kareem and James.

"He's a fine-looking boy, Vegas. Looks just like you."

"Yeah, he does. Doesn't he?"

The minister nodded. "Have you given any thought to letting me teach him privately? I can make a man out of him."

"I talked to his mother about maybe letting you tutor him for a year; then, if he's ready, sending him to the school."

"Fantastic. He'll be my most prized student." Minister Farah looked so pleased with himself, and somewhere deep inside of me, an alarm bell started ringing.

"Well, with that being said, I'll see you gentlemen soon," he said.

"Sure thing." I gave him a halfhearted smile.

"Man, you better watch out," Daryl said with a laugh after Minister Farah was gone. "I think the minister is planning on making your kid his own." He was joking, but I was afraid it might not be too far from the truth.

Sonya

55

"You're doing a great job. You fit right in like you've been a regular member of the staff," said Louisa, one of the Duncans' housekeepers. When I'd checked on LC an hour ago, Louisa had helped me change his bedding. A conversation we started in the laundry room had carried on into the kitchen, where I sat watching her sweep and mop the kitchen floor while we chatted.

"Thank you so much," I said politely, trying not to sound insulted. I wasn't there to be a regular member of the staff; I was there because I was a member of the family, or at least I would be soon, now that Xavier's body had washed up on Jones Beach two days ago. With him being pronounced dead, I was free to marry Junior and officially become a Duncan.

"Miss Sonya, Miss Sonya!" I heard a little voice calling before I saw the miniature body it belonged to. "Miss Sonya." Mariah came bursting into the kitchen.

"What is it, Mariah?" I said. "And slow down. The floor is damp, and you might fall and get hurt."

"I need a glass of water."

"Water," I said, standing. "You're making all that ruckus over water?" That must have been one parched child. Probably worked up a thirst running through the house like that. When I was little, I only got excited to beg for soda or juice.

"Not for me," Mariah said. "It's for Pop-Pop. He wants some water."

I halted halfway to the refrigerator, turning to look at her. "Mariah, were you in your grandfather's room?" I said, gently scolding her. That little girl loved her grandfather so much that she wanted to be in there with him all the time.

"Yes," she replied sheepishly.

"Mariah, remember, you're not supposed to bother your grandfather. He needs his rest." London didn't want Mariah seeing her grandfather that way. It would cause her to ask more questions than her young, inquiring mind was already asking.

"But he wants some water."

I held the little girl's hands as I thought about how to approach this. I didn't want to say the wrong thing. She was just a child who dearly loved her grandfather. Children make up imaginary friends all the time, so I didn't find it strange that she was playing a little game involving her grandfather. After all, he spoiled the girl rotten. Of course she would want to pretend he was awake and telling her how special she was. Just like old times. She was taking it a bit far with the whole water thing, though.

"Mariah, your grandfather can't drink water from a glass. There are tubes called IVs that are giving him water."

"They must not be working, because I was just talking to him. He said he wanted water."

Looking down at the little girl, I realized that she seemed quite sincere. A feeling went through my body. I looked back at Louisa. She shot me a look, along with a shrug of her shoulders, that suggested maybe I should go check things out. Was it possible the little girl wasn't playing a game of make believe at all?

"You wait right here, Mariah. Let me go check on your Pop-Pop." I let go of her hands and exited the kitchen.

The closer I got to LC's room, the more anxious I felt. By the time I reached his door, I was doing a light jog.

The door was cracked open, probably left that way by Mariah when she came looking for water. I slowly pushed the door open and walked over to LC's bed.

"Water." His voice was weak and hoarse. He looked at me, his eyes pleading.

At first, I stood there in complete shock. I had to blink a few times to make sure I hadn't allowed my imagination to get the best of me. "Mr. Duncan," I mumbled.

"Water," he repeated.

"Dr. Whitmore . . ." I said it in a normal tone at first, but then I found myself running out the door and yelling for the doctor the same way Mariah had been yelling for me. "Dr. Whitmore! Dr. Whitmore!"

I saw him rushing down the hall. "What is it, Sonya?"

"It's Mr. Duncan. He's conscious."

"What?"

"He's talking." I moved out of the way as the doctor hurried into LC's room.

He walked over to the bed to see for himself. "Mr. Duncan, can you hear me?" He took LC's wrist to check his pulse.

LC nodded and blinked, struggling to keep his eyes open.

I had to go get the family. I couldn't let them miss this.

"Miss Chippy! Miss Chippy!" I called out. There I was, acting like a kid again. My shouting caused such a stir that practically every family member in the house came running to see what was going on.

"Sonya, what's wrong?" Miss Chippy said. She looked terrified. No doubt she was expecting to hear terrible news.

I smiled, letting her know there was nothing to fear. "It's Mr. Duncan," I said excitedly. "He's awake."

"What?" She placed her hand on her chest and leaned against the wall to steady herself.

"Awake," London said as she brushed past us quickly to go into the room. Miss Chippy and I were right behind her, followed by Orlando.

"He asked for a glass of water," I told her. "He's not just awake, but he seems to be alert."

"Daddy," London said, throwing her hands over her mouth. Her eyes filled with tears. Harris entered the room just in time to comfort his wife.

I looked to Orlando, who was choking back tears of joy. His face looked more relaxed than I'd seen it in weeks.

No one's emotions, however, matched the depth of feelings displayed by Miss Chippy. Dr. Whitmore moved to the side to allow her a moment with her husband. Tears poured from her eyes as she walked over to LC, placing her hands gently on his face as she leaned in to give him a kiss that communicated the strength of the deep, abiding love they shared.

He'd been in a coma for almost a month now. No one knew when, or if, he'd ever come out of it. This moment proved that LC Duncan wasn't the head of this family for nothing. It was going to take more than a couple of bullets and a coma to keep him down.

"LC," Chippy said softly, taking his hand.

He opened his mouth and croaked out, "Water."

Chippy smiled as if he had just said the most beautiful word she had ever heard. She looked over her shoulder at all of us. "You heard my husband," she said, then looked lovingly back at LC. "Get my husband some water."

Discussion questions

1. Who is your favorite Duncan?
2. Is Vegas as bad-ass as you expected?
3. Was Junior wrong for walking out on the family?
4. Did X's rats creep you out?
5. Were you afraid when LC got shot?
6. Were you upset that Connie died?
7. Who do you think shot LC?
8. Have you ever been in the situation where you might have to pull the plug on a loved one?
9. Did you feel bad for Marie when Nevada was introduced?
10. What do you think of Nevada, and where would you like to see him fit in future stories?
11. Did X get what he deserved?
12. What did you think of Bernie the Jew?
13. Who is sexier, Paris or Sasha?
14. Who did you feel was the real villain of this book?
15. Do you like Chippy's role?
16. Would you like to see a love triangle story between Daryl, London, and Harris?
17. Do you think Sasha and Elijah could have made it as a couple?
18. Do you think Rio stepped up?
19. What are your feelings about Minister Farah?
20. What did you think of the ending?

Coming Summer 2015

GRAND OPENING
(LC, Lou & Chippy's Story)

Once Upon a Time in the South

I'll never forget the sound of that organ and the sight of Mrs. Beasley, the sweet, elderly lady almost too blind to play it. Four people were in attendance that day, but none of them were my family. Not even a best man for me. My collar was too tight, making it hard to swallow. It took all my control not to reach up, yank my necktie loose, undo my top button, and ask for a glass of water. Yeah, I was uncomfortable and thirsty—and this was one of those churches where air conditioning wasn't checked on the option box.

But doing any of that would've been disrespectful of me during what was to be a joyous occasion here in the house of the Lord. And I was always the respectful one, the responsible one. At least that's how the moms and grandmothers around town always referred to me.

Lavernius Duncan.

The schoolboy.

"Not like those other two," they would hiss under their breath.

One brother felt the world was always conspiring against him. The other one felt he owned the world.

Me? I was here simply trying to survive in it.

"Do you take this man to be your lawfully wedded husband? To have and to hold? For richer . . . or for poorer? In sickness and in health? 'Til death do you part?" he dramatically asked the veiled bride, each rehearsed question and subsequent pause eliciting a chuckle from the intimate gathering, while twisting my already nervous stomach even more.

"Yes! I . . . I do," she gasped, futilely holding her tears at bay in this moment she'd probably rehearsed a million times in front of the mirror. Sure, this wasn't exactly how she'd planned it either, but the end result was the same: She'd be a bride. I held her hand firmly in mine, doing my best to remain strong.

It's going to be okay. This is right. This is what you want, I thought to myself.

"And you, Lavernius," the Reverend Johnson, happy to be presiding over his best friend's daughter's wedding, began. "Do you take this lovely woman to be your lawfully wedded wife? To have and to hold? For richer or for poorer? In sickness and in health? 'Til death do you part?"

As everyone turned to me, it was so quiet that you could hear a mouse fart.

"Lavernius?" the Reverend prodded as my fiancée looked into my eyes, tears now fully formed and running amok down her delicate cheeks.

I knew what I had to say. And what I had to do.

I wasn't like my brothers.

"I—"

1975
Lavernius "LC"

I checked the simple, black Timex watch on my wrist while pretending I was playing the trumpet with my other hand. Kool and the Gang's "Jungle Boogie" was on the radio and just getting to my favorite part. You know, where the horns first kick in. Too bad one of the speakers was damaged and crackled with static each time I tried to turn the volume knob past three. DJ Tony Mitchell was spinning the best music in town on GROOVE 770 AM. Before long, he would be out of tiny Hillcroft, Georgia and working the request lines at FM stations in the big cities like Atlanta or Birmingham. He was just that good.

"I don't feel comfortable about this," she said, nervously wrapping her hand around my shaft, peering over the old van's cracked and faded dashboard. I'd parked us in the corner of the lot, away from anyone else, which gave us some privacy.

"Nah. You're good. Keep going," I replied to my fiancée, Donna, coaxing her to get back to business. Besides, I was still doing the air trumpet to Kool and the Gang. *Get down, get down. Get down, get down.*

I planned to drop Donna off at home after class, but she promised me something special if I let her tag along. I knew that the reason she wanted to come along was because she didn't trust my brother's influence and wanted to mark her territory and remind him that I was taken and not free to cat around like him. Not that I would have even looked at another girl, because my brother and I were cut from an entirely different cloth.

Shoot, I felt lucky that a girl like Donna had even given me a second look. She was nothing like the girls I had grown up knowing. For one, she was really classy. Donna's father was a doctor, and she came from three generations of college-educated professionals. Her father graduated from Morehouse, and her mother from Spellman. In my family, I was the only one that had graduated from high school, and now I was in my third year of college.

Donna and I met in high school, and she was adamant that she could not even consider a guy who didn't have college in his future. Instead of admitting that I had never thought about higher education, I buckled down and set myself on track to be the kind of man that she could see herself with. Thanks to Donna, I had become a better man, and I loved her for it.

"Ouch!" I yelped as her hands suddenly felt like sandpaper on my dick. "Put your mouth on it. It's too dry," I said, trying to convince her to do a brother a solid.

"I'm not going to do that, and certainly not in a parking lot," she said, rolling her eyes at me like I had lost my mind.

"Baby, please, just put your mouth on it to get it wet," I pleaded with her. The look she gave me had me regretting saying anything.

"I would never disgrace my family name by acting like some low-rent tramp. My parents would disown me," she shot at me. But I was too far down the road to cut my losses.

"Donna, I love you. And I need you," I cooed, hoping to get her back in a loving mood.

"LC, I know the kinds of girls you're used to, but most of them don't know the names of they babies' fathers. How dare you try to put me in the same category as the kind of girls that do that." She gave me a look of absolute disgust before continuing. "So if you want me to be like them, then I suggest that you go find you one of them." She slid away from me, real upset. Shit! I had gone too far. I put myself back in my pants and tried to comfort her.

"I am so sorry. I would never want you to feel that way. You are everything that I want in a woman. You're my dream. Please don't be mad at me." I gave her my puppy-dog-trapped-in-the-doghouse face, hoping she'd forgive me. Thankfully, she broke out into a smile, and my heart felt a hundred pounds lighter.

Within minutes we were laughing and cracking jokes, and though that felt good, a blowjob would have felt so much better. I hoped that after we got married Donna would feel more comfortable and give a brother some head, but I knew better than to say anything about that. Hopefully, she'd be up to it later, and that meant sex without any extras. Loving Donna taught me that you can't expect everything, and so I reminded myself I was lucky for what I had—and that was a good woman.

By my guess, my brother Lou's bus was thirty minutes late to the Trailways station on the edge of town where we waited. My boss, Mr. Mixon, was gonna have something to say about my being late to work—especially this late—and also for taking his van to run the errand. But I'd smooth things over; I always did. Besides, where else he could get someone who catered to the customer like me and who worked so cheap? My business acumen and hard work made me "invaluable and indispensable," as my professor at Hillcroft College—the tiny historically black school that catered to the area's underserved "colored folk"— would say.

It was another thirty minutes before the bus that bore Lou pulled into the station. Things never ran on time around here, and I'm surprised Lou put up with the hassle, since he had a car. It was a super bad Chevy Monte Carlo with a tricked-out V-8 he wouldn't let anyone else touch, even though I was the one who painted it for him and made sure it ran so well. His trips up to New York were the rare occasions when he didn't want to attract attention, and with good reason. Of my two brothers, I was the only one who had chosen to walk the straight and narrow.

By the time Lou stepped off the bus and onto the gravel outside the station, Donna had already blown me off . . . literally, leaving me in a mellow mood. I would need it once my brother's mouth started running. Let's just say that he and Donna were not each other's favorite people. Only thing that they had in common was me.

I exited the van, telling Donna to remain inside, then walked over to meet Lou. I wanted to prep him to be nice to her and to not get pissed that I had brought her along. Outside the bus, the smell of diesel fumes clung heavy in the air, reminding me of my job back at Mixon's service station and garage. My brother and I slapped hands, giving each other five, followed by the "black hand side" before sharing a hug.

Although Lou and I were around the same height, he out-weighed me by about fifty pounds of muscle. That's not even speaking of the fly threads and shoes he loved to sport, which I never could afford.

Lou had been gone a month this time, tending to whatever relationships he was trying to cultivate beyond Hillcroft. From his demeanor, I guessed he was successful.

"Still workin' at the gas station, huh, college boy?" he joked, flashing that smile of his nestled beneath his full moustache and untouchable afro. His eyes scanned my oil-stained shop coveralls only briefly before moving on to survey the people around us. Lou could be here, but his mind always seemed to be operating somewhere else. This town made him restless, and he wasn't afraid to let it show.

"Yep. It's an honest job," I replied, trying to cut my brother with words that I knew would merely bounce off his impervious ego. But they did bring his attention back to me as we waited for his luggage to be unloaded from storage beneath the bus. I had a good idea of what he brought back with him from his trip up north.

"I'm honest with my work too, boy. No preconceived notions about what I do," he said, playfully slapping me across the back of my head. From inside the bus, a girl in the window was frantically waving to get his attention.

"A friend?" I asked as I looked at the girl with high cheekbones and long, straight hair like she had some Indian in her family. She looked to be younger than me.

"Yeah. You might say that," he replied, offering up a mouthful of teeth and a disingenuous wave to appease her. "She on her way down to Tallahassee. Parents back in Philly can't manage her no mo'. Goin' to live with her grandma is what she said. I actually thought she was *quite* manageable. Especially when we stopped back 'round South Carolina. Pussy so good it needs its own name—first, middle, and last."

"Uh-huh. Watch you wind up in jail over something you can't talk your way outta. That girl is what? Sixteen?" I said, shaking my head.

"Nah. She's seventeen and a half, and a damn good half too. And I'll leave jail to Larry. For somebody who lies so well to all these women he's juggling, he sure hasn't figured out how to use it with the law," he said with a hearty laugh, referring to our brother, the middle one.

I joined in on that, knowing it was true. Larry was one unlucky motherfucker, and quick to blame it on someone else when the world came crashing in like it always did.

The bus driver, following his list, pulled out a large, olive-green Army duffle bag and a Samsonite suitcase for which Lou produced his claim ticket. Knowing Lou, neither his bus ticket nor his ID was in his real name.

"Here. Let me get one of those," I requested as I reached for my brother's duffle bag.

"Nah. I got it, scrawny. You tryin' to be as skinny as JJ on *Good Times*?" he clowned, stepping in front of me. "Take the Samsonite. Don't want you catching a hernia, boy."

Out in the open, I knew better than to question Lou about the contents of the duffle bag in front of the driver, especially since I wasn't going to like the answer. Let's just say that Lou preferred to take chances with his freedom and had no problem carrying drugs across state lines. I did, so I just took the Samsonite like he told me, and we walked to the van waiting across the street.

"Damn, LC. You need you some of your own wheels instead of fixin' 'em all the fuckin' time," Lou said, frowning at his transportation from the bus station. Whatever the van's original color was, it was long gone. In its stead was a dulled coat of powder blue with rust fully showing on the back end of the old Ford. I used it to pick up parts from the auto supply store and, in exchange for keeping it running, Mr. Mixon let me use it from time to time. "You might like that job, but you ask me, it's just another kind of indentured servitude.

"Don't worry 'bout me, bro. When I graduate from college, I'll have my own garage," I said and made sure that I wasn't in striking distance of Donna. This was one thing we disagreed on, but I felt certain she'd come around.

"That's what I love about you, li'l bro. You got plans. Stay that way, because not everybody's cut out to be a risk taker," Lou remarked, absent any bullshit.

"Well, when I have my shop, Lou, you can work for me," I stated, puffing out my chest with pride. I was going to be helping out my family and know it would make our parents up in Heaven proud.

"Me? *Work for you*?" my brother remarked, his nose crinkling as we stopped to the rear of the van to stow his luggage. "No offense, li'l bro, but that'll be the day. In case you hadn't noticed, I'm not the manual labor type."

As I swung the rear doors open, light flooded the van's bleak interior. Donna peered back at us from the front bench seat, her eyes adjusting.

"Oh. Hey, Donna," Lou chimed in, shooting me a dirty look. He plastered on a fake smile, acknowledging my fiancée as he threw his duffle bag in back. I got why she didn't like him, but I couldn't quite figure out why my brother was not a fan of the woman I loved.

"Hey, Lou," she replied like she had smelled something sour. Normally Lou had women falling all over him, even our female relatives, but that wasn't the case with Donna. "Sweet Lou" is what they called him. Or maybe he started calling himself that. Hard to say, but it stuck.

"How was Queens?" I asked him to take my mind off silly, bothersome thoughts.

"Talk about it later," he responded curtly.

"It's just Donna. She's okay," I reminded him. I had no idea why he was acting all secretive around her. It's not like they ran in the same circles. Besides, everyone in town assumed we'd be married one day, so she was virtually family, both mine and his.

But virtually wasn't the same as real.

"Nah. No bitch is 'okay,' jive turkey," he snapped, a growl popping up outta nowhere.

"Hey!" I snapped back, my annoyance evident on my face. "You're home. Show some respect for the lady."

"Sorry, bro. No harm," Lou apologized, light returning to his demeanor as he retrieved a black fist rake from his back pocket and tightened up his 'fro. "Now let's get outta here. We'll talk after you drop her home."

Reluctantly, Donna moved over and made room for Lou as he climbed into the van. They could barely mutter three words to each other, making me realize what a bad idea this had been to bring her along. Who could blame me for wanting the two people I love most in the world to also love each other, or at the very least get along? But today that would not be the case.

Driving away, the three of us huddled in the front as if it were Scooby Doo's Mystery Machine, but without the fun and games. I knew that Lou would have a fit if I didn't drop Donna off first, but it would have served him right if I didn't. The longer I made him pretend that he didn't mind her company, the bigger the chance of me having to hear about it later. He thought that being my big brother meant he knew what was best for me, but he'd have to understand that I wasn't a little kid anymore who needed him to look after me. He certainly didn't get a vote when it came to my girl. He just needed to give her a chance, and with time I would show him that he was wrong about Donna. I had to, because despite us getting on each other's nerves, we were all we had.

On the highway to Dr. Williams' house—Oh. That's Donna's father's house, by the way. He was the most successful black man in the biggest five counties around, if not more—we didn't say much. Donna stared straight ahead, ignoring my brother. Lucky for me Lou was keeping focused on the radio. "The Hustle" was playing, and he began whistling along and bobbing his head to the song, probably imagining himself back in some swanky Manhattan discotheque being "the man" or something. I figured that once Donna and I got married we'd take a trip up there together. That way she could keep an eye on me.

She would have pitched a bitch at the thought of me following Lou to the Big Apple. Donna had been there before to visit the Statute of Liberty, but something told me that her New York and the one Lou visited were completely different. I had to admit that even though I was a small town guy, I did want to see what New York was all about.

"What time you gotta be to work, bro?" Lou asked as GROOVE 770 went to a commercial, probably not really caring.

"An hour ago," I answered, cutting my eyes as I shifted the van in an effort to get it over forty miles per hour. I wasn't one to push my luck like this with Mr. Mixon. Even though I had a scholarship to attend college, my wages allowed me to buy my books and live a somewhat satisfying life. There was no way Donna would be dating some broke-ass buster, so I tried not to become one. She liked a man who showed initiative and could take her to dinner at the kinds of places her family had been frequenting for years. Her fancy taste could be stressful on my wallet, but I sure liked to see her happy.

As we drove down the road, there were trustees from the nearby jail, picking up trash and stuff. One of them, in his orange jumpsuit, which looked cleaner than what I wore to work, saw the van coming and held up a hand, a shit-eating grin across his face. A sheriff deputy sat in the back of the truck with his shotgun, alertly watching over him and the others. As we passed, I laid into the van's weak horn, making the deputy a little nervous. The one who waved recognized us and smiled as we drove by.

"How much longer he got?" I asked Lou about a mile down the road, almost as if Donna weren't with us.

"At least a few months," he solemnly replied, referring to how much time our brother Larry had left on this, his most recent jail stint.

"He's such a loser. It's hard to believe he's related to the two of you," Donna said as she turned and stared out the back window at Larry slowly fading in the background.

2

Al

At the intersection of FM 1405 and East McKinney, we waited for the steady stream of big trucks to pass by. The air conditioning wasn't blowing cold enough for me in the back seat, and the car not moving didn't make it any better. The shipments of large pipes and valves rolled out the gate toward parts unknown, shaking the Chevy Nova we were in. The rumble didn't seem to bother the two men seated in front, but the silence in the car led me to nervously check my watch. Today was to be a big day, and I didn't want to mess up on account of being late.

All of this activity was on account of the US Steel plant. A lot of hungry mouths being fed because of oil pipelines in Alaska or somethin'.

Once the trucks were gone, we were again on our way. A mile down the road, we turned into the next open gate on the right and proceeded toward a large warehouse complex big enough to hide anyone or anything.

"We're here, Al," the driver, Manny, said as he stopped the Nova in the parking lot of one of the warehouses. He was chattier last weekend at the club in Houston, when he drank too many brews and asked me if I wanted more work. Apparently I'd caught the eye of some smart folk.

I wasn't at this warehouse for a pipeline job, though. I was here for a promotion. If Manny wasn't lying, this was my chance to move up and make lots of money.

Miguel and the man he called his cousin led me from the car, sandwiching me in the middle of them like I was somebody important. His cousin wore his black cowboy hat tilted low over his face, with equally dark sunglasses hiding his eyes like he was afraid of the sun. Normally I'd be worried, but if they wanted to kill me, they didn't have to drive this far to do it.

After a double knock by Manny, we entered the office door. Inside, a bunch of men who looked like they belonged on a farm or ranch stood idly by, joking around while wielding shotguns. Their arms weren't for handling cattle, and whatever crops they "managed" paid more than corn or soy beans. I was sure there were several more of them outside that I didn't see.

One look at Manny's cousin and they motioned the three of us through an interior door leading deeper inside the warehouse. No turning back now.

Dead center was where all the action took place. Behind large sheets of plastic that doubled as makeshift walls, several cars and vans were being carefully loaded by elderly men and women who looked as if they had lived hard lives. In my mind, I began counting the armed men around us and memorizing their positions. Just in case. Around Houston, I liked to carry myself like a million bucks, but inside these walls, I knew that I needed to act humble.

A muscled older man no more than five foot five, with long black hair and a thick moustache, looked to be in charge. As he clipped the end of a fresh cigar, he turned to acknowledge us.

"Al!" he belted out as if we were friends. "Please. Have a seat," he instructed me as a single chair was waiting behind him. Talk about a hot seat. He was military and very formal when he spoke; probably educated up north. Even while being polite, his voice was threatening, like he was used to not being questioned. Those with questions probably asked them no more.

I listened and sat my ass down, knowing how to play the game.

"That bumbling idiot Gerald Ford is President now," the man in charge said, obviously having no love for him. He went so far as to imitate the President's fall down the stairs of Air Force One, which we'd all seen on the television. "But this DEA that Nixon started has us concerned. We don't know if they're serious about drugs like they were about alcohol during the Prohibition Era, but perhaps that is good for what we do. Just a few years ago we were worried that marijuana might be legalized, but of course it wasn't. Nevertheless, we must always plan for the future. And that involves expansion and forging new alliances."

From my seat, I listened to his history lesson, nodding like it was the only thing that mattered. But I also watched a team of younger men busy switching out license plates on several cars as if on an assembly line. I saw the New Jersey plate on the car closest to me and smiled. They must've known I could drive—and fast.

"Do you know why you're here?" he asked, seeing what really held my attention.

"No," I replied, feigning ignorance as I repositioned myself in the chair. I suddenly hoped I wasn't here as a lesson myself.

"You represent the new breed who can blend in, and that is why you've been given this opportunity. That is an asset, *Al*," he lectured, stopping to chuckle. The other men followed his lead and laughed even harder at my expense.

But they could laugh at me all they wanted. Unimportant, jealous fools were what they were to me. I was the one being given the opportunity to run with the wolves, to prove I deserved more than just peddling joints in nightclubs and bars.

I focused on the shiny new Gran Torino I was about to have all to myself. I imagined the highways opening wide for me, like the actor Steve McQueen in *Bullitt,* dealing out justice from behind the wheel. Except that was a Mustang Steve McQueen drove. Well, I could have one too one day, but for now the Gran Torino would do. And if they let me keep it, who knows how much pussy I could get around here.

"You want me to drive the Torino for you, no?" I asked as I dared to stand up. With my sudden move, I heard one of his men chamber a shell into his shotgun. My employer motioned to them it was okay and smiled wildly at me.

"Oh. That's not what you will be driving," he stated. He had his men pull the plastic down from around another car. This one had a Jersey license plate too, but was quite different.

"A Country Squire," I muttered aloud as I grimaced over what I was being shown. It was an old station wagon. Not a new Gran Torino, but a fucking station wagon, complete with wood panels along the sides. It was like something you'd see on *The Brady Bunch* for all those fuckin' California kids and their stupid dog. But even theirs looked better than this monstrosity.

"That. That is what you will be driving for us, Al." He cackled gleefully as he let a puff of cigar smoke blow into my face. "It's good, no?"

"But . . . I don't understand, sir," I began as respectfully as I could. This had to be a joke. "It's a station wagon. I will look like a fool."

"What? You thought we would let you go out there in a flashy racecar? You are already too flashy with your pretty hair and gold chains. We're sending you to deal with the head Italians, but not in a car that will attract the attention of the police or this new DEA."

"What do you mean, sending me?" I questioned, no longer hiding my annoyance. Reckless, I know. "I thought I was making a normal run."

"Oh, you are, Al. We're delivering a healthy sample of our best crop to the Mafia in New York. You will be in charge of getting the shipment to Sal Dash, a low level lieutenant with their families, as an overture for future cooperation."

"Why me?" I asked, genuinely stunned by the responsibility I was being given, but at the same time bursting with pride.

Neither Manny nor his cousin had said a thing since we arrived. Instead they stood off to the side as if deaf. I guess they knew better than to give me a heads up.

"We've been watching you, Al," he answered, motioning for me to sit back down. I quickly complied. "We've seen you in the discos, and we see how easily you can blend in with any group. Manny says you are a charmer, so you can bullshit your way out of certain situations."

"Well, I do what I can." I smiled, suddenly feeling my normal confidence return.

"The families in New York don't know about our venture. These are delicate times as we try to branch into the Northeast, which they control. And if the Northeast Italians discover us encroaching on their territory, it will be unfortunate . . . for you. Understand?"

"I . . . I don't know about this," I mumbled, no longer comfortable or as confident about my latest job opportunity as when I strutted in there. But I had parents and sisters that I helped to support. They depended on the money I made to keep my sisters in school and not working in some sweatshop. As much as I feared the road ahead, the idea of winding up another mouth to feed worried me more.

"So, you think you can handle it, or do we need to get another man for the job?" his voice thundered, as he questioned my ability to handle the assignment.

"I will return from New York with every dime you've been promised," I swore to the men who were now watching me too closely.

"Good, because to disappoint us would prove fatal," my boss assured me, his tone steel and ice.

Also Available Now

To Paris With Love

Paris

1

My first three years at school taught me more about life than I could ever begin to learn in the outside world. I had sopped up those lessons like a hungry bitch going in on a plate of biscuits and gravy. And now, with graduation right around the corner, I would be the student awarded the grand prize for most accomplished. That's if I got to graduate, because bitches like this one kept challenging my last nerves.

I tightened my grip around her neck, pulling her into a headlock. She whipped around and flipped me over her head, onto the ground. In seconds I was up on my feet, crouching like a caged animal ready to strike again. Her hand shot out, coming down on my shoulder. The pain shot through me but there was no way I'd let her be the first one to finally take me down. I had an uncontested track record of wins. I kicked her in the solar plexus and kneed her in the jaw, causing three of her teeth to fall to the ground. I grabbed her in a bear hold, bending her arm behind her back until her short gasping breaths grew almost inaudible, making her drop the weapon at my feet. Still holding on to her I slid my hand to the floor and retrieved the Glock 9.

"*Ggamdungi*," she spat the words at me.

"*Shang nyun, Sheba-nom!*" I responded then jerked her arm harder, causing her to squirm in pain.

"Fuck you too, bitch!" She spat the words at me.

"Oh, so now you speak English? 'Cause I prefer to be called a beeyotch in English and not your slanty-eyed language!" I schooled her. Although my orders were not to cause physical harm, I wasn't feeling particularly generous. Last fool to use the N-word on me couldn't walk for a week and will probably never be able to impregnate a woman. I swiftly clocked her on the side of the head.

"*Paris!*" Yosef, my instructor, a former Israeli rebel fighter, grabbed me tightly from behind, his fingertips boring into my shoulder blades. The pain forced me to let go of Jae Kim, who fell in a heap on the ground and passed out. She probably fainted at the sight of her missing teeth.

A group of students gathered nearby, ecstatic to watch the spectacle.

"Knocked her the fuck out!"

I heard two palms slap together in a high five.

"Bam! Just like that."

"Damn! I told her not to mess with Paris," I heard one girl say as Jae Kim stirred near her bloody teeth.

"I wouldn't. Chick is fuckin' lethal," another added, then received a rousing round of agreement from the other girls.

It occurred to me that this would be a good time to practice passivity and restraint, but my head and my badass attitude were out of alignment with my reality. *Fuck him, her, and the rest of these motherfuckers. I won this exercise fair and square.*

"I won!" I yelled out. There was no way they were going to mess up my record.

"Why do you do these things?" Yosef, the gorgeous six foot four inch, 240-pound Israeli instructor admonished me. He smacked me hard on the neck. "How many times do I have to speak to you about your inability to follow orders? Have you lost your fucking mind? Look what you've done."

I could hear the sound of my own heavy breathing as I tried to contain myself so that I could respond appropriately instead of what I really wanted to do, which was curse his ass out.

Yosef wasn't much older than us, but he was the one person in the school who I truly respected. Not only was he built like a Mack truck but he was also capable of killing you with his bare hands without giving it much thought. I knew better than to piss him off too much because he could make your death look like an accident. It would take me years to know all of his secrets, but during our "private" lessons I made sure to get extra instruction, which somehow turned intimate over the past year. He wasn't the first man I'd ever slept with; however, he was the only one who put fear in my heart. As much as I pretended to hate, it I found it sexy as hell. Most men who acted all tough got the pussy and promptly turned into pussies. But not him; he kept sex and work separate, and right at this moment he was all business, which basically meant I was fucked, because I'd never seen him this upset.

"You need to gather your things and get to the headmistress', office," he said as he led me through the tunnel that connected to the catacombs and back into the main building. It was the perfect place to flip this shit in my favor. I darted ahead of him, stopping and blocking his path.

"Yosef, she started it," I whined, flirting with him. He held up one finger, silencing me. Damn, even deep in the shit he made me get all moist and turned on. I leaned closer to him, brushing my lips against his neck.

"Please."

"Paris, you are such a hellion!" he snapped at me.

"Isn't that what you like about me?" I slid my hand over the outline of his penis. It quickly hardened under my touch. "Instead of sending me to the office, wouldn't you prefer me putting my lips on this?" I rubbed his growing dick, motivating him to cave.

An hour later I found myself sitting in front of the headmistress, Madame Joan Marie, as she gave me her version of a come-to-Jesus talking-to. Yosef got the goods and still sold me out.

"Do you realize what you have done? Ms. Kim is from one of our most important families in South Korea. Imagine the conversation I will be having when her father arrives today. Do you want to explain to him why his daughter needs extensive oral surgery?"

"No, Madame," I answered submissively.

"Young lady, you are among the best and brightest students to ever cross the threshold of our establishment," she continued in her thick French accent. "Rarely have I gleamed such raw potential in a person your age but you are also your own worst enemy. You act as if rules only apply to others. And no matter how many times I've talked, you continue to disobey orders and protocol, and now you have proven to be a danger to others."

"Madame, I am so sorry for my behavior. It really was an accident," I lied, trying to sound as apologetic as possible so I could be on my way. I was ready for my vacation to begin.

"Mademoiselle Duncan, I believe that you believe that your apology is genuine. Then again, you always sound sincere after you've crossed a line. Unfortunately, the very next moment you rush headfirst into more conflict. I cannot allow you to continue to remain a hazard to the other students and to yourself."

She stood back, studying me. I tried to appear as vulnerable and defenseless as possible. If only this had been a man I'd have talked my way out of it already, but women didn't always get my charm. Finally she shook her head, resigned. "I must contact your father."

My bad attitude deflated and her words set off loud, scary bells in my head. *Danger! Danger!* "Nooooo!" The panic rang out in my voice. Anything but that. My father would have my head, and that would only be the beginning of my demise. "I promise I will change. Please give me another chance to make you proud. To make my father proud. Please, Madame," I begged and pleaded. This time I meant every word because I had never been more desperate. If my dad knew that I was over here in Switzerland showing my ass and messing with his name it would be bad.

"You will have to change both your behavior and your attitude," she continued.

"I will. I promise."

"I sincerely hope that my decision to give you one more chance will not be wasted."

"No, Madame." I leaned up and gave her a quick squeeze, something you just didn't do with these Nordic types. She looked shocked. Shit, I would have dropped to my knees and had my first try at cunnilingus if it would have prevented her from calling my father.

"Good! Now we are done with this unpleasant conversation." She opened the door and led me into her outer office, where a group of students were gathered in front of the fire.

I joined her, partaking in the roaring flames, tapping my foot on the wooden floorboards beside my matching Louis Vuitton luggage. I threw on my designer sunglasses and quarter-length fur despite the heat being produced by the fireplace. Felt good to be out of my school uniform, so I bit my tongue and kept my impatience to myself while the jealous hoes who were my classmates looked on. They'd never be as fly as me and they knew it. Nor would they know how close I came to being a former student.

Psh . . . finishing school.

Luckily, my electives—while not my raison d'être, but my reason for being here—were da bomb dot com.

"Mademoiselle Duncan, you will be sure to enjoy yourself back home in the U.S., no?" Madame Joan Marie asked as she kissed me on both cheeks. Right before removing my sunglasses and placing them back in my hand. Of course, she meant the opposite of what she and her big-ass smile said. You had to look beyond that and into those tiny, cold eyes of hers. She wanted me to behave myself back home. Rein a bitch in 'n' shit.

"Oh, I will most definitely enjoy myself," I replied, meaning exactly what I motherfuckin' said. Couldn't wait to get out of here and back in the NYC, specifically Jamaica, Queens where my family lived and ran things like motherfuckin' bosses. Yeah. To sleep in my own bed, eat some less bougie food, and see my fam would be all to the good.

Oh, yeah. And some good American dick, too. Don't get me wrong. These Euros could eat some pussy like nobody's business, but I missed the rhythm real niggas had back home when they were layin' it down.

But that could come later. For now, I really missed my family. And that was most important in this fucked-up world: Family.

There was my daddy, Lavernius Duncan, who everybody called LC, head of Duncan Motors, the largest African American–

owned car dealership chain in the tri-state area. My beloved moms, Chippy, had his back and was the rock of the family. Held it down for me and my four brothers: Junior, the big diesel one who was loveable as fuck; Vegas, the heart of the family whom I would die for; Orlando, the calculating one whom I would have to think about dying for; and Rio, my wild and crazy twin who I lived for. Oh, and my older sister London was part of the family too, but the less said about her the better. She and her lawyer husband, Harris, already thought their shit didn't stink, *but now that she was pregnant?* Fawk. Would never hear the end of it. Was almost enough to make me want to remain in Europe over break.

Almost.

Once I touched down back home, I'd just have to be civil. Steer clear of her, Harris, and the demon spawn in her gut.

Besides, it was only a month after all. Then back here to complete my schooling.

"Is your family sending a car for you, Mademoiselle Duncan? Or will you need transportation arranged?" Madame Joan Marie asked before she turned her attention to the next departing student, this Croatian bitch with bad skin. Madame Joan Marie liked everything to run with Swiss precision. And when it didn't, heads rolled.

The text I'd been waiting for came through on my phone, leading me to tune her ass out momentarily.

"No, Madame. My ride is here now," I said as I looked up at her, flashing my first genuine smile of the day.

"Very well, mademoiselle. Adieu," she commented as she took a slight bow and gracefully stepped aside. Funny that she never referred to me by my first name. Probably thought being named Paris, after a city, was *ghetto* or sumthin'. But not ghetto enough to refuse our money.

Had been counting down all week to this moment. So with a deep sigh of relief, I stepped, luggage in hand, toward the thick reinforced doors strong enough to survive a bomb blast. The inconspicuous school in this town, not far from the border of France, was on a lake bearing the same name. Until my parents sent me here to Neuchâtel, I only knew of this town for the Swiss chocolates they sold in America.

But my school was no Willy Wonka experience. No Oompa-Loompas around here. And creepy men in top hats and coats would get got.

Place was originally a hospital until, back in the late 1800s, it was converted into a school for the betterment and civility of young ladies like me, whose parents had the money and desire to have them molded into so much more.

Leaving the toasty confines, I pulled my fur close to shield me from the cold rush of air on a sunny day. Just as the text said, a car horn to my right alerted me to the all-black Citroën C6 rolling in my direction down the slightly uneven Rue du Pommier. If I knew my daddy, he probably had it armored. I couldn't contain myself and waved frantically, dropping the poise and polish drummed into my head twenty-four seven over the past year. I hoped LC had made the trip across the ocean to surprise me. I couldn't wait to show him the new me I'd become and what I'd learned from my instructors.

Standing in the cold air I spotted Jae Kim being comforted by her fine-ass British hottie, who attended the male equivalent to our school in the next town. We exchanged bitter, hostile glares when I noticed him checking me out. Instead of continuing down the steps, I stopped for a moment and a smile spread across my lips. When I finally approached them on the first landing of the steps I saw a look of confusion flutter across her face.

"Bye, Jae. Have a great spring break," I offered in my most conciliatory voice. "You heading back to Korea?"

"Don't you speak to me, you fucking bitch!" She glared then turned her back to me to punctuate her seriousness. But he shot me an apologetic smile. I stepped to him.

"If you didn't have such shitty taste in women I'd consider giving you some." I reached into my pocket and handed him a card with my phone number on it. "Just in case your taste improves," I finished, the sounds of them arguing followed me down the stairs.

When the sedan rolled to a stop in front of the school, I didn't wait for the driver to exit. Instead, I scrambled down the remaining brick steps and up to the car window where I tapped on it with my fingernails. Through the tint, I could make out a silhouette that had to be my daddy's.

As the passenger lowered the window, the driver exited and went about gathering my bags to place in the trunk.

"Hello, Paris," the voice said, taking me aback that it wasn't my daddy's.

"Orlando," I muttered dryly at the recognition of my brother, clad in a navy blue suit with shiny O.D. cufflinks that adorned his crisp white cuffs. "Where's Daddy?" I asked as he discarded a cigarette out the window while blowing smoke out his nose. Orlando was trying too hard to fit in with the cool and the chic out here. He had a woman seated on the side of him who looked to be Italian and probably didn't speak a lick of English. I guessed it was a high-priced whore whom he'd arranged to spend time with. I paid her no mind.

"Well, hello to you too," he replied with a grin certainly meant to piss me off.

"What do you want?" I asked my brother as the driver slammed the Citroën's trunk shut then opened Orlando's door for him. Bitch was getting cold and they wanted to play games. As Orlando exited, he allowed the driver to place his wool overcoat on him like he was a stone-cold pimp. The brunette stayed inside the car, never daring to look at me.

"C'mon, take a walk with me," Orlando said with a motion of his head.

The Citroën slowly trailed us in the distance as me and my brother strode along the lake on Quai Phillippe-Gaudet. As a little Smart car buzzed by, even I had to admire the postcard beauty of this town. But this was cutting into my free, time and Orlando wouldn't come all the way here just to take a stroll with me.

"Why aren't we on a G5 by now?" I pressed Orlando, who'd been much too quiet.

"Because you're not going back home."

"Huh?" I said, stopping dead in my tracks. "Oh, that's some serious bullshit!"

"At least not this time," he added, taking two more steps before looking back at me. "You know London's at the end of her pregnancy?" he said as both of us resumed walking, albeit much slower this time.

"Yeah. So?" I spat out, irritated at Orlando's mention of my older sister.

"Your sister's having some health issues, Paris. LC wants you to wait. Just stay away for a little while longer. Until the baby's delivered. Every time somebody mentions your name it's like her blood pressure spikes or something. You can see it in her eyes. Pop knows how y'all two are when you're together."

"London's still upset about that ex of hers? Damn. That didn't mean shit and I was younger back then. 'Sides, she should be thanking me for saving her from his lame ass."

"No. It's not just London's issue with you," he said, pausing to ensure our car was still trailing us. His disdain and disgust for that whole mess back when I'd visited London in college, especially my part in it, still showed. "Things are also unsettled over the stuff that went down with Vegas." He mentioned my second-favorite brother and the family peacekeeper. "Delicate times."

"And you're just swooping in to take over for the throne, ain't ya?"

"Your feelings for me aside, you need to shut the fuck up and listen," Orlando growled. "Instead of coming home this trip, we want you to stay in Europe. Got a resort for you in Spain. Five stars . . . just how you like. Sun and fun, so it's right up your alley. But try to stay low-key. We have enemies all over, so we don't need you broadcasting who you are. Reservations are under 'Paris Wimberley.'"

"Spain, huh? And if I choose to go home instead?" I pushed, challenging my older brother. Fuck. I'd already planned my first twenty-four hours back home. Me and Rio were gonna get fucked up, go clubbin', then compare notes on the men we'd selected for the night. Thoughts of spring break were what got me through these last few months. But now?

"This was LC's decision. So he would be very disappointed in you," Orlando replied, meaning Daddy would go ape shit and cut off my funds. Or worse. "Any more smart aleck questions?" my brother added after gauging the look of fear on my face.

"Yeah."

"What now?" he said gruffly as he motioned our car over to pick us up.

"Can I get a new wardrobe?" I asked, batting my eyelashes.

Orlando frowned, consternation etched on his face as he no doubt wanted to object. "No! You've supported the rising stock prices for high-end designers long enough. Deal with it," he bellowed.

"Then you wouldn't mind me telling LC how you're spending your money on this trip . . . and at home. At least I have some material shit to show for my money. All you have are memories of nasty cum stains on some fake-ass titties bought by the last john," I said, setting his ass straight.

Notes

Notes